Torbjørn's Gold

The Secret of Isle Royale

By

John Eric Nystul

Edited by Carl James Anderson

Cover Artwork by Tom Anderson ©
Hadley House

Singing River Publications

Map of Lake Superior

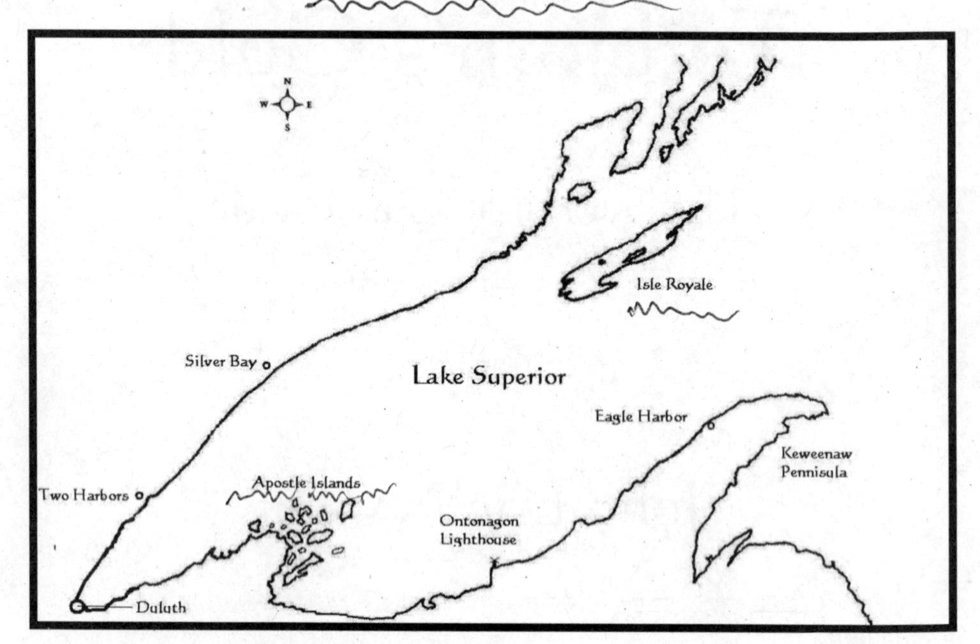

Acknowledgements

I would like to thank my late dad, Jack Nystul, who exposed me to reading and book collecting and for introducing me to great classic adventure novels. Thanks to my mom, Lois Nystul, for constant help and support and for always 'being there'. She read an early copy of the manuscript. She told me stories of her grandfather, Jens Egeland, a major inspiration for this book. Thanks to sisters Nancy Nystul and Jane Vaughan, brother-in-law Jim Vaughan, and mother-in-law Katie Kelly, who gave insightful input and support. I would like to thank my children, Kari, Anna, and Erik for encouragement. They helped mom while I wrote in the basement until the wee hours. Thanks and gratitude to my publisher, Chris Moroni at Singing River Publications, for an opportunity to see one of my dreams come true. Carl Anderson's editing insight carved the detail out of my massive manuscript, and he worked on layout details, such as maps and diagrams.

Lastly, I want to thank my wife Kris, for giving me much needed encouragement and showing enthusiasm for this project. Her corrections and suggestions for the manuscript were needed and treasured. She gave me the faith to finish this project. Without her, this book would not have happened.

Singing River Publications

Printed in Canada

ISBN 0-9789870-0-4
International ISBN 978-0-9789870-0-8

Published by:
Singing River Publications
P.O. Box 72
Ely, Minnesota 44731
www.singingriverpublications.com

Map of Isle Royale

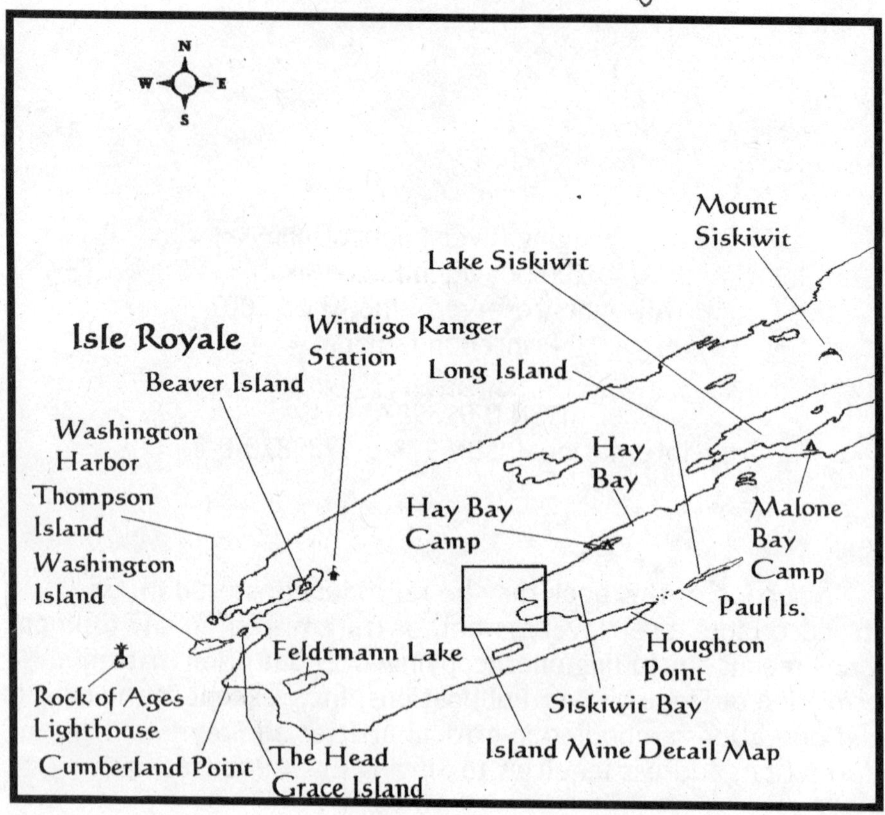

Torbjørn's Gold is a work of fiction. Names, places, characters, and occurrences are the products of the author's imagination or are used fictitiously. Any resemblance to actual events, locales, or persons, living or dead, is entirely coincidental.

About the Author

John Eric Nystul is a second generation Norwegian-American. He was born in Minneapolis and grew up in St. Louis Park, MN. He is a graduate of the University of Minnesota, and works as a real estate appraiser. John has been sailing and chartering out of the Apostle Islands on Lake Superior for over 20 years. He lives with his wife, Kris, and his children, Kari, Anna, and Erik, in Chanhassen, MN.

Chapter 1

Have you ever had the feeling you were just about to die, and you couldn't do anything about it? Your life flashed before your eyes and you said to yourself—so this was it? This was how I was going to die? Would it be painful? Would it be quick?

I glanced out at the vast liquid nightmare from the helm of my small sailboat, which bounced up and down like a toy in a whirlpool. The helm was not responding. The sky and water were one, dark and eerie. The horizontal rain was pouring down in sheets, stinging my cheeks and exposed hands. So this was what a storm was like on Lake Superior! I saw a wall of water above, just about to smash down—surely enough to capsize the boat. The water hit, and I was totally immersed. I opened my eyes and saw green water, and felt the freezing cold. Everything seemed to be in slow motion. So this was it. Then I felt a jolt from my safety harness and the sailboat and I were upright, above the water. Incredible!

That was what it had been like for the past two hours. Two hours of the most gut-wrenching Hell I could imagine. The storm reminded me of the sea stories I heard from my uncle Olav about my great grandpa, Jens, whom I was named after. He was born near Arendal, Norway in 1850. At the age of twelve, he went to sea. He wasn't the oldest son, so it was unlikely he would inherit the small family farm. So he, like his father, and his father before him, went to sea. Grandpa Jens started out as a cabin boy, then cook, and eventually ended up as a first mate. My uncle Olav told me Jens sailed all over the world for more than ten years, visiting far off lands and sailing in all kinds of storms. He faced death on many occasions: scampering up the rat lines and reefing sails in a pacific typhoon; facing ice storms in the Baltic; and getting shipwrecked off the coast of Florida. On that last occasion, there had been a horrendous storm and most of the hands were lost.

The captain, too, went down with the ship. Grandpa Jens was picked up by a steamer bound for New Orleans. The story goes that he got a labor job hauling goods onto ships at the harbor so he could earn enough money to sail back to Norway. The job didn't pan out and he found himself working on a sugar plantation for a few months. He missed the sea and ships so much that he found employment on riverboats and barges on the Mississippi river. Eventually he found himself in Wisconsin, where he discovered the Great Lakes. He signed up as a common sailor on a small schooner on Lake Michigan, and within a few years became the first mate and eventually the captain and owner. By the mid-1870s, though, he found himself beleaguered in another storm, this time on Lake Superior. His ship sank and he barely escaped death for the fourth time. I think that's when he came to the realization that ships weren't the life for him, even though he loved the sea. He ended up homesteading in the Red River Valley of Minnesota.

As I surveyed the colossal waves crashing down all around me and felt the soul-piercing wind gush through me, I felt the presence of Death somewhere out there on the deck—maybe concealing himself behind the mast with his anxious red eyes, ready to take me away to the realm of the dead.

I remember my uncle telling the story of when Grandpa Jens was in the North Atlantic in the early 1870s. A large squall suddenly came down on them, and the crew was ordered to take down the sails, but the rapidity and fierceness of the storm prevented them from securing the topsail, which ballooned in the brutish wind and made the ship wobble from side to side. The captain assembled his men and asked for a volunteer to climb up and secure the sail in the face of imminent death. Immediately a voice was heard, '*Jeg skal prøve!*'—I will try! It was my grandfather. He scampered up the lines and, while dangling upside down with his legs over the spar, tied up the topsail. The family legend may have gotten a bit embellished, but just think of the courage—or just plain stupidity—of climbing up the lines in the middle of a fierce storm where, with one miscalculation, you would fall to a certain death! I wonder if Death was hanging around the spars that night, disappointed because Jens Halverson got away from him—that time.

•

A few hours passed, and the storm gradually subsided. I had changed my wet clothes for dry ones, and was back at the tiller. I looked around and realized the stars were out. There was a slight southeastern breeze gently brushing against my face. I was alone in the cockpit. I had checked on the crew about an hour ago and couldn't get over the glazed looks on their faces—I think they don't believed yet that they were not dead. They survived, and somehow Jens pulled them through. It was a bit lonely in the cockpit; my only visitors were the far off lights in the sky and on the coast, and a gentle lap of waves against the bow. I gazed around the vast, dark horizon. The lake was amazingly beautiful.

I raised the main sail and tried to find some wind. How far had we been blown off course? I glanced at my watch and saw it was four A.M. I adjusted the main sail and started a new leeward tack. How could all of this have happened? What a crazy whirlwind existence these past six months had been! I felt a smile of defiance appear on my face when I thought of what my boss would think of me, out here on the lake, on this foolish adventure of mine. I remembered how I pleaded with him to let me take two weeks of vacation in a row.

I don't really care anymore. I was sure I had been—or would be—fired. Good, I should have woken up years ago and realized what a mistake that job was. I think deep down I knew, but I was way too frightened to do anything about it. Well, now I finally did something. But something went askew. I thought I had anticipated all the contingencies. But I was wrong—as usual.

Everything was going according to plan until we had that unexpected visitor. Thank God for the waves. Just at the right moment, the wind and the waves made him lose his footing, and I had taken action. For reasons I can't really understand, my crewmates weren't as excited about my actions. They were all down in the cabin, resting. I don't think they wanted to see me for a few hours. I got a little upset and I may have flown off the handle a bit. I may have said things I shouldn't have, but I was angry. I think there were a whole bunch of issues that had been percolating to the surface for the past two weeks. After my little tirade, I was a little surprised to see the reaction on the faces of my shipmates. Brian just looked at me in disbelief and Nora had a look of frustration and hurt.

But I had more important things to worry about. I had to get this sailboat safely back to Madeline Island, and be on my toes the entire time. I had to complete this mission of mine. Failure was not an option anymore. I had to prove to Brian, Paige, my boss, my parents, my adversary, and yes, even Nora, that I could complete a quest, something that took a bit of daring and risk.

Another hour slipped by. The lake was still calm. I hadn't heard a word from below. I didn't know what I would say when they did come up. Maybe I should apologize. I didn't know. I glanced out to the eastern horizon and saw a hint of dawn. Every minute brought us closer to Madeline Island, where this whole nightmare would be over. I took a deep breath. I could think more rationally now, although my mind was still racing. It was spinning around all the events of the past few days. What was I doing here? Why had I put my friends and me through so much danger? What was I trying to prove?

I gazed out again at the lake. She seemed so bewitching now. A mild wind kissed my face. I looked to my right and saw the distant outline of the island. I looked to my left, and saw what I thought was the Keweenaw Peninsula coming into view. I saw more lights out there that weren't there a few minutes ago. Quickly, I ran down into the main cabin and looked at the radar screen. A small blip was there.

Chapter II

My little story began one uneventful Friday morning in the middle of May. It was quite an ordinary early summer day, the clouds were high and puffy, and it was bright and crisp. I had stayed up too late the previous night reading a wild Hammond Innes novel—the British author who wrote about desperate, on-the-edge men, falling into life or death situations, mostly in the uttermost outposts of the world. Well, at three a.m., Mr. Innes had me sailing in the North Atlantic, with one hand on the helm of a splendid sailboat and the other around a beautiful woman agent. I just had to finish the book. It was that good.

I was violently shaken awake three hours later by my obnoxious alarm clock that went off at its usual six a.m. I was upset that I had lost my dream and couldn't remember what the woman looked like. I turned off the alarm and thought to myself: was the book last night so good that I only got three hours of sleep? I concluded it was, so I rolled over again and fell back asleep. Sometime later, I was jolted awake by the familiar sound of the front door of my apartment closing—it must have been my roommate. Doesn't he usually leave for work about 15 minutes later than I? Looking at my clock told me I had to be at work in ten minutes! My boss would be waiting to go on some appointments!

Ten minutes later, I ran down the two flights of stairs and out onto the street where my Saab 900 was parked. The inside of my windshield was full of morning dew, so I quickly tried to rub it off with my shirtsleeve, but I wasn't successful. I started the car and took off in a fury down Lake Harriet Parkway. I was driving east into the sun and my windshield immediately fogged up again, so I had to rub off the dew with my already damp sleeve. Same result. I turned onto a somewhat busy street, praying that I could make out all of the oncoming traffic through my fogged up and potentially dangerous windshield. I glanced at my fuel indicator. It was below "E" and I wondered if I would even get to the office. No time to get gas, I had to wing it somehow. Great.

When I finally got to my office, I was an hour late. Norm was pacing back and forth near my cubicle as I walked in. I wanted to tell him a story, like I had a flat tire on my car or I got into a small accident, but I thought he might catch me lying so I told him the truth. He rolled his eyes and started muttering something while he walked into his office to get his briefcase.

"Let's go, Nilsen," he said as he started walking toward the door. "You drive." I got my car keys out of my pocket and then I realized that my car was on double E and I could only probably drive a few miles before I would run out of gas. The look on Norm's face when I told him my car's fuel situation spoke volumes. He shook his head and motioned for me to follow him to his car. It was a ten year old Plymouth station wagon. I got in and we took off from the parking lot. I looked around the inside of the car. The seats were really worn and there was a crack on the dashboard. It was old and smelly, with pop cans and candy wrappers on the floor, and coffee stains on the front seat. Talk radio was on the airwaves. Norm immediately turned the radio off. I think he didn't want me to know what radio station he regularly listens to.

The first of the two inspections was of an ex-crack house in Minneapolis. A church about a block from the house bought it from the city for a dollar. The city had kicked out the renters and condemned the house. The church had a lot of their members help gut the place and then remodel. A single mother with five children who was a member of the church bought the house for $30,000.

The neighborhood was going through a renovation of sorts. While there were still plenty of houses boarded up, and many rental properties in poor condition, many other houses were being updated and a lot of the old, condemned houses were being torn down and new ones were being built. Young professionals with families had started to move into the neighborhood and the percentage of home ownership was significantly increasing.

When we were about two blocks from the property, Norm said, "Look at those guys just hanging out. Don't they have anything better to do? Don't they have jobs?"

I was about to tell him about inequality and the lack of justice to some people with limited resources, but under the circumstances, I thought I'd better keep my mouth shut. 'Who the hell do you think you are to make judgments like that about people you don't even know?' I thought to myself. It was obvious the man had limited abilities. I took a good long appraising look at my boss. If I were to see him on the street as a stranger, I would think there's really nothing special about this guy. He's just a typical guy, on the wrong side of forty with a receding hairline who wears cheap suits with nerdy shoes and has a haircut and glasses that must have gone out of style twenty years ago. The only thing he has going for him is that he knows how to appraise houses. He's very good at his craft and what's worse, he knows it. My father always said that the most dangerous kind of person is a very smart person who knows he's smart. He says that these smart people think they can 'strut sitting down.' Well, if it wasn't for that one thing, I don't know where Norm would be in life right now.

Pastor Robinson was waiting for me at the doorway when we drove up to the house. I ran out of Norm's car and went up to shake the Reverend's hand and I apologized for being so late. He was very gracious about it and told me he planned to stay here all morning until all the repairs were completed. The sale of the house was closing this afternoon and some minor finishing touches were still needed. He took me on a little tour of the property. It was in marvelous condition compared to the first inspection a few months ago. When I completed my final inspection, I thanked Pastor Robinson again and told him that he and his parishioners had done a wonderful job remodeling the house. I told him that I would call the mortgage company and inform them the property had cleared the final inspection and they could close this afternoon.

I walked back to the car and got in. Norm sped off and yawned. After he drove a couple of blocks he asked, "So how was the dump?" I looked at him in amazement. I couldn't believe he just said that. He didn't even acknowledge that Pastor Robinson existed or what good work he was doing in the community. He just assumed that since the house was in this neighborhood, it must be a dump.

I said without thinking, "At least someone gets to live in a remodeled house, and there's no more crack house in the neighborhood!" Norm turned to me with a puzzled look. He recovered a split second later and then an arrogant smile appeared on his lips. He rolled his eyes and turned back to the street.

We didn't say another word until we got to our next inspection. It was on Lake Minnetonka in an affluent area about sixteen miles west of Minneapolis, but in reality it was another galaxy away from the last house.

I had to admit, I felt pretty good about what I said to Norm. It was the first time in five years I've expressed a differing opinion on any subject. In the past, I was too afraid to say anything. I always wanted to get along with this guy because there might be an advancement opportunity. But today something changed. I enjoyed that startled look on his face and the fact that he hadn't opened his mouth in the past thirty minutes.

"How much did this baby go for?" Norm asked as we drove up to this enormous house that had just been erected on the shores of Lake Minnetonka. He looked like a kid on Christmas morning. The sight of all this wealth, power, and prestige was just too much for him. Norm had found his nirvana. I opened the file. By the time I looked up the figures, he had driven up to the driveway. "The property was appraised for $4.5 million."

"Whoa, baby! Can you imagine?" He had a huge grin on his face and he looked up to the sky, dreaming that he was living in this palace. "What's the square foot finish on this puppy?" He was practically foaming at the mouth now. Down boy, I was thinking. I looked at the appraisal report and said, "23,450 square feet with a 2,200 square foot heated, eight car garage."

"So what does this guy do for a living?"

I said "I heard that he started some type of finance company."

"Whoa, baby. What a country!" Norm jumped out of the car and quickly walked over to the builder, who had been waiting for us for some time. Norm shook his hand and patted him on his back. He acted like they were long lost buddies. They walked into the mansion, hand in hand as I got out of the car and tried to take a picture of the palace. I had to walk a block away to get the whole house in the frame of the camera.

I started my inspection by walking into the three-story foyer. There were workers all over trying to finish the last minute touches. This house was also closing this afternoon. I then walked into the kitchen, living room, sun-room, study, master suite and then into the large indoor pool. I thought I was at the Holiday Inn or something; the indoor pool was that large. I then walked into the basement and saw the family room, media-theater room, exercise room with sauna and steam rooms, and then into the gymnasium with a regulation basketball court. The last part of the inspection was the eight-car garage and the 2,000 square foot caretaker apartment. The one thing that kept on pounding in my head when I was walking around this palace was that I heard only two people would be living in this house, give or take some servants or caretakers. Do you think they would ever see each other in a house this size?

After an hour or so, I had to corral Norm, who was having such a wonderful time with the builder going through the house. It was like trying to get a small child to leave Disney World. I reminded him of his afternoon engagement. "Oh yes. Thank you Nilsen. Mr. Kelly, I want to thank you so much for this little tour. I had a lovely time."

The builder smiled and said, "So, you'll pass the inspection?"

I was about to say 'yes' when Norm interjected, "With flying colors, Mr. Kelly."

We got back into Norm's car and drove off. We only said a few words to each other on the way back to the office. I think Norm was getting excited to tell his golf buddies about the house we were just in. Two things entered my mind. First, I got a big kick out of Norm's reactions to the little Minneapolis house and the big Lake Minnetonka house. He didn't even care if Pastor Robinson ever existed but he wouldn't have missed seeing the big house if his life depended on it. My second thought was to ask the owners of the large house if, no matter how rich they are, how they could justify living in a house that large. The house on Lake Minnetonka was over twenty-nine times larger than the small house in Minneapolis and cost 150 times more. The house on the lake had a garage 275 percent larger than the entire size of the main floor of the Minneapolis house. Talk about diversity in America!

•

We got back to the office about 2:30 and I was a little nervous because I didn't want to take the blame for Norm being late to his golf outing. The rest of the afternoon drifted by in a haze of boring tasks, but my mind wasn't on them. When I finally noticed it was ten minutes past five, I threw all of my papers into my briefcase and quickly got out of the office. It was quitting time, and I had to meet my roommate and some friends in Uptown for happy hour.

Chapter III

Ah, the weekend had come at last! I fumbled around my messy car and found my 'Friday after work' mood tape. As I drove off in the direction of the bar, I heard The Jam's Paul Weller's Rickenbaker playing *Here Comes the Weekend*, followed by the Clash's *48 Hours,* and then, *In the City* by The Who. Finally I could take a deep breath and relax. I shoved away all of today's events, and thought how great a beer would taste. Driving down the freeway I couldn't help but feel good, even though the traffic was at a snail's pace. There's something about Friday afternoons. It's my favorite time of the week. My spirits lifted even more when I found a parking place only a block away from the bar—that's pretty lucky for me. Maybe the day's mood would change.

Lately, my roommate, Brian McGinnis, and I have been making it a habit to have a drink, or two—okay, maybe three—every Friday night at this cool bar in the Uptown area of south Minneapolis. Brian told me that his girl friend, Paige Morgan, would be stopping by for a few bumps. Secretly, I was hoping that Paige's roommate, Nora, would also make an appearance. She was the kind of woman who made me talk in incoherent and incomplete sentences every time I was around her. In short, she was the woman of my dreams. The problem was, last I heard, she was dating some local TV weekend sportscaster. Someone way out of my league.

I walked through the door and was bombarded by cigarette smoke and loud chatter. The place was packed and all the tables were occupied. I glanced around the room to see if I recognized any familiar faces. No such luck. There was a mixture of young professional types with their ties undone guzzling down beer and staining their white starched shirts. Most of them were disagreeably loud, slapping each other on the back with insipid laughter. There was also the older student crowd, dressed in blue jeans and sweaters, smoking cigarettes, drinking beer or wine, huddled in deep conversations. I could hear the low hum of music playing in the background as I stepped up to the bar and ordered a Belgian beer. I loved this place. They had an inventory of more than two hundred beers from around the world. I told myself that I was going to try every one of them. I was presently at the B's and making my way to Zambian beer—if they had it. I took a few long and serious gulps of my beer and walked over to an unoccupied area of the bar and waited for Brian. Then I heard someone say, "Hi, Jens. How are you doing?"

I turned to my left and saw Nora Janson addressing me. She was standing there in a business suit with an empty wineglass in her hand. She was a sheer vision of beauty—tall and athletic, a dark blonde with streaks of gold. I was caught off-guard and blurted out something stupid. She smiled and asked, "How long have you been here?"

"I just got here." There was an uncomfortable pause. "How long have you been here?" I finally asked.

"Ten minutes. I'm meeting Paige. We're going to a bachelorette party tonight."

"Oh," I said. Come on Jens; think of something to say that sounds halfway intelligent. Anything. I looked around the bar and saw a booth opening up. Three people were leaving. "Do you want to sit down?" I asked as I pointed toward the booth.

"Sure," she said, as she started to follow me toward the booth. We were just in time, as another group standing nearby started to make a move toward it. We seated ourselves and I flagged down a waitress. I ordered the house red wine for Nora and a Canadian beer for myself. There was another uncomfortable pause, and I made eye contact with her. She smiled and asked how my job was going.

Nora and I have a little history. We met soon after I moved in with Brian. Nora and Paige are best friends and have been roommates for the past few years following college. Brian and Paige had been an item for two years now. We met at a New Years Eve's party about a year and a half ago. We hit it off immediately. I found out she was from Edina, which is an affluent suburb just south of where I grew up in St. Louis Park. We found out we had a lot in common; we both come from a Norwegian background—she was also half Swedish, but let's not dwell on the negative. Like me, she was quiet and shy, and she was a runner. She grew up in a family of lawyers and was in law school. As the party progressed and we consumed more alcohol, we got friendlier and friendlier. In fact, we couldn't keep our hands off each other. We danced and drank, danced, and drank some more. We started making out by the time of the New Year's countdown and the traditional New Year's kiss. We went upstairs and found a vacant bedroom and started messing around. I can't quite recall what happened next—but we both fell asleep and woke up the next morning with messy hair and clothes and that dreaded morning breath. We both were completely embarrassed by the entire situation. Neither of us had ever been so irresponsible. Since then, there has been an uneasy tension between us. I was so upset with myself because I thought we really had something going there that night, and it could have turned into something special. But I blew it—again.

I lied and told her how I was enjoying my job. I then asked her how law school was going. She informed me that she had a semester left and then she was going to intern at her dad's law firm. We finished our drinks, and I asked if she wanted another. She thought for a long moment then and said, "Sure." I flagged down the server and ordered another house red and a Czech beer for myself. When the drinks came, Nora took a sip and asked, "Where could Paige and Brian be?" as she glanced at her watch.

I looked right into Nora's gorgeous blue eyes. I think there were a lot of subtle, hidden messages in our body language, but I couldn't tell for sure. I quickly looked away and I think I blushed. She has a beautiful, almost reserved smile that makes her nose, which has just a sprinkle of freckles, kind of wrinkle. She also has a nervous habit of taking a fallen strand of hair, with her hand, and putting it behind her ear. I loved that about her. I wanted to ask if she was still seeing that TV sports personality, but I was too shy. Why couldn't I ask her if she was still seeing that guy? Maybe they broke up. Maybe I could get up enough guts to ask her out. Then I thought the hell with it. I don't care if she is still seeing him. I can still ask her out, right?

I was just about ready to open my mouth when I heard, "So there you guys are! Where have you been hiding?" It was Brian. He smiled and gave me a wink. Nora and I were both defensive about it and explained we were here the entire time. Brian laughed and waved his hand to Paige signaling that he found us and to come over. Paige flamboyantly walked across the bar toward our booth. Many men in the crowded bar stopped their conversations and stared as she crossed the room. She looked like a fashion model and had the attitude to go along with it. She had long legs, wore the latest high-end clothes, and had a swagger that could make men cry. I couldn't help but think that if I wasn't Brian's roommate, she would never give me the time of day. Not even a look. I was in the little league, and she was the 'big show.'

Now I can recall Brian saying something about Paige growing up in the affluent suburb of Wayzata but there was something hazy about her family and upbringing. All I know is that two things really annoyed me about her. The first was her fascination with money. I can't tell you how many times I've cringed when I heard her say: "Yes, I know them, they're so filthy rich they don't know what to do with all of their money." The second thing is that the only correct way to do anything was how she did it in New York City. I guess after college, she made the pilgrimage to the Big Apple to become a world famous fashion model. It didn't go too well—I understand. She came back after a few years with her tail between her legs, but she did develop an attitude. She loved everything about the city and we had to endure her monotonous New York stories. She would always start off by saying "Well you know, when I lived in New York..."

Brian ordered drinks. They joined us, and we all started talking about the week we had. Well, I should say that the three of them were talking about their week. I kept quiet. I didn't want to bore them. The waitress delivered our drinks, and I took a long hard swallow of my Danish beer. I was thinking of how I could somehow get Nora alone and ask her out when I heard Paige say, "Nora, it's time for a bathroom break. Come along now." Nora smiled and started to get up. It really bugged me how Paige would order Nora around. "We'll be back later boys," Paige said as she got up and followed Nora to the restroom. We watched as several heads turned at the bar as the women walked by.

Brian smiled and said, "Nilsen, there truly is a god." I nodded my head, and he continued, "So?"

I looked at him and said, "So?"

"So, how did it go? Did you have a good talk? Did we give you enough time?"

"What do you mean... enough time?"

"Come on Nilsen, get with the program. If you can believe it, Paige suggested we take our time to get to the bar and maybe the two of you would meet and talk to each other and get to know each other again."

Brian had a smart-ass grin on his face, and I knew what he was alluding to with that word—'again.' "It was Paige who suggested it? You've got to be kidding. Huh. So she does know I'm alive?"

"Funny... very funny." Brian's face changed to a more serious tone and he said, "Jens, Paige and I are getting a little worried about you. When was the last time you went on a date?"

"Probably six months ago. Don't you remember? You set it up. I think her name was Jill or something," I said.

"Oh yeah," Brian replied, "She's a friend of a friend of mine from work. How did it go? I can't remember."

I smiled at him and said, "The dinner was fine, but we had to leave the movie theater early when her stalker ex-boyfriend started yelling at us."

"Oh, yeah. That was it. What happened next?"

"I can't believe you don't remember," I said, mildly offended. "They had an argument in the parking lot. Then, all of a sudden they apologized about how terrible they were to each other and how much they missed each other and kissed and made up. They left me in the parking lot. I went back to our apartment and watched an old movie." Brian still looked like he had clouds in his eyes. "You got their wedding invitation in the mail last week. There're getting married in July."

Brian started laughing. "Oh, yeah, that was it. You see Jens, that's why we wanted you to talk to Nora."

"Aren't I just wasting my time? Isn't she still seeing that TV sportscaster?"

"Nope, they're history."

"You're kidding! What happened?"

"Nora caught him in too many lies. She knew the relationship wasn't going anywhere. Plus he's as thick as a brick. He can read a teleprompter okay, but you can't have an intelligent conversation with him. If you can steer him away from talking about himself, he doesn't know what to talk about."

"That's great news," I said a bit too enthusiastically. "But why me? There are surely other guys."

"Hey pal, don't you remember? I'm going out with her roommate. Let's say that maybe some conversations between the two of them have been steered in your direction. The problem is that in a few minutes they're going to that bachelorette party, so you don't have much time to ask her out."

I was about to ask him how I could do that when Nora and Paige sat down in the booth. Boy, talk about pressure. I started a conversation with Nora when the song *Can't Hurry Love* by Phil Collins came on. Several couples walked down to the small dance floor in the center of the room and began to dance. "Let's dance," Brian blurted out to no one in particular. Nora said yes right away and Paige looked at her watch and said, "I don't know if we have enough time before we have to go."

"Come on Paige, just one song," Brian said.

"All right. One song. Then we have to go. Come on Nora, let's dance." We all walked down to the dance floor. I'm not usually the dancing type. But, put a few beers in me and if I have the right motivation—Nora—then I can get down and boogie. We paired up and started dancing to the tune. Nora was a good dancer, and I was trying to keep up. I was trying to enjoy myself, but I knew I only had three minutes or so to ask her out. I was trying to think of something to say when I blurted out, "You know, I really want to apologize for acting the way I did at that New Year's party." I couldn't believe what I just said, but I had to get it off my chest. I really felt that bad about it.

Nora said, "What did you say? I can't hear you, the music is too loud!" Great, I can't believe this. I was about to say forget it, but something inside me made me say it again. This time I got up real close to her left ear. I took in the delightful aroma of her perfume, and repeated what I just said. She smiled and shook her head, "I'm the one, Jens, who should apologize. I felt awfully horrible about the entire thing."

That went fairly well. I was just about to pop the big question when the song finished. Paige looked at her watch and said, "Nora, look at the time! We've got to go. First, the restroom.

Let's go." They marched to the woman's room and went in. I followed them to the door and stood outside ready to catch her on her way out. I told myself I was going to ask her out, no matter what. I stood out there for a minute and then realized that I've had four beers and hadn't visited the men's room. I had to go in a really bad way. I couldn't hold it any longer. I quickly walked into the men's room and relieved myself. I looked around the room and was happy to see that I was alone. I washed my hands, looked into the mirror and wasn't impressed with the reflection. Plain and average came to mind. I think I looked stuffy—a guy who didn't like to take too many chances. I shook my head and told that somewhat stranger in the mirror, you can do it, you can ask her out. I looked in the mirror and started to rehearse what I should say...

"Ah, Nora, I was wondering, if you don't have anything to do next week, then maybe you would like to go out for dinner?" No, that's not good enough, I told myself. Glancing in the mirror, I said with a little more attitude, "Nora, why don't we get together next week and have dinner. We'll catch up." Yes, I told myself, that was better. I looked around the room again, to make sure that there was no one looking at me and said to the mirror in my best James Bond voice, "Nora, babe. What's up? How about you and I, dinner tonight, and then we can make some beautiful music together." I was pointing to the mirror while I was saying it. This guy came walking in, in the middle of my little rehearsal and gave me a strange look. I ran out of the men's room with my head down.

I quickly walked back to the bar, forgetting about Nora leaving so soon and looked around. She was nowhere to be seen. They must have left. My heart was pounding as I walked over to the dance floor, then our booth, and then the front door. I saw Brian ordering another beer. I walked over and asked, "Are Nora and Paige out of the women's room yet?"

"Where the hell have you been Nilsen? They waited around to say good-bye, but it got to be too late and they really had to go. Nora asked me to say good bye to you."

My heart sank. Great, did I do it again?

Chapter IV

"Don't tell me you didn't ask her out! What were the two of you talking about while you were attempting to dance?" Brian said as he shook his head. I got the small dig about my dancing and I could detect frustration in his voice.

"We were just talking, I guess. I was trying to work up my way to ask her out but the song ended so quickly, and then she and Paige ran into the restroom." Brian had turned toward the bar and was paying for the beers halfway through my sentence. I figured he'd probably heard of all of my lame excuses and was becoming tired of them. He motioned for me to come with him, and we walked over to a little opening in the crowded bar. As the night was progressing, more people were filling up the place.

"Brian, I've had a really bad day. I was late for work."

"So?" He had a puzzled look on his face, "And your point?"

I shook my head and took a sip of the crappy domestic beer Brian had just bought.

"You know, Jens, lately I've been worried about you. I can remember a few years ago, when we first met, you were always cracking these cheesy jokes and you always had a stupid smile." He winked and smiled a bit—he had a habit of winking when he had a few beers. I smiled back at him and wondered what he meant. He was kidding, right? Somehow, I could tell though, that deep down he meant it. "You just don't seem to have fun anymore. You just seem like you're going through the motions. What's wrong?"

I was just about ready to pour out all of my feelings and emotions I'd experienced that day, but managed to squeak out, "I don't know. I just seem to be in a funk lately."

I couldn't help but feel how lucky I was to have a roommate like Brian. On the surface it appeared that we had nothing in common. He is an Irish Catholic, I'm a Norwegian Lutheran; he is from Wisconsin, a Badger fan, and worst of all a

Packers fan. I'm from Minnesota, a Gopher fan, and a Vikings fan. If that wasn't bad enough, he's a lawyer, and a damn good one. He has a very good sense of style and taste, and the women go crazy for him. Charisma oozes from every pore. He had a great personality too, the kind were everybody wanted to be around him. He was a fun guy. He had an air of success and confidence. I, on the other hand, had a hard time putting clothes together, and my hair was always messy. Women don't notice I exist. I feel an air of insecurity and failure follows me around.

When we go places together and just happen to be in the company of women, or we just walk by them, they always give Brian a second look, never me. He is tall, at about six-feet-four inches, and has sparkling dark green eyes and wavy, thick dark hair. His cheeks and chin have a hint of a Celtic look with a rugged, chiseled quality. I, on the over hand, mostly had bad hair days. I'd wake up and my hair was always greasy. Rarely did I have days when my hair looked good. The clothes I wear just hang on me. They always look rumpled and sad like a street person wearing the same clothes for weeks on end. I'm about six feet tall and have light brown hair and blue eyes.

We met at a mutual friend's party. A whole bunch of guys were standing around talking about music. The conversation was turning to various rock and roll bands, genres of music, and a variety of musicians. There was this tall guy telling us that the best song on the Rolling Stones *Goats Head Soup* album was *Wild Horses*. Well, as we all know, that song is on the *Sticky Fingers* album. I had to straighten this guy out. I had to admit that he gave a compelling argument of why he was right and had the whole crowd on his side. It finally took the owner of the house to find those two albums from his record collection and straighten everything out. Brian admitted he was wrong and we started talking more about music. We liked all the same bands. We just sort of clicked that night. We also have the love of history in common. We would spend many late nights discussing the ramifications of various events in history.

Brian McGinnis was born in Milwaukee and had gone to law school at the University of Minnesota. He had just gotten a position in a big time law firm in downtown Minneapolis. I was working as a real estate appraiser, and my office was in a large office park in Bloomington. I was finally moving out of my parent's house—I couldn't afford to live in an apartment on the starting pay of an appraiser—and was looking for a roommate. We found a charming old apartment overlooking the shores of Lake Harriet in south Minneapolis. The rent was expensive, but Brian convinced me that in the long run it would be worth it.

Our conversation was waning a bit. I thought it was a great chance to ask Brian something that was gnawing at me. I said out of the blue, "Brian, are you happy? When you get up every morning and you look at yourself in the mirror, do you say—Damn, I'm happy today. Do you say: 'I love my career, my girlfriend, and my life'?"

"Well," he looked at me strangely like I had just asked him the most personal and embarrassing question anyone had ever asked anybody. "I guess so, yeah sure... yes. I guess you could say I'm happy. If you mean if I have a fulfilling and exciting career and if I have a girlfriend that I really care about and one day may marry. Then yes, I am happy. Why do you ask, Jens?"

I shrugged my shoulders, and said: "I don't know, just curious, I guess." I felt a little embarrassed. I didn't think that was the reaction I wanted to hear from him. Damn, so I guess he really was happy. I guess that there really are people who can look themselves in the mirror and say that. I wasn't about to tell him about the feelings of sheer hopelessness I had today at work.

"Come on, Jens, what's going on in that quiet and deep mind of yours? What's eating you tonight?" I sighed and thought—what the hell? So I told him the events of the day, starting with why I stayed up so late last night, how I was late to work, my discussions with Norm, etc. When I was finished I looked at Brian's reaction. He appeared quite sincere.

"So that is why I asked you if you were happy, because I know for sure I'm not."

The waiter interrupted us and asked if we would like anything else. I looked at my watch; it was already 8:30. I asked for a pitcher of water. We would be driving in an hour or so, so we decided to stop drinking the brewskis.

"Okay, Jens, if you really want to know, I don't think I'm happy. It's more like contentment. I'm content that I have a good job; I have Paige and so on. I think you can't classify happiness as a condition. It's more like an event. I'm happy for a short period of time and then the next day, reality sets in and I'm content. Do you understand what I'm trying to say?" I nodded. "I was told ever since I was a small boy that I was going to be a lawyer. My father is a lawyer, my uncle is a lawyer, and my brother and sister are lawyers. I didn't think I had much choice in the matter. I majored in political science in college, like my brother and sister, and got good grades. So law school was just the next logical step. Now I can probably think of five other things that would interest me, but the chips were all in the favor of being a lawyer."

"What did you really want to do?"

Brian smiled. "The Milwaukee Brewers' baseball radio play-by-play announcer."

"Cool," I said.

"I know. But I just didn't have the balls to stand up against my family," Brian replied. "So now I'm content being a lawyer."

"My dilemma, Brian, is that I have a real problem making a good decision. Sure, I can make up my mind on everyday decisions on what clothes to wear, what to eat and all that. It's just the really big decisions like a choice of career, or what school to go to or what girl to go out with. Those big decisions are the ones that I always seem to get wrong. Like I was thinking today at my desk, what happens if you choose your career and spend a lot of time and money on achieving that career? So you get that job and everything is fine and dandy, for awhile. Then one day you wake up and think, oh my god, what have I done? You can't stand your job or the people you work with. But by then you're married, have two kids, a mortgage, a couple of car payments and have to go on an expensive winter vacation every year to try to impress your neighbors and co-workers. You wake up and find out you're stuck and you've dug a hole so deep you can never crawl out of! Then what do you do?"

"You die!" Brian said half laughing and half realizing a bit of truth to my statement. "Welcome to the American way of life."

"You got that right." I said, relieved that I finally got that chain of thought out of me. It might have taken me a few years to realize this.

"You know what though, Jens? You're a lucky guy."

"How's that?"

"Because you have realized the realities and tragedies of the human condition and you're only twenty-eight years old. You don't have a wife, kids, mortgage and all the other things, so you won't fall into that trap."

I shook my head and smiled. "You've got to love that Irish optimism."

Brian smiled, gave me a wink, and then looked at his watch and said, "It's time to go. I've got to get over to Paige's place."

I was happy Brian was staying over at Paige's place. I wanted to get back to the apartment, put some sweat clothes on and relax. Sometimes I wondered why the two of them didn't find a place together. I know that they're both extremely religious and wouldn't think of moving in together unless they were married, but they still spent about two nights a week together. They're keeping up appearances, but fooling no one.

•

I woke up the next morning, groggy and feeling sorry for myself. I looked at the alarm clock; it was 11:00 a.m. I walked into the front sunroom of the apartment and sat down in my favorite reading chair and gazed out over Lake Harriet. My apartment was like so many others in south Minneapolis, a three-story walk-up, built in the 1920s with a spectacularly, overpriced view of the lake. The place smelled old and musty; it reminded me of the smells in my great aunt's house—old and orderly. Everything had its correct place—its own symmetry. The ancient and uneven hardwood floors would creak every time you walked on them—burglars beware.

The sunroom, with a row of windows, occupied the front portion of the apartment, with the living room, dining room and kitchen taking up the middle. In the rear were two bedrooms and a bathroom—complete with claw tub. The rent included a one-car garage, which Brian snatched up, along with the larger of the two bedrooms. In return, I got exclusive rights to the sunroom, which I turned into my den. I had no problem waking up at two a.m., walking out in my bathrobe, braving minus twenty degree weather in the dead winter and warming up my car so it would start in the morning. It was a small price to pay for my den. I loved the whole concept of a den, a place where I could have quiet and be alone with my book collection. I have an old desk and an old reading chair. Completing the room, I have a cabinet that holds my map library. I can hardly move around in this little space, but it's best to have everything in one room.

I grew up reading and collecting books. My father loved to read and had a vast collection. Every other Saturday morning we hit the used book circuit and sought out that special edition of a book or tried to complete a collection of an author's life's work. I love to read classics. My den is my refuge from a rough day at the office, where I can immerse myself in inquiry. I love reading an adventure novel with an open atlas by my side, following along all the exotic places described in the book.

In my cluttered den, I have five bookcases of various heights, all full of books and occupying the entire windowless wall. I call it *The Kingdom of Spirits* after the book collection of the poet Karl Weismann, in Rølvaag's novel *The Boat of Longing*. Some days, when I'm sitting in my chair, I just glance up at all those books, full of so many tales of the human condition. They're trying to explain why we exist. Some days, I'm almost overwhelmed thinking about it.

I also have a series of framed prints hanging in my den's limited wall space. There are eight prints in various sizes by the Norwegian painter, Edvard Munch. They're part of what he called *The Frieze of Life.* He said: 'No longer shall I paint interiors with men reading and women knitting. I will paint living people who breathe and feel and suffer and love.' What I like about him is that he tried to capture on the canvas some kind of emotion. My favorite print is called *Evening on Karl Johan's Street*. It sends chills down my spine every time I look at it. I'm overwhelmed by the bleakness of the painting and the walking skeletal masses with blank stares strolling in unison down the sidewalk. They're dressed in drab clothes, half dead in their predictable lives. I remember Munch also said, 'For as long as I can remember I have suffered from a deep feeling of anxiety which I have tried to express in my art. Without anxiety and illness I should have been like a ship without a rudder.' Are you starting to understand what it's like to be Norwegian yet?

So I sat in my lonely reading chair staring out at Lake Harriet. The clouds had rolled in, and it had become a dreary and dark, overcast day—kind of like how I was feeling. I could see rain coming out in the distance. Brian was at Paige's house and probably wouldn't be back until late evening. I started to reassess, in my mind, all the decisions I had made and why so many of them were poor. But, as Brian had said, I was just twenty-eight years old. I did have my whole life in front of me. I knew I had to start making major changes.

Chapter V

I have always wondered what it would be like to celebrate the Fourth of July from an immigrant's point of view. I recall my mother telling me the story of my Great Grandfather Jens' routine of every morning, rain or shine, raising the American flag up a flagpole on his farm and briefly standing at attention. I think he was grateful for all the freedom and opportunities he had in this country which he never would have had living in the old country in the latter half of the nineteenth century. I think my dad felt the same way, he just never showed it. After his father and brother were murdered by the Nazis, his remaining family had nothing. The Nazis, in retaliation for their close relationship to the resistance movement, burned down their house, took away the deed to their property, and destroyed their car. The only option left for my father, uncle, and grandmother was to come to America, start a new life and try to forget the past.

My childhood was very uneventful. I remember that my family was never too poor or too rich. I was never too dumb or too smart. I went out for sports, but I was never a star. I never fumbled the ball in football, but I never scored a touchdown either. I was never picked first at a pick-up game in the neighborhood park and I was never picked last. I hung around a somewhat popular crowd, but I was never the most popular. I was part of the vast suburban landscape—like camouflage, you had to look hard to find me.

When my dad emigrated a few years after World War II, it was a time when everyone had to look, act and sound the same. Everyone wanted to be American. They all wanted to shed their ethnic idiosyncrasies and become true blue American patriots. My father, however, never shed his singsong accent and stayed very Norwegian.

I pulled up next to my dad's 1985 *Riviera* convertible in his driveway. I was at my parents to celebrate the Nilsen's annual

Fourth of July picnic. We have a barbeque on the backyard deck, and then watch the fireworks. It's a twenty-five year tradition.

We spent a pleasant couple of hours eating and talking over Norwegian traditions, and then walked out onto the deck, waiting for the fireworks at the nearby park to begin. At one point, my sister Sigrid looked at me. I had been unusually quiet all day and I think she detected the funk I had been experiencing lately. She was thinking about something. "You know Jens. There's this old Norsky at the nursing home. Everyone is afraid of him. He's in a wheelchair and just mumbles to himself in Norwegian. He doesn't speak English, and the nurses have the hardest time with him. He curses and throws food at them. He's just an old cantankerous coot."

"That's very interesting, Sigrid," I said. "Why are you telling me this?"

"Because, I thought that maybe you could come over and visit him. You speak Norwegian. Maybe the two of you could get together and shoot the breeze."

I took a deep breath and thought to myself, why in the world would I want to waste my time with some old cantankerous Norsky who would swear at me in Norwegian? "What's his name?" was all I could muster to say.

"Torbjørn Ruud," Sigrid said. "And watch out. He's a real pistol."

Just then the first fireworks exploded overhead. I turned to Sigrid, who was looking up at the fireworks and said, "I'll think about it." Without turning her head she said, "Good. I'll set up a visit with him next week."

•

The next week was fairly mundane. I inspected a few houses each day. On Saturday morning, I got up early and jogged around lakes Harriet and Calhoun. I was just about ready to dive into a Desmond Bagley novel when the phone rang. It was my sister Sigrid, who told me she had set up a visit with Torbjørn at 10:30. I tried to think of any excuse not to go, but failed. I said I'd be there. The nursing home is in an older neighborhood a few miles south of downtown. The morning was clear and bright, and I could tell it was going to be a hot early July day. I parked my car on the wide boulevard and strolled into the lobby, walked into a waiting elevator and pushed the button for the sixth floor. I'd only been in the nursing home a couple of times to visit Sigrid. I hated this place. I hated the smell that permeated it. I couldn't stand being around all those old, feeble, lonely people waiting to die. I hated that a lot of those good, decent, hard-working people got shuffled off to this nursing home and many of them went through their entire life savings in a matter of a few years to stay at this expensive resort. I admired my sister, though, for being able to work with them.

The elevator door opened and I headed for the nurse's station in the middle of a large lounge and cafeteria. I passed various blue blooded, white-haired corpses in assorted stages of death. The more alert ones followed me with their eyes. Some smiled and mumbled things under their breath. I had to walk around a woman who had to be in her late nineties. She was mumbling in a low toothless voice: "Mama? Mama? Where are you Mama?"

"I'm looking for Mr. Ruud, please," I said to the old battle-axe nurse who was standing behind the desk. She had a stare that could make General Patton shake in his boots. In fact, she was built like a Patton Tank, with large round shoulders and a square jaw and stubby fingers sticking out of tree trunk arms.

"And who might you be? A relative or a friend?" she said, as she became very interested in me all of a sudden.

"Neither," I said, as the nurse frowned and looked a bit puzzled. "I'm Sigrid Nilsen's brother, Jens. Sigrid thought that I should come down and visit with him."

The nurse smiled and had a glow in her eyes as if to say, 'Fat chance you'll get anywhere with that grouch.' She said in a quiet voice, "You know he doesn't speak a stitch of English."

"I know. That's what Sigrid said. I can speak Norwegian."

"Oh really? Well, what do you know," she turned and started to walk toward the side hall. She motioned with her arm for me to follow her. We walked down to the end of the hall where there was a large window looking out over the busy street below. Next to the window was an old man in his eighties, sitting in a wheelchair with a blanket wrapped around the lower part of his body. My first impression was of a pathetic, lonely and bitter man. He had a big round face with white, thick eyebrows and a mostly bald head with a little white hair around the edges. His blue eyes were glazed over as he watched all the activity down on the street. His mouth looked like it was stuck in a permanent scowl. I couldn't tell if he was angry or just constipated. He wore an old plaid shirt that was buttoned to the top. His pants were held up by red suspenders.

The nurse tried to get his attention. Either he was far off in some distant memory or he was just ignoring her. She grabbed his shoulders and started to shake him.

"Torbjørn? Torbjørn, are you all there? I've got a visitor for you today," she said, in an overly loud and obnoxious voice. She ceased shaking him and pointed toward me. He had a puzzled look on his face and then he turned and looked at me. A flash of fear ran through his eyes, like he had just seen a ghost.

"This is Mr. Nilsen, Sigrid Nilsen's brother. Do you remember Sigrid telling you that you would have a visitor today?" The nurse said slowly and again, too loudly. Mr. Ruud had a puzzled look on his face and then he raised an arm and pointed down the hallway. He then pointed to his eyes. "I think he wants his eyeglasses," the nurse said. "Could you wheel Mr. Ruud down to his room and give him his eyeglasses?"

"Sure. No problem," I said, as I grabbed the handles behind the wheelchair and started pushing him slowly down the hallway.

"Good luck, Mr. Nilsen," the nurse said as she started off in the direction of the nurse's station. I could have sworn that she said, "Because you're going to need it," under her breath as she turned and walked away.

There were a few awkward moments as I pushed him down the long hallway. I had no idea where his room was, so every time I came to a door I slowed way down. When we were about to pass the fifth door, I heard Mr. Ruud grunt. I stopped, and he pointed into the room. The room was small and stuffy and it had a smell you had to try to get used to, if you know what I mean. It reeked of old things. On top of his dresser he had, like many old-time Norwegians, a small shrine that reminded him of the 'old country.' It consisted of a small Norwegian flag on a thin wood pole, Luther's large catechism—in Norwegian, of course—an old black and white photo of an old couple—whom I assumed were his parents, an old photo of a house sitting next to the ocean, and a portrait of King Olav V.

Mr. Ruud pointed to the top of a nightstand where his reading glasses lay. I grabbed them and gave them to him. He quickly put them on and started to examine me from head to toe. After half a minute, he took off his glasses and gave out a big sigh of relief. I evidently wasn't the person whom he thought I was. He composed himself and then, using his arms, wheeled himself over to the small window.

"*Hvorden ha du det Herr Rudd. Jeg heter* Jens Olav Nilsen." I introduced myself to him in Norwegian. The only response I got from him was another grunt. He turned toward the nightstand and lifted a lid to an ancient record player. He turned it on and put down the needle to the first song on the old record. He then turned to look out the window and had a glazed-over look in his eyes. He was far off somewhere in time or space. He acted as if I wasn't even there. I just stood there, mesmerized by the scene that was unfolding. After the song played for awhile, I recognized it. It was the old and melancholy song called *Vandringsmenn Synger* or the Wandering Singer. I liked the sadness and loneliness projected from the singer's voice and also the harmony. After it was finished, Mr. Ruud woke up from his little daydream and played the song again.

After the third time hearing the song, I felt that this was getting ridiculous. I walked over to and turned down the volume so we could have a little talk. For some reason, I've always enjoyed talking to older men. I think it's because I really never had a grandfather that I knew. Older people lived through a lot of history and had a lifetime of accumulated wisdom.

I think he was surprised that I was still in his room. I opened up the bag that I had been carrying and said, "I thought you might like to have some *lefse* and herring later on. I'll just put them on your dresser." I had stopped at a Scandinavian deli on the way, thinking some Norwegian food might make him happy. He looked at the food. I think he didn't know how to react to an act of kindness. He just stared and didn't say anything.

"Where in Norway where you born?" I asked hoping to break the ice by asking questions. He just looked at me like I was from Mars. I bravely continued, "My father was born in Brunkeberg, Telemark and came over here after the war." I think I detected a little glimmer in his eyes when I said Telemark. It looked like he was about to say something, but then thought better of it. "My mom's granddad was born near Arendal." Torbjørn gave me another stare. I could tell I wasn't getting anywhere so I said, "Well, I guess I'll see you next week when you're in a better mood." I got up and started for the door. As I was walking out, I heard a faint voice.

"I don't suppose you could get a little butter and maybe some sugar for the *lefse*?"

I went to the kitchen and got a slab of butter, a knife and sugar. When I got back, we both had three pieces of *lefse*. He told me he hadn't had *lefse* since last Christmas.

"I was born in Skien, Telemark. That's the city where Henrik Ibsen was born. Did you know that?" he asked. I nodded my head.

"Have you read any of his plays?"

"Yes I have," I said.

"What's your favorite play?"

"I think I like *Ghosts* and *When the Dead Wake* the best," I replied.

"Ah, good choices. My favorite is *The Lady from the Sea*." He took a bite from his *lefse,* looked up at the ceiling, adjusted himself in his wheelchair and said, "When I was ten years old my family moved from Skien to the coastal town of Brevik on the *Langesunds Fjorden*. My father was a fisherman and a farmer. He would be gone half the year fishing in the North Sea, catching cod by the ton. Then the other half he would try to plant some crops on that rock of a farm we lived on. By the time I was eighteen my older brother Odd and me went off to sea to help our parents pay the bills. So for five years Odd and I sailed from Europe to America to Asia on a bunch of tramp steamers."

I told Torbjørn about my great grandfather Jens going to sea in 1862 and how he had sailed all seven seas. He appeared to be interested in my story, but I could tell that he was getting sleepy. He would close his eyes for a few seconds and then suddenly wake up with a snap of his head. Nurse Thorson came into the room and was amazed that I was still there and even more amazed that Torbjørn wasn't being cantankerous. She smiled and said, "Torbjørn, time for your pill and nap."

I looked over at Torbjørn. As he realized the nurse was in the room, he immediately became belligerent and started complaining. I got up and told him I'd see him next week. He looked at me and gave me a subtle nod as I walked out of the room.

As I was waiting for the elevator door to open, I heard this hoarse, lonely old voice say: "Sir? You there. Sir? Yes, you there. Say sir, have you seen my mother?" I could see from the corner of my eyes a ninety-plus year old woman in a wheelchair creeping over to me. The elevator door opened, I turned to her and said as politely as possible, "No Ma'am, I'm afraid I haven't."

Chapter VI

I decided to call Nora on Tuesday night and ask her out. You would think that by the time you were in your late twenties, calling women to go out would be fairly routine. Well, not in my case. For one, I hate talking on the telephone. It was getting to be about seven p.m. and I hadn't rallied up enough guts yet to call her. Finally I dialed. As I heard the phone ring I prayed to God that Paige wouldn't be at the other end. It rang a few more times; I thought the message might go on when all of a sudden I heard Nora's voice.

"Hell ... Hell ... hello, Nor ... Nor ... Nora?"

"Yes?"

"Ah, this is Jens Nilsen calling."

I heard her chuckle and then said, "Oh I'm glad you gave your last name because I know so many Jens." Oh, my God, I thought to myself. How stupid was that? Uncomfortable pause.

"Yes Jens? Did you want something?"

Okay, here I go, "Ah ... yes, I was just wondering if you'd be interested in going out to dinner on Saturday night?"

"Oh, I'm sorry I can't." Oh my God, I thought, this couldn't be happening.

"My old college roommate is coming into town on Saturday and I promised her that I would take her out. We haven't seen each other for over two years."

"Oh ... I see. Well ... Okay, I was just wondering."

"Jens?"

"Yes Nora?" I said dejectedly.

"I can go out on Sunday night, if that's okay?" YES!

"Yeah, that will work. Great. How about I pick you up around seven-thirty?"

"That would be fine. I'll look forward to seeing you."

"So will I. Well, I guess I'll see you later. Good-bye."

"Good-bye Jens."

•

When Saturday morning finally rolled around, I went jogging around the lakes and visited Torbjørn. This time, instead of taking food, I brought along an old record called *Songs of the Norwegian Fjords*. I knew how much he enjoyed listening to that one song, so I decided to bring this old record of my grandfather's. There were two songs I especially enjoyed, *Hils Til Dem Derhjemme—Give My Love to Those at Home*—and *Barndomshjemmet—My Childhood Home*. There was something mysterious and sad in the artist's voice that haunted me. Sure they were sentimental, but they had another quality to them which is hard to explain. Somehow, I felt closer to my grandfather every time I listened to those songs. I remember what my cousin Mickey said about our dads that really stuck with me. He said that immigrants, like our dads, never really fit into American society. They had thick accents and strange traditions. If they had gone back to the 'old country,' the Norwegians would call them Americans, because they would have picked up Americanisms and lost some of their native tongue. So our dads, like so many other immigrants, never really felt that they fit in anywhere. I thought Torbjørn felt the same way.

When I got to the nursing home, Torbjørn had already finished his lunch and was waiting for me near the elevator. He was very curious about the old record and pointed immediately to his room. I pushed him to his room and put on the record. A smile enveloped his face when he heard the music. I knew he was in a far away time and place, perhaps Skien, or on the North Sea. I saw a single teardrop roll down one of his cheeks and I quickly looked away. I didn't want to embarrass him.

After listening to both sides of the record, Torbjørn gave a big sigh and said in Norwegian, "When I was a young man in Norway, I grew up on the coast." A warm smile came over his face. "My father was a fisherman in the winter and a farmer in the summer. But the land we lived on was a bunch of rocks, don't you know? We couldn't grow a thing, so me and my older brother Odd went to sea to help Mama and Papa pay the bills." I didn't want to tell him that he had already told me this last Saturday. I asked him what year he went to sea to get some indication of how old he was. He vaguely alluded to the beginning of World War One, so I concluded that he was born around the turn of the century and was on the wrong side of his eighties. More old songs were playing on his ancient record player and Torbjørn became quiet and melancholy.

After an hour or so I could see that Torbjørn's eyelids were heavy and he was having a hard time keeping them open. I thought my visit was about over, when out of the blue Torbjørn asked me what I was doing tomorrow. I was taken aback and told him that I wasn't doing anything during the day. Then it hit me. Every July, there was a picnic and festival in Minnehaha Park called Norway Day.

"Do you want to go to Norway Day tomorrow?" I asked, quite surprised at myself. He looked at me strangely, and his face was kind of contorted. Then a wide grin appeared on his face and there was a genuine twinkle in his bright blue eyes.

"You see," he began, "I don't get around much, on account of my leg." He pointed down to the blanket that was always wrapped around the lower half of his body. He lifted the blanket up to reveal that his left leg was missing below the knee. I tried not to show my astonishment. I was so busy worrying about his temperament that I didn't think about what was under that blanket. I was about to ask him how he lost his leg, but thought better of it, he would probably tell me in his own time.

"I would consider it an honor to take you to Norway Day tomorrow," I said. "I'll pick you up around nine so we can get to the outdoor church service that starts at ten."

"Church service!" Torbjørn said, quite alarmed. "Why the hell do I want to go to an outdoor church service? I haven't gone to a church service in over thirty years!"

"It's in Norwegian," I said, surprised at his outburst. "Won't it remind you of the old days in Norway?" He frowned, and I could see that he really didn't want to go to the service, but I think he felt he better appease me. After all, I was taking him there. After a few seconds of deep thought he nodded his head in agreement.

•

Arriving early the next morning at the nursing home, I was surprised to see Torbjørn dressed and ready to go. I had no clue on how often he got to leave the home; however, judging from his enthusiastic disposition, I figured it was hardly at all. He reminded me of how excited I used to get as a child, opening gifts on Christmas Eve. The anticipation, the waiting for the grown-ups to wash the dishes after a wonderful meal of *lutefisk*, mashed potatoes and meatballs, *lefse*, and fruit soup. Then we had to all gather around the piano in the living room and sing hymns and carols. I would always wish that we would only sing the first verse of all the carols, but inevitably, we would sing all of them. Then and only then did we sit around the Christmas tree and get the chance to rip open our presents. I look back now and wonder if I could ever re-create that feeling.

I signed Torbjørn out at the main nurse's station and wheeled him to the elevator. As the automatic doors in the lobby opened, bright sunshine invaded Torbjørn's pale cheeks. He brought his hands up to his face to shield his eyes from the intense rays. I looked at the sky and noticed it was going to be a perfect summer day. I imagined Torbjørn must have felt like he was escaping a prison cell, because his face was beaming like a little leaguer hitting his first home run. I felt a little awkward picking him up and placing him in the front seat of the car, but things went fairly well. I put his wheelchair in the trunk and in no time we were off.

Suddenly a large, older model sedan turned in front of us. I had to slam on my brakes and swerve to avoid hitting it. I instinctively swore and looked over at that driver. It was a man who must have been in his 90s. He was probably driving to church, and appeared blissfully oblivious to anything around him. I had seen, out of the corner of my eye, Torbjørn's head almost hit the dashboard. Luckily he was wearing a seatbelt. He was steaming mad and blurted out, "You would think an old-timer like that would have the damn sense not to drive anymore!" Now it didn't shock me that he was upset over the incident, but what did shock me was that he had said it in English. Torbjørn immediately put his hand to his mouth when he saw my reaction.

"So Torbjørn", I said, "Is that some kind of far western Norwegian dialect that I'm not aware of? Or could it be you speak English just as well as I do?"

He sat there for a few seconds gazing out at the houses as we drove down the street. He turned and looked at me. "All right, the cat's out of the bag," he said with a mischievous twinkle in his eyes. I wondered to myself just how many secrets this mysterious man really had.

Torbjørn continued, "You see, I get so tired of listening to that old hag nurse. She's always complaining to me. She's worse than a nagging wife. I pretended that I don't know no English when I got to the nursing home so they would leave me alone. It's worked pretty well so far, don't you think?" I had to admit it was clever. "You mean, when they say all those bad things about you, you understand everything?"

"Everything," Torbjørn said, as he let out a little chuckle. We both laughed a bit as we went driving down one of the old broad avenues in south Minneapolis. "You have to promise me not to tell anybody about me speaking English. Let me have my little fun. I don't have much of it anymore," he said, as he got that far-off look again.

"What English?" I said as I smiled at him. "You old dog you," I said under my breath as we both started to laugh again.

•

When we got to Minnehaha Park, the benches around the main pavilion, where the outdoor service was going to take place, were already filling up. I parked the car fairly close by and wheeled Torbjørn to a nice shady spot just in time for the opening hymn. I grabbed a program and opened it to the service.

The first hymn was *Oh Master, Let Me Walk with You.* I gave Torbjørn the program so he could follow along and sing. His singing left something to be desired. He was singing so loudly that little children in front of us turned around and stared at him. I was getting a little embarrassed by the fourth verse when even middle-aged people were turning around trying to find out where the racket was coming from. Thank God that after this verse, the pastor went right into the confession and forgiveness of sins. I knew that this was supposed to be an ecumenical worship service, but it was Lutheran through and through. I guess majority rules.

From the church program, I learned that the minister was a Reverend Buslett, a pastor at the Norwegian Lutheran Memorial

Church, or *Mindekirken,* in south Minneapolis. Built in 1925, the church was founded by the Norwegian-American community in order to preserve the Norwegian language. During World War I there was an anti-ethnic movement and all the established Yankees were very suspicious of any foreign language being bantered about. As a result, the Norwegian churches were pressured to start having their worship services in English so the Norwegian-Americans would 'fit into' mainstream American society. To be fair, many second generation Norwegian-Americans also wanted English language services because their knowledge of the mother tongue was waning and they were becoming more Americanized. However, there were still some who resisted this movement, and so the Norwegian Lutheran Memorial Church was formed by stubborn Norwegians. The *Mindekirken* followed the Norwegian State Church liturgy. I had only been to the church a few times, the last being the *Syttende Mai* celebration a few years back. I always got a real good feeling walking into the church. I always felt a sense of connection to my ancestors and the past.

I started to think why I was so into my heritage. Most of the friends I'd grown up with were a mixture of nationalities and could have cared less where their grandparents came from. It just wasn't cool to hang around your family and ask questions about where your family was from and what their traditions were all about. I think I really got into my heritage because I wanted to be just a bit different.

Finally the sermon was over and all that was left was the benediction and final hymn. I think Torbjørn got a kick out of the service.

"Now what?" Torbjørn muttered as he rubbed his hands together and looked around the park.

"Well," I said as I was trying to remember how this festival was set up in the past. "I think there are arts and crafts over here and all the food is over there," as I pointed to a few small vendor and display booths.

"Excellent. What are you waiting for boy, push me over to the food!" Torbjørn and I both stuffed our faces full of *lefse, varmepolse*— a hot dog rapped in *lefse*—and *torsk*. I then wheeled him to the arts and crafts displays. He was particularly interested in the Ingebretsen's booth that had many books about

Norway for sale. He pointed to a book and told me he had known the man who wrote it.

"Who was he?" I inquired.

"Knut Haukelid. He was one of the heroes of Norway during the war and occupation. He helped sabotage the heavy water plant in Telemark."

"The heavy water that would have given Hitler the atomic bomb before the Americans?" I asked.

"You're damn right. He helped blow up the plant and the barge train that was transporting the heavy water to Germany. It derailed Hitler's whole atom bomb program."

"Let's buy it," I said, "I would like to learn more about the occupation during the war. My dad, uncle, and grandfather were all in the resistance movement in Telemark."

"I was in the movement, too. I went back to Norway after the occupation to help kick out those damn Germans." I bought the book and wheeled Torbjørn back toward the pavilion just in time for the *barnetog*—a kind of children's parade. Torbjørn became a little choked up when he saw all those little kids, some in *Norsk Bunder*— Norwegian folk costumes—marching up and down the aisles and waving little Norwegian and American flags. After the children's parade, the master of ceremonies started the program. The Norwegian Consul General gave a short speech, followed by a Norwegian-American U.S. congressman from Minnesota, followed by a few more local Norwegian-American politicians. The highlight was an all-male chorus group from Norway called *Berlevåg Mannsangforening*. There were about thirty gray-haired gentlemen wearing identical black suits with black bow ties and white sailor's hats. They started out singing a hypnotic tune called *På Sangens Vinger* and, after a few more tunes, they sang *Ailt E Stampa* and the audience almost brought down the place with a thunderous applause.

A local Norwegian-American folk band, complete with two accordion players, performed after the male chorus. They played old immigrant songs. After awhile, a few benches in the front of the pavilion were removed and some couples started to dance. Torbjørn was so moved by this that he turned and asked an elderly woman in a *Norsk Bunde*, who happened to be sitting next to us, if she would like to dance. She gave him a startled look and glanced down at his wheelchair.

"Don't worry, I won't bite," he said with a mischievous smile. He wheeled himself to the middle of the dance floor and the older woman followed him. He turned his wheelchair around and faced her. He raised his arms and grabbed hers. She started swinging her arms and her hips. Torbjørn had a huge grin on his face and started moving his arms around. It was a real sight, let me tell you. I didn't know whether to laugh or hide. The song appeared to go on forever, but finally it ended and most of the dancers started to sit down. The band started to play a lively tune. Two young, attractive women walked up to Torbjørn and started talking to him in Norwegian. They looked like they were college exchange students. I saw Torbjørn nod his head and then one of the women grabbed the back of his wheelchair and started moving him around like he was dancing while the other grabbed his hands in front of him and started to dance. They were making quite the scene and people started clapping and stomping their feet in a large circle around them. Torbjørn glanced over at me and gave me a smirk, and started to raise his eyebrows up and down. Boy, I thought to myself, some people get all the breaks. This ordeal lasted for two songs. When the second song was over, the two young women gave Torbjørn a kiss on the cheek and disappeared as quickly as they had appeared. I walked over to Torbjørn, shaking my head.

"Why weren't you out on the dance floor with those lovely ladies?" He asked me with a surprised look. I looked at him and didn't know what to say. "I guess you were out there stealing the show, and I didn't want to intrude on your dance number."

"I suppose you're right. It's hard to keep the young ladies away when you've got the charm and charisma I've got." He said with a hint of a wink.

Norway Day was beginning to wind down, and I could see by Torbjørn's face that he was getting tired. I wheeled him to my car and we took off toward the nursing home. On the way, he wanted to show me the old neighborhood where he used to live.

"Here, turn down this street... no, not that one... this one." He pointed toward Cedar Avenue and Washington Avenue. This area was known as *Snoos* Boulevard and was a neighborhood for many Scandinavian immigrants about one hundred years ago. He told me that when he first came to this country, he lived in an old rooming house with his brother Odd. We then drove by an old building that was being used by a plumbing supply company. He said that he worked at that building many years ago. It used to be a tavern and every night, after closing, he and his brother Odd swept the floors and cleaned the bathrooms. He started to reminisce about other buildings in the neighborhood. I subtly looked at my watch because I had a hot date with Nora and I didn't want to be late. As we turned toward the nursing home, Torbjørn told me about when he came to America. I was about to ask him if he could save the story until my visit next Saturday. His story, though, was so compelling that I forgot all about the time...

Chapter VII

I sat down on the little chair next to Torbjørn's bed and quickly looked at my watch. I hoped that his story would be short; time was ticking away and the last thing I wanted was to be late for my date with Nora. Torbjørn was wiggling in his bed and trying to get comfortable. I was just about to tell him that I really had to go when he asked me if I would be so kind as to get a thirsty old man a glass of water. I sighed and got up and quickly dashed into the bathroom and got him a drink. I sat down again and watched him slowly put the glass to his mouth and gulp down the water, making a dreadful noise. He drank the glass and then took a deep breath and cleared his throat.

"Okay, where were we?" he said as it looked like he had finally settled into the bed and was somewhat content. I was just opening my mouth and was going to steer him in the right direction when he said, "Oh yes ... I was going to tell you what happened once I jumped ship, so to speak, and came to this country." Torbjørn took a deep breath. He spoke in English, carefully choosing his words.

"I decided to come to America because my older brother, Odd, told me that jobs were plentiful here." He pointed to the ground, "He told me that if you worked real hard, stayed out of trouble, and saved your money, you could become rich. He also told me that I could make more money in one day in America than I could make in a week being a sailor. Odd had quit sailing a year before and came over to this country. He had a great job in Minneapolis with real potential and he had one waiting for me. After working ten years at sea and having hardly any money to show for it, I decided to take him up on his offer. When my sailing stint was over, I took the next available ship over to America."

"When was that?" I asked, hoping to pin down some more dates.

"Let me see... it must have been in the mid to late twenties. So, I landed at Ellis Island and journeyed to Minneapolis and met my brother there." Torbjørn stopped for a second, looked up at the ceiling, ran his hand through his white hair and continued. "When I saw my brother for the first time in a few years, I thought, what a sight. He looked like he had been sleeping in the gutter for a few days. He had greasy hair, tattered clothes, and at least a two-week beard. I tell you, he gave me such a fright."

"What happened to the great job he had lined up for you?" I asked becoming mildly interested in the story, although always keeping one eye on my watch.

"Well, the lazy bastard got drunk at a local tavern, don't you know. Odd had been drinking all day and that night when he went to work, his boss told him he wasn't sweeping up hard enough. Odd told him to go to hell. Well, the boss and two others threw Odd out on the street and told him never to come back. The kicker was that Odd lived in a little one room place above the tavern. His boss also threw out all of his belongings—which weren't much—and he had nowhere to go. Luckily, we were able to stay at the YMCA for a couple of weeks while looking for a job."

"Did you find anything?"

"In time, we found more work than we needed. You see, Odd had this friend named Tor Mikkelsen. This character thought he was a real tough customer. He had lived in Chicago before coming up to Minneapolis. Let's just say he hung around a lot of mobster types in Chicago. Mikkelsen thought that he could come up here, throw his weight around and control the town in no time. He saw how the Sicilian crowd controlled the underworld in Chicago, and thought to himself, why can't the Norwegian crowd control the underworld in Minneapolis?"

"The Norwegians? You have got to be kidding," I blurted out. The story was getting more interesting.

"You're God damn right, the Norwegians," Torbjørn said with a serious face. "Mikkelsen thought he could come up here, hire a few thugs and start controlling all of the Norwegian businesses. So Odd and me started to work for this Mikkelsen character and we started leaning on the smaller Norwegian businesses. We got caught up in it and worked a few years in the business until we could find legitimate jobs. Odd and me got tired of scaring the pants off of all those poor old Norwegian farmers and workers who couldn't rub two cents together."

I had to admit the thought of Sven and Ole walking around the streets of Minneapolis in the 1920s acting like gangsters was a bit too much for even my wild imagination. I could just see this Mikkelsen guy, acting like a Godfather, ordering his thugs to break kneecaps if the store owners didn't pay him extortion money. I had to see where this tall tale was going, so I egged him on.

"So how long were you a thug, I mean, working for Mikkelsen?"

"A couple of years. We earned enough to buy a small two-bedroom house in south Minneapolis. The job wasn't too bad. Sometimes things would get a little messy, some bones were broken and some skulls were cracked. All in all, it wasn't too bad. Nobody got hurt unless they behaved bad."

Just then a nurse walked in to check on Torbjørn. Without missing a beat, he switched to Norwegian.

"So you said you did this until you got your feet on the ground. What did you do after that?" I asked him in Norwegian.

He looked at the nurse, who was about to give him a pill and said, "Odd and me started a little grocery stand. We called it O T Grocery. Do you get it? O for Odd, T for me, and then grocery. It kind of rhymes in English."

I smiled and nodded to the nurse as she walked out. I turned to Torbjørn and said, "Where was this O T Grocery located?" If the place ever existed.

"It was in a small building just off *Snoos* Boulevard. It's torn down now. The freeway runs right through where it used to be," he said. He shook his head in and started cussing under his breath in Norwegian. "And they call that progress. Odd and me bought a second-hand flatbed Ford and, early every morning, we would drive out to an old Norsky's farm and get fresh milk, butter, eggs, vegetables, and the like, and bring it back to the city. We were known around town as the store with the freshest groceries." He then paused a bit and a big smile enveloped his face. I could see that it had been a happy period of his life. "But, don't you know, we started having a problem with that Mikkelsen character. We weren't going to take any crap from him."

"What did he try to do to you guys? Extort money from you? Did he try to run you out of town?" I was so into this story right now that he had me in his back pocket. Torbjørn also knew that he had me. He was totally in control. He smiled at me and glanced at his watch.

"Didn't you say you had a date with a young lady tonight?"

"What?" I asked, trying to get my thoughts out of the clouds from sixty years ago and back to the present. I glanced at my watch. It was seven o'clock and I had to pick up Nora in half an hour! "Oh, my!" I said. "You're right. I've got to go. Can we finish this next Saturday?"

Torbjørn smiled. "Go ahead, Jens. I've got nothing but time on my hands. By the way, I want to thank you for the day. I had a really good time." I dashed out of the nursing home, got into my car and sped off down the street. I was keeping one eye out for police cars and the other on the speedometer, trying not to get too carried away. I was wondering how I could get home, take a quick shower, and then make it to Nora's place in... I glanced at the clock on the dashboard... twenty-two minutes. I also couldn't get Torbjørn out of my mind. What was up with those stories, and why was he telling them to me? Was he just a lonely old man confessing his life story or did he have another purpose? One thing was clear—he was no fool and his mind was sharp. He had really pulled the wool over the eyes of everyone in the nursing home, even my sister.

•

At 7:55, I arrived at Nora's. I quickly parked my car and ran to her front door, trying to figure out a good excuse for being so late. I couldn't come up with any. I rang the doorbell and waited. It was quiet—too quiet—inside. All I could hear was the beating of my overly excited heart. I waited a few more moments and rang the doorbell again. Maybe she got upset waiting for me and took off somewhere with Paige. I nervously rang the doorbell a third time and then thought I should have waited a bit. If she is home, she now probably thinks I'm desperate. While I was waiting, I could see my reflection through the small front window on the door. I was shocked. What had happened? I knew I had to rush to take a shower and dry my hair, but this was ridiculous. My hair was so flat and geeky. I looked at my shirt and noticed I had buttoned it incorrectly. It was off by one. I started unbuttoning my shirt when the door opened and Nora was standing there.

"Hi. I thought you forgot about me. Come on in," she said with a smile. I heard myself starting to give excuses and apologies left and right when she interrupted and said it was no problem. She asked if I cared for a beer and led me to a chair in the living room.

"Sit down and make yourself comfortable. I'll be right back," she said as she headed for the kitchen. I plopped down on the chair and corrected the buttons on my shirt. I then gave out a big sigh of relief. I think it was a bit too loud because Nora asked "What was that?" from within the kitchen.

"Nothing," I said cursing myself again. I started to look around the room. The duplex was built in the 1930s and the living room had hardwood floors and an elegant fireplace. The place was large. It was in a very trendy neighborhood in south Minneapolis, about two blocks from Lake Calhoun. I knew the rent had to be expensive.

"Is this okay?" Nora said as she handed me a bottle of *Ringness*.

"Oh yes, it's perfect," I said a bit too enthusiastically. I took a long hard swallow of the beer as she walked over to a couch and sat down with a glass of red wine in her hand. I couldn't help but stare at her. She was wearing a comfortable sweater and skirt and had her dark golden hair pulled back into a ponytail. I was trying to think of something halfway intelligent to say, but my mind went blank. There were a few more moments of awkward silence, when all of a sudden she said, "So how was your day today, Jens?"

I took another quick swig of the Ringness and started to tell her about Torbjørn and Norway Day. She appeared mildly interested in what I was saying, and she asked sincere questions about Torbjørn and the nursing home. I had consumed the beer far too quickly and Nora got up and got me another. We talked a little more about Torbjørn, and then I asked her how her internship at a downtown law office was going. As she started to talk about her work, I happened to look at the time on the antique clock sitting on the fireplace mantle. "Is that the correct time?" I interrupted her in a bit of a panic.

"Well yes... last time I checked. Why?"

"We have dinner reservations in five minutes."

"Well, we better get going, then," Nora said in a matter-of-fact tone. I agreed and we rushed out the door. As we were driving to the restaurant, I wondered what kind of impression I was making on her so far. I didn't think it was a good one.

For some reason, I always take first dates to a place that is a bit out of character for me. Tonight was no exception. Although I like only a handful of seafood delicacies—my ancestors would be ashamed of me—I took Nora to Captain Nemo's. It has a reputation for having the best seafood in town. I love the place because it is so dark and mysterious. There is a small aquarium built into the wall of each booth and a large floor-to-ceiling aquarium in the center of the restaurant. I love the way the light flickers on the walls and floor from the reflection of the water in the aquariums. I also love the subtle music in the background.

Captain Nemo's is in an old flour mill building near the Mississippi River a few blocks from the Minneapolis central business district. The building blends in so well with the surrounding buildings that people have a hard time finding it. I guess the owners like it that way. We arrived at the restaurant a full half-hour late. The receptionist had given up our reservation and we had to wait an additional twenty minutes in the Chartroom Bar. We passed the time by sipping red wine and watching the lobsters being taken from a tank on the side of the bar. Nora and I ate dinner in a cozy booth, tucked away in the corner of the restaurant with the light flickering from the built-in aquarium. I was feeling a bit daring so I ordered a clam and octopus appetizer. I detected a bit of surprise on Nora's face and I even may have impressed her with my choice. Little did she know that that was one of the wildest foods I had ever ordered. We tried the appetizer, and I made a mental note to myself to never order it again. Nora ordered a French seafood dish and I, of course, had Torsk for my main entrée. We talked and enjoyed each other's company. The time went amazingly fast.

As we talked, I found it a bit ironic that we grew up about three and a half miles from each other, but never saw one another. We went to different schools, shopping centers, and churches; had different friends, etc.

"Did you go to the University of Minnesota, Jens?"

"Yes," I answered.

"Did you like going to such a large school?" she asked.

"In retrospect, no. I lived at home for over half the time to save money. It seemed like I commuted to school every day like going to a job, fighting rush hour traffic and all. I never really felt that 'college experience.' You went to St. Olaf, didn't you?"

"Yes, and I loved it. Half of my friends today are the friends I met there."

"That's where my hero, O.E. Rølvaag, taught and wrote books."

"That's right. Didn't he write *Giants of the Earth*?" she asked.

"Yes he did, but I think his masterpiece was *The Boat of Longing*, about a young Norwegian immigrating to Minneapolis at the turn of the century. The book was incomplete though, and I think Rølvaag was going to write a couple sequels to that book, but he died of heart failure in his mid fifties."

"Yes, it was so long ago. I think there's a small restaurant named after him off campus near St. Olaf," she said thoughtfully.

•

After dinner we walked along the Mississippi River Parkway, crossed the Hennepin Avenue Bridge to Nicollet Island and sat on a park bench with a beautiful view of St. Anthony Falls. The lights from downtown illuminated the river and the falls, and we both just took in the sight.

After a few moments, I turned towards Nora. "You know, I've been meaning to ask you, why are you so interested in France?"

She smiled and said, "I learned so much about France when I went to the University of Paris my junior year in college. You see, I have a French aunt; she's married to my dad's brother. He's in the Foreign Service, and I got to stay with them every summer when I was in high school. I then enrolled at the University of Paris my junior year in college."

"Wow, that's impressive. How many times have you been to Europe?"

"Let's see, I think, five times. Nope, wait, yes, there was the first time when I was ten and went with my family. Six times. How about you Jens? How many times have you been to Europe?"

I gulped hard and tried to think of some rational and practical reason why I, at twenty-eight years of age, had never been to Europe. I think my face was turning red and beads of sweat were forming on my forehead. "You know, I've never gotten around to getting there yet. My cousin and I were all set to go after I graduated from college, but I got this job offer, you see. I just couldn't pass it up and I thought that I would have plenty of time to get there, but you know, funny, I just haven't gotten there yet, but, I'm going there pretty soon..."

Nora smiled and I awkwardly put my arm around her shoulder and we both turned our heads toward each. I looked deeply into her dark blue eyes and we kissed. We then sat there for a couple of quite and peaceful moments until Nora said, "Nicollet Island reminds me so much of La Cité in Paris. You've got to go there, someday, Jens, it's wonderful." She turned to look at the illuminated falls again and said, thinking out loud, "You haven't lived until you've seen Paris." She then suddenly realized what she had said and turned to look at my face. "I'm sorry Jens, I wasn't thinking."

"That's quite all right. I believe you... You haven't lived until you have seen Paris... and a whole lot of other places in the world for that matter."

Chapter VIII

The next week was incredibly busy. I had more than enough appraisal assignments to keep me out of trouble. I felt a bit uncomfortable though, when I got back to the office in the afternoons after my inspections. The back of my head burned as though someone was staring at it. My cubicle is visible from Norm's office, and I could feel him judging me. I knew my monthly production was way down and my turn-around time had practically doubled. Norm couldn't figure out what was wrong.

I, of course, knew what was wrong. Nothing. Instead of my job consuming ninety percent of my time and my mind, I now had other interests. It was a relief to leave work and not bring it home and work late into the night. I much preferred a date with Nora or a visit with Torbjørn. The only things that suffered were my finances and a sure career track to mediocrity in lower middle management. I didn't care.

•

Nora and I had a date on Wednesday night, and I had my customary Saturday morning visit with Torbjørn. I decided to take Torbjørn down to the Mississippi River Parkway for a walk. It was such a beautiful day, and we had to take advantage of it. While I was pushing his wheelchair down the parkway, Torbjørn pointed out that under the Tenth Avenue Bridge was a shantytown called the Bohemian Flats. The neighborhood consisted of old, two-room shotgun shacks where many immigrants came to live over sixty years ago. It was right next to the Mississippi River and was prone to flood every other spring or so. By the early 1930s the city had torn down the entire shantytown in the name of urban renewal. I wheeled him over to a park bench almost underneath the bridge and I sat down. Torbjørn took a deep breath and continued his story.

"When Odd and me came to Minneapolis, we lived in a small old shack which we rented from a little old lady from Nordland. It was just about here." He looked up at the bridge and then pointed to a place about fifty feet from where we were sitting. "It was quite the dump, don't you know, but we couldn't afford anything nicer." I looked to where he was pointing and tried to imagine what this well manicured park must have looked like as an old shantytown sixty years ago. "Yes sir. I remember looking up at the bridge every time I would walk out of the house. I would often wonder if I would make it here in this country, like all the people up there on that bridge and above the bluffs in the nice neighborhoods."

"How long did you and your brother own that grocery store?" He looked at me and smiled with his bright eyes. He knew I was hooked and I think he enjoyed that a bit.

"Let's see now. I think it must have been at least five years. We started off with the vegetable stand and that got to be real good and busy. We got the reputation of having the freshest vegetables at a reasonable price. We worked hard and finally saved enough money to buy a small bungalow up on the bluff. Odd worked hard and got off the sauce, and things were going real good, see? Then we bought into the grocery store when the owner, Old Man Johansen, got sick and died."

"Did you have to worry about Mikkelsen and his goons?" I asked.

"Ja, for sure. That bastard Mikkelsen was around all right. He was scaring the pants off of the older folks and the green-eyed immigrants. He demanded a cut of all the businesses in the *Snoos* Boulevard area. When he came to us and demanded money, we told him to go fly a kite, if you know what I mean. Odd and me weren't afraid of him. We did, though, have to watch our backs. A couple of times he would send out his goons late at night and break our windows and tear down our doors and ransack the place. We would just repair the damage in the morning and act like nothing had happened. This would get Mikkelsen really steamed, if you know what I mean."

I nodded, and Torbjørn took a deep breath. I could see that he didn't want to go on with his story. Pain and sorrow swept his face. "It was about this time that I noticed a pretty little thing come around to buy our freshest food. She worked as a domestic for some high-brow Yankee family in Kenwood. Oh, Jens, I hope sometime in your life you'll get the same kind of feelings for a woman I got when I saw her come into the store! She was like a breath of sunshine brought down from heaven." He stopped for a moment and looked out at the expansive Mississippi River. We sat there quietly for a few minutes. I waited for his little reverie to pass and then asked him: "What was her name?"

"Ida... Ida Anderson. She was an American, you know. Her parents were born in the old country, but she was an American through and through. She was working as a domestic during the day and going to teacher's college at night. Well, time went by and one day when she was in the grocery store, I got the courage to ask her out for coffee. She declined, of course, and blushed. She said she would love to go out for coffee, but since she was still living at home, she had to have permission from her father. Ida told me that her father was a minister and the only way I could get permission to go out with her was to go to her father's church for Sunday worship service so he could get to know me. Now normally I wouldn't put up with that foolishness, but Ida was a real catch, see. So I agreed to go to her church next Sunday. That would be a bit tricky, though, because I hadn't been to church since I was a young boy in Norway. For personal reasons, God and me had parted ways. But getting cleaned up and going to church for an hour was a small price to pay for the companionship of Ida."

"I sat in the back row where all the bachelor men fell asleep during the sermons. Ida, of course, sat in the front row with her mother and other sisters. I don't think she even noticed I was there for the first couple of weeks, but her father sure did. He would give me dirty looks during his sermons when he was talking about sinners and drunkards. A few weeks later, I subtly worked my way up to the middle rows of the church. I even started to listen, a bit, to the sermons. I would also give as much as I could when the offering plate was passed around. After church there would always be coffee and donuts in the basement. Ida and me would slowly make our way to each other and have pleasant little chats, always under the watchful eyes of her father.

"After about six months of this, I finally got the courage to ask permission to take Ida out for coffee. He asked me what my intentions were with his daughter. I replied that I was a hard-working Norwegian who owned a small grocery store and my intentions with his daughter were honorable and pure. I also told him how I had strayed from the fold for the last couple of years, but since I learned so much from his sermons that I was now ready to accept Jesus Christ as my savior. I remember seeing a smug smile on his face, like he had won another one over to the cause. I don't know if he believed my lies, but maybe he was glad that I had to play this little game, or maybe he was happy to feed one less mouth every day. I don't know."

"Well to make a long story longer, after about a year and a half of courtship, Ida's old man finally agreed to marry us. We honeymooned at a small lodge on the north shore of Lake Superior." I sat back on the bench and took a deep breath. When I first met Torbjørn a few weeks ago, I thought he was a pathetic, lonely old man who had never meant anything to anybody—and here I find out he had a wife.

"Did you and Ida live in the same house you and Odd bought?" I asked.

Torbjørn looked at me, stretched and then yawned. "Boy, what time is it? I'm getting awfully tired and a little hungry. How about I stop this little story, and we can take it up again when we meet next Saturday?"

•

After work on the following Tuesday, I went for a casual run down the Mississippi River Parkway. The humidity made my run extremely difficult, and I had to dash home for a swift shower to get ready for my date with Nora. Our relationship was getting to the point of seeing each other twice a week. We tried to get together on Tuesdays or Thursdays, and one day on the weekend. Just as I was stepping out my door to drive over to Nora's place, I bumped into Paige coming to visit Brian. We exchanged polite conversation and then I walked down to my car. While I was driving to Nora's place, I got to thinking why Paige and I just didn't click. For the most part, we were polite and could tolerate each other, but we seemed to be worlds apart. I found it fascinating that Brian apparently saw something in her that I didn't. I've tried to figure out why she annoys me so much. Maybe it's the way she comes off as so 'with it.' She appears to be superficial, a down-right blue-blooded snob, and too deeply into high fashion and money for my taste.

When I got to Nora's place, she insisted on driving. She wanted to take me out on a French date extravaganza. We got into her Renault *Le Car* with the oval "F" sticker placed in the lower right portion of the back of her car. I liked that, because I had an oval "N" sticker on the back of my car. She took me to a little French haunt on Grand Avenue in St. Paul. The place was so *chic* that I was surprised they let me in. Nora ordered—in French, of course—some kind of veggie dish *de jour* for her that probably had five calories and some type of French beef dish for me. After we were done eating, I shot a glance around the restaurant to take in the ambience. I came to the conclusion that the place was a bit too intimidating for me. The restaurant was filled with well-dressed, cultured people. Some were even wearing French berets. I could hear witty banter and conversations about Voltaire, Camus, Sartre, and Balzac. I focused in on the table directly behind us. The group of two women and two men were smoking up a storm, drinking red wine from juice glasses and discussing scenes from one of Moliére's plays. I felt like interrupting their discussion, and asking them what they thought of the Vikings' chances of going to the Super Bowl this year, but thought better of it.

After dinner Nora drove us to the University of Minnesota Film Society and we watched some early 1960s French film with English subtitles directed by François Truffaunt. If I thought the people were intimidating at the French restaurant, this theater crowd was downright scary. I felt like I stuck out. My clothes were too square and too suburban for these urbane, sophisticated cats, and I wasn't wearing a scarf around my neck or thick rimmed glasses. The movie theater was ancient and damp, and there was the aroma of Turkish cigarette smoke permeating the air. I was happy when the lights went out and I could relax and start munching my popcorn.

We talked about the movie on our drive back to Nora's place. I fibbed, just a bit, about how much I enjoyed the film.

Nora explained certain subtle allegories and subplots about the movie that I hadn't noticed. I wondered if we had seen the same film. Oh well, I heard Orson Wells say once that you had to see a good movie at least three times to really get the meaning of it. I walked her to her door and gave her a long and lingering kiss under the porch light. She invited me in and I couldn't resist. We sat together on the couch in the living room, engaged in a pleasant conversation, shared some wine, and enjoyed being together. I ended up spending the night, and if I can steal a phase from Torbjørn, we had a wonderful time, 'if you know what I mean.'

In the morning, while I was driving home, I thought to myself that no matter what I did with that woman, I enjoyed it. No matter how pompous the restaurant or the film, I just took pleasure in being with her.

•

The next Saturday morning, I took Torbjørn to the same small park on Nicollet Island overlooking St. Anthony Falls that Nora and I enjoyed a few weeks ago. It was one of my favorite places in the Twin Cities. I loved the view of the river, the falls, and the Minneapolis skyline. I pushed Torbjørn's wheelchair down a sidewalk and gave him a full view of the Mississippi River. It was August, and even though it was early in the morning, I could tell it was going to be a scorcher. There were numerous joggers darting by us on the pathway. I watched the swift current flowing south. I spied an empty bench next to the river with an exquisite view. I pushed Torbjørn's wheelchair next to the bench and then I sat down. The sky was bright, clear and cloudless. There was a gentle breeze off the river that tenderly kissed our faces.

"Ah..." said Torbjørn in a relaxed voice. "Isn't this just wonderful, Jens?"

"You bet it is."

"The beauty of it all!" He said, with his hands waving in the air. He looked at me with his devilish grin and said, "You young folks just don't understand. You're always running around looking for something to do. You're always in a hurry. You never just sit back and take in the whole moment."

I didn't know where he was going with this, but I could tell he was in one of his talkative moods. I wanted him to continue his story about the 1930s and Ida. He sat there for a few minutes, taking in the scenery. I took a deep breath and then said, "So after Ida and you got married, did she move into your house?"

He looked at me for a few moments and then said, "So how did that evening go with that girl a few weeks ago?" I was taken aback. It was the first time he had asked something about my personal life. "You mean Nora?"

"Yes... Nora, Nora Janson, I believe. Is she a nice Norwegian girl?" He said as his eyes twinkled at me and he smiled again.

"She's half Norwegian and half Swedish."

"Oh, well, at least she's half perfect. Did you have a good time?"

"We had a great time. In fact we're seeing each other twice a week now."

"Good. Could she be the one, Jens?"

"Possibly. I enjoy being with her and I think about her everyday."

"You don't say! Well, I hope something good happens between you two." He was quiet for a few moments and then said, "So you want to know more about an old man's past, do you? An old man who has lost everyone he has ever cared about and now is all alone in this world." He said this almost under his breath as he looked out onto the river. We watched a barge slowly navigate down the river and into a lock.

"Ja, after me and Ida got hitched, we moved into the little two-bedroom bungalow. Odd had fallen into his bachelor ways many years before. The two of them couldn't stand living under the same roof, so I bought out Odd's half of the house and he moved out. Ida had the place looking like the Taj Mahal, if you know what I mean. Ja, we had a good life together, Ida and me. In a few years she got her teaching degree, and she started teaching grammar in the Minneapolis public schools." Suddenly a look of sorrow enveloped Torbjørn's face, and it appeared that he was deciding whether he should go on with his story. He looked up at the sun. The temperature was definitely rising. I thought he was thinking it was too hot, and that he wanted to go back to the nursing home, but he continued. "Our little grocery store continued to prosper, but Mikkelsen and his goons were coming by almost every day, poking around the place, and demanding we pay them protection money. We told him to go to hell. He retaliated by having his goons break more of our windows and even having them beat up some of our best customers. He was starting to hurt our business. We had to do something."

Torbjørn paused again and I think I detected his bloodshot eyes starting to water and then he said, "You see, Mikkelsen started parking his fancy car in front of the school where Ida taught. He would sit there in his car and wait for her to leave the building after school. He pretended to be a gentleman and bought her flowers and things and asked her out for supper. Ida, of course, just tried to ignore him, but he was persistent. Ida was a shy girl and she knew how upset I would be if I found out Mikkelsen was making a move on her. So, she never told me about Mikkelsen's shenanigans. I guess she figured Mikkelsen was trying to get back at me by bothering her, and she didn't want him to succeed."

"How long did he harass her?" I asked, getting angry myself about Mikkelsen.

"Oh, I heard it went on for about a year. It must have been just terrible for her."

"How did you hear that?" I asked.

"I heard from some of the boys I worked with when Odd and me were working for Mikkelsen. Some of those guys were okay, and we kept in touch with just a few. They also told me that he was getting too greedy and his territory was too large and he was stretching himself too thin. He was getting sloppy, drank too much of the hard stuff, and had a big mouth. You know the old saying, give a Norwegian a few drinks and he'll tell you everything you want to know. So anyway, one cold and snowy January night in 1934..." he paused, let out a deep sigh, and tears starting building up in his bloodshot eyes. "...it was cold, real cold you see, and Ida was walking out of the school on her way to the corner to get picked up by the streetcar. Mikkelsen was there of course, waiting for her; he had been drinking and was in a feisty mood, if you know what I mean. He slowly drove his car next to her on the sidewalk. She saw who it was and started walking fast toward the streetcar stop. Mikkelsen rolled down his window and yelled out, asking if she wanted to get into his nice, warm car. She ignored him and started walking even faster. He got real mad, you see, and drove the car up onto the sidewalk and cut her off. She had to stop quickly so the car wouldn't hit her. Mikkelsen quickly opened up the car door, got out and threw her into the front seat. He took off like a bat out of hell with one hand on the wheel and the other holding Ida down, as she was trying to get out of the car. He was like a madman, speeding down the street, slipping and sliding on the icy streets. Poor Ida was putting up a good fight, struggling with that monster while he was trying to make advances on her."

Torbjørn had such an utter look of sadness it was hard to look at him. Looking back at it now, I'm sure it was good for him to get this story out. It had probably been locked inside of him for more than fifty years. I was most likely the first to hear it in over half a century—or maybe ever. Torbjørn sighed again, dusted off more cobwebs in the basement of his mind, and went on.

"Ida was squirming back and forth while that bastard was touching her. He was going real fast down Hennepin Avenue. Somehow, Ida found the door knob with a free hand and opened it and then jumped out."

I looked at Torbjørn in shock and amazement and couldn't quite comprehend what he had just said. "You mean she jumped out of the car while it was speeding?"

"You're God damn right. She wasn't thinking clearly. She must have wanted to get away from that monster as quickly as possible."

"What happened, was she all right?"

Torbjørn wiped tears off his cheeks. His eyes were more bloodshot and his face was beet red. I could feel a tear running down my cheek as well. "The eyewitnesses said that the second she jumped, a streetcar coming from the opposite direction ran over her, dragging her more than a hundred yards to her death." He said. Sobs that had been trapped inside of him for so long came pouring out. I hugged him and started to cry, something I hadn't done since I was a small child.

Chapter IX

I drove Torbjørn back to the nursing home at about 4:30. His story had been so intriguing that the time had just flown by. I felt extremely guilty about coaxing him into telling me that story. I didn't realize that it was going to be so emotionally exhausting for him. When we got to the nursing home, I helped Torbjørn into his bed. He fell asleep almost immediately. I sat there staring at him for an hour or so. I was afraid to leave because I felt that something might happen. I looked at my watch and saw that it was 6:00. I had a date with Nora. I got up and walked over to the nurse's station and told the nurse on duty to please check on him regularly because he seemed weak today and not himself. She assured me that she would, and then I left. As I drove over to Nora's duplex, I couldn't get the image of Ida's death out of my mind. To think that shriveled up, insignificant old man that no one cared about could have had such an interesting and tragic life.

•

Nora and I went out for a quick bite to eat and then went to a mega-plex theater to see the latest blockbuster movie. Nora had to go out of town early the next morning on some business, so I dropped her off early and told her that I would call her when she got back on Sunday.

My apartment was quiet when I got home, Brian's door was shut. This meant Paige was spending the night at our apartment, and I was supposed to be quiet. I walked into the bathroom and brushed my teeth and then walked into my room and put on my pajamas. I went into the living room and noticed the phone message light was on. I pushed the button and heard my sister Sigrid's voice on the tape. Now what?

"Jens? Are you there? If you are, please pick up the phone. I know it's late. Oh well. I hate to call you so late... but it's Torbjørn. We think he had a heart attack or stroke or something.

We just don't know yet. The ambulance rushed him to the county hospital. He's in the intensive care unit. Sorry for leaving a message like this. I'm really frazzled right now. I guess it doesn't look good. Love ya. Bye."

I quickly got dressed and drove over to the county hospital. It was, of course, after visiting hours and the night nurse gave me a hard time about seeing him. I lied and told her that Torbjørn was my great uncle and I had just gotten the news of his illness. This seemed to work, and I think she felt a little sorry for me. She told me I could walk down the hall and look through the little window in the door to his room but I was, under no circumstances, to go into the room. I peeked through the little window. Tubes ran every which way in and out of him. He looked calm and was breathing regularly, but the color on his face was very pale. He looked like a man who was living on borrowed time. I can't recall ever feeling sorrier for anyone. The night nurse came by and asked: "Do you want to spend the night at the family hotel complex? We can get you a cot and a little privacy," she said, as I think she was feeling sorry for me again. I thought for a few moments and then said, "Sure, I can do that. Where do I go?"

Ten minutes later, I found myself lying on a hard cot and staring up at the ceiling. I was sharing a semi-private room with two middle aged men who were snoring up a storm on either side of me. I was wondering what the hell I was doing.

I woke up the next morning feeling tired and with an extremely sore back. I threw some water on my face and walked down the hallway to see Torbjørn, fearing the worst. The night nurse was gone and a more personable nurse had replaced her. She informed me that Torbjørn was doing fine and showing signs of improvement, although he was still very weak and had not yet woken. "I'm sorry, sir, he will not be taking any visitors today," she said in a very direct tone. "So how are you related to the patient?"

I was about to lie to her too, but thinking the better of it, I decided to tell the truth. "I'm a good friend of his. I visit him every week at the nursing home,"

"Does he have any living relatives?" she asked as she was holding up a clipboard, reading some information the nursing home had sent over. I was about to tell her all of his relations have passed away when she said, "It looks here that he has a nephew, a Mr. Brett Ruud who lives... uh... it looks like his whereabouts are unknown," she continued, half talking to herself and shuffling the papers. "I'll have to try to track him down and inform him of his uncle's condition." She walked back to the nurse's station and picked up the white pages and started thumbing through them.

Torbjørn had never mentioned a nephew. I guess I never asked him, but still, why didn't he say anything about him? Could it be Odd's son?

•

On Monday, I went to work after I found out that Torbjørn hadn't awakened. I didn't have any inspections, so I stayed in the office trying to catch up on old reports. I worked hard, as I was trying to avoid Norm's disappointed stares.

When I got home that evening I decided to do a little investigating on my own to find out where this Brett Ruud lived. I didn't have any telephone books, so I decided to call information. I was surprised when the phone operator told me there was a Brett Ruud in the city of Otsego, and gave me the number. I started to pace back and forth in the living room. I was getting really nervous. I hated using the phone, but for the good of Torbjørn, I decided that I had to call Brett. I felt it was the right thing to do. I dialed the number and heard the phone ring a couple of times. A woman answered it. She had a nice voice, but it was weak and timid. I identified myself and asked if she was related to Torbjørn. She started to say something when a ruff, husky voice interrupted her and said, "Who the hell is it?"

"I don't know." I heard the woman say in an embarrassed voice. "He says his name is Jens Nilsen."

"I don't know anybody by that name. It's probably some asshole salesman. Hang up the phone." There was a slight pause and then I heard the man yell, "Hang up the fricking phone, woman!" Then I heard a click.

I tried to call back a few times, but no one answered. I figured that the crass man was none other than Brett. Boy, was he a piece of work. I didn't like his voice, or the way he treated that woman. I had to admit, though, that this relative of

Torbjørn's intrigued me. I really thought I should let this guy know of Torbjørn's illness. I decided next Saturday I would take a drive up to Otsego and have a visit with Mr. Brett Ruud.

Every night after work, I visited Torbjørn. His condition hadn't changed. He just lay in that hospital bed, peacefully asleep. I took some of my work to his room and sat in the chair next to him. I don't really know why I did this; I just wanted to be there when and if he woke up.

•

On Saturday, I found myself cruising up to Otsego, which was so far away from Minneapolis that it wasn't the end of the world, but you could probably see it from there.

After what seemed an eternity, I found Brett's street in Otsego and pulled up on the gravel driveway to the house. It was a corrugated metal trailer in tired condition. I thought I might have taken a wrong turn and ended up in the Appalachian Mountains. It appeared to have been built in the early 1960s and had green painted shutters that were rotting away. Most of the screens were torn and lazily flopping in the wind. The only entrance was an old wood deck that had concrete blocks laid down on some of the broken and missing steps. There was an old and battered picnic table in front. In the middle of the yard was a 1960s Chevy on blocks, rusting away. The engine was all torn up and parts of it were lying on the weed-infested yard. On the other side of the home were three ancient disassembled snowmobiles. The whole place reeked of neglect and poverty. I could see two young kids playing in the yard. I slowly got out of my car and walked over to the front door. I waved at the little kids, but they just stopped what they were doing and stared at me.

I knocked on the front door a couple of times. I could hear some muffled noises coming from the house. I knocked again. Then silence. I could see a pair of eyes staring at me through the little window on the steel door. The door slowly opened and a handsome woman in her late twenties appeared. She was holding a baby who was busy sucking on a bottle while another small kid was clinging to her leg.

"Can I help you?" she said. I recognized the voice from the previous phone call.

"Is Brett Ruud home?"

"No, I'm sorry, he's not. He's at an all-day softball tournament. I'm his wife. Is there anything I can help you with?"

I smiled, took a deep breath, "Well... I just wanted to let Brett... and you know that Brett's uncle, Torbjørn Ruud, is very ill and in the hospital. I tried to call the other night, but there must have been some kind of misunderstanding."

She looked at me with a blank stare. Uncomfortable pause. Then she said, "I don't understand. Do you want to try to sell me something? Because if you are, I'm sorry, I'm not interested. "

I tried to not get irritated. "No, no, no, I'm not trying to sell you anything. Torbjørn Ruud, who I understand is Brett's great uncle, is very sick. He's the one who lives in a nursing home in Minneapolis."

Suddenly, a light appeared to go on. "Oh... you mean Great Uncle Torbjørn. He's Brett's grandfather Stig's brother." So, more of Torbjørn and Odd's family did come over from Norway, I thought to myself. "Yes, that's right. That makes sense," I said.

"Is he really bad?" she asked with a sincere look on her face. "Do you think he'll make it through?"

"I don't know. He still hasn't woken up from a heart attack. It doesn't look good." I bit down on my lip, I think that sounded too harsh and I didn't want to alarm her. There was another uncomfortable pause. I didn't know whether she was going to let me into her house or slam the door in my face.

"My name is Jens Nilsen," I said trying to break the awkward silence.

"Oh... I'm Holly... Holly Ruud," she smiled and looked down at the floor. She looked like she didn't know whether to invite me in or not. I got the impression she was wondering if her husband would think it would be appropriate to let me in. "Oh... won't you come in?" She pointed me toward the small dinette table in the kitchen. I sat down on a small, dirty chair. She walked over to the kitchen and asked if I'd like some coffee.

"No thanks. I never touch the stuff," I said. My dead Norwegian relatives would roll over in their graves.

"Suit yourself," she said as she poured herself a cup. I quickly glanced around the trailer home. It was a mess. The breakfast cereal bowls were still on the table with bloated and soggy cereal all over the table and floor. Dirty dishes from a few days ago were piled high in the kitchen sink, and crumbs of old food lay out on the counter top. The walls were marked with dents and black shoe marks and some were decorated with crayons. There were children's toys laying all over the floor and furniture. The entire house was swimming in the aroma of day-old dirty diapers.

Holly sat down in a chair and took a long sip of her coffee and said, "So, are you a relative of Brett's?"

"No," I said. I described how my sister, who works at Torbjørn's nursing home, introduced me to him and how we became friends.

"That's nice," she said as she took another sip of coffee. There was another longer pause. I looked into her eyes. She looked like she was a very attractive and vibrant person at one time, but child bearing and marriage to Brett had taken a toll on her mind and body. "So how did you meet Brett?"

She smiled and said, "We've known each other for years. We went to school together. I guess we started dating in the ninth grade." She pointed to a picture on the wall of a very attractive cheerleader and a young man in a hockey uniform. "That picture was taken when we were juniors in high school."

I noticed a photo next to it that showed them wearing formal attire and they had crowns on their heads. They must have been king and queen of their high school homecoming. She sighed and said, "We were the most popular couple in high school." It was a matter-of-fact statement and not necessarily bragging. "I think we peaked too early." She said with a slight grin. "I got pregnant when we were seniors and we got married right after graduation. Charley came last June. This is our sixth." She patted the baby she was holding with her free hand and waited for a response from me.

"I see," was all I could muster. "I have an older brother who had the same thing happen to him in high school."

"Did he get her pregnant?"

"No, but they got married the fall after they graduated."

"Are they still married?"

I hesitated a bit and then said, "Well, they just got a divorce about a year ago."

"It can be really tough when you get married so young. Brett and me have had our ups and downs," she said with a tinge of regret. "Life isn't bad when Brett has work and he stays away from the drinking. Right now he's working and just bought a new truck."

"What does he do for a living?"

"Construction. I know it ain't a fancy job, but it can pay pretty good sometimes."

Just then we heard a scream come from outside. We both jumped up and went to the door. One of her sons was pulling the hair of one of her daughters. Holly yelled at them to stop fighting. They ignored her and kept on fighting.

"Do you mind?" She said as she handed me the young child in her arms and walked out of the house. I held the child loosely as its big blue eyes stared at me. I had time to look around the house while she was scolding the children. So this is how the other half lives, I said to myself. I noticed that the only other decorations on the wall besides the dents and the scuffle marks were dead stuffed heads of animals from what appeared to be Brett's hunting expeditions.

Holly sent the two children to their rooms. "Sorry about that. The older they get, the harder it is for me to control them. They can get kind of wild."

I told her that it was perfectly understandable. She again offered me something to drink. I accepted a can of pop. I think she was warming up to me now, because she started to talk about her life with Brett. Maybe she was just lonely and was happy to talk to another adult. She sat down on the chair, and I handed her back the child. The other child was still at her leg, hanging on for dear life. "Brett has his good days and bad days, just like anybody else, I suppose. I think that underneath it all, he's a very fine man. It's just that he's had a lot of bad luck in his life and he's got an awful temper." I remembered his temper on the phone when I called the other day.

"Well I'm sure you know he lost his dad a long time ago," she said, acting like I knew Brett.

"No. I didn't know that."

"Oh yes. When he was about seven or eight years old," she said as she gave me a puzzled look. "His mother died about six years ago. Smoked too many cigs. She got lung cancer. Died just like that," she snapped her fingers.

"I'm sorry to hear that." I didn't know what to say. "Do you know about Brett's grandfather Stig, or his brothers, Torbjørn and Odd?" I said, trying to subtly get some information about them.

She looked up at the ceiling and started to think. "Um... No, not really. Let's see... I think Brett's grandfather died before he was born. I think the same with Uncle Odd. I remember we invited Uncle Torbjørn to our wedding, and I asked him at the reception about how Stig and Odd had passed away. He acted like he was real upset and said he couldn't remember. I just thought he was a crazy old man and left it at that. Later, he told me that they had both died in a car accident." She looked up at the ceiling again and started to think. "You know? Now that I think about it, it's kind of funny."

"In what way?" I asked.

"Well, some time after the wedding, Brett and me were talking about his family and he told me that his father had said that Odd and Stig died in a boating accident. Again, I didn't think anything of it because I thought that Torbjørn was a little crazy and old and he had just forgotten about how they died."

I made a mental note to ask Torbjørn how his brothers died. I wanted to tell Holly that Torbjørn wasn't crazy.

"That's one of the reasons why I think Brett is always so angry. He thinks the world is out to get him," she paused again. We sat in silence for a few moments. Her eyes were beginning to tear up and she continued. "Brett grew up real poor and didn't have a father. His mom was an alcoholic and couldn't keep a job for very long. The only thing Brett was good at was sports. The coaches all said he was gifted. That was going to be the ticket out of this lousy life. He was really good in hockey. The University of Minnesota was going to give him a full scholarship. But, that's when I got pregnant, and Brett had to quit school to support us." Her voice was cracking up now and tears came poring out of her flushed red face. "I was the one who blew his chance to get a college education or, who knows, even have a career in the NHL."

I blurted out without thinking, "It takes two to tango. It was just as much his fault as yours," I said trying to comfort her.

She forced a smile and said, "That's what all my friends say, but I think I forgot to take the pill a couple of times. Brett says that I intentionally forgot to take it so I would get pregnant and then he would have to marry me." She got up from the chair, set the child she was holding on the floor and said, "Will you excuse me for a second?"

I nodded and she quickly walked into the bathroom and shut the door. The baby instantly started to cry and so did the one who had been clutching at Holly's leg. I didn't know what to do. I couldn't believe I was here. I couldn't believe that a half an hour ago I was a complete stranger to this woman, and now she had poured her heart out to me. Why did I ever come here and get involved with all this? I was just about ready to get up and walk out the door when a man walked through the front door.

He was a tall and wiry man in his late twenties and must have been at least six foot four. He had golden blond hair, parted in the middle, in a 1970s style. His eyes were very blue and they had a shifty quality to them. His hands were large and well weathered and calloused. He had a cat-like bounce in his step as he walked over to me. He was wearing a softball uniform with a liquor store logo on the jersey. He gave me a quizzical look and said, "Who the hell are you and what are you doing in my house?"

I stood up and introduced myself. As I started to explain why I was here, I could see him looking me up and down. He was sizing me up as a man. He looked like a man who was very competitive and domineering and wanted to be in control of all situations. By the look on his face, he didn't think I would be any threat to his supremacy. I told him that Torbjørn was gravely ill and in the hospital.

"Is he going to live?" he asked with a skeptical look on his face. He seemed more concerned about my being here than if Torbjørn was ill. He gave me this look like, okay pal, why are you really here? What's in it for you? Do you know something about Torbjørn that I don't know? Does he have any money stashed away somewhere? The conversation wasn't going very well. I was doing all the talking. He was listening very carefully and absorbing every word I was saying.

Just then, Holly walked out of the bathroom. A look of surprise jumped into her face. She froze and reverted to the woman I first met. She was timid and looked down at the floor. The two young children stopped crying when they saw him and had the fear of God in their eyes. The atmosphere in the house changed entirely when Brett entered. Uneasy tension seeped into the room.

My impression was that Brett could not care less about the health of his great uncle. He again asked my name and where I lived. He wanted to know what I did for a living and how I found out that he was a relative of Torbjørn's. The whole situation was getting creepier. I finally got up the guts to tell him that I had an appointment in Minneapolis that I had to get to.

He smiled and said, "Please keep us posted on Uncle Torbjørn's condition, won't you? What hospital did you say he was in? We'll have to visit the old man in a few days."

I saw myself out and walked quickly to my car. As I drove away, I had a bad taste in my mouth. That was a horrible experience. Why did I do it? Somehow, I thought this little visit might come back to haunt me.

Chapter X

Torbjørn's condition improved significantly in the next few days. He finally woke and was as feisty as ever. Since he didn't appear to be in critical condition anymore, and had a pulse, they kicked him out of the hospital. I saw him the next day at the nursing home. As I came walking into his room, he was having an intense, one-sided conversation with a nurse about the quality and quantity of the food in the home. The nurse's response was to shake her head, since Torbjørn still kept up the façade of speaking Norwegian.

"So why have you honored me with your presence today, Herr Nilsen?" Torbjørn said in Norwegian the second I walked in. The nurse saw her opportunity to exit the room and bolted out. "Tell me Nilsen, am I about to die, and you're the one elected to tell me the news? I know that quack doctor of mine don't have the guts to tell me, so out with it. What's the news?"

"You tell me, Torbjørn. I didn't talk to any of the doctors, so I'm in the dark. By the looks of it, though, if you don't listen to the doctor you might not have long to live."

"Ah, that damn doctor tells me to eat more healthy food and take them crazy pills." He pointed to a bottle of pills on the nightstand. "Can you imagine? Me taking them damn pills. I'm never going to take that medicine again. Huh, popping pills just because my ticker is a little weak and tired. For land sakes."

"I'd listen to the doctor if I were you," I said, as I sat down in a small chair next to his bed. "So how are you feeling today?"

"Fit as a fiddle. In fact, I need some fresh air. How about you taking me somewhere where I don't have to stare at four walls and I can get some good scenery, if you know what I mean?" I didn't know what he meant, but I nodded anyway.

"I'll have to run that by the nurse, you know. You just got out of the hospital."

"Do you have to talk to that old battle-ax? Can't you just sneak me out the back?"

"I could, but don't you think I might get into trouble doing that?"

"Ah. Nobody cares if I'm here or not. They won't even notice I'm gone," he said. I did run it by Nurse Thorson. She wasn't too keen on the situation, but I think from the looks of the other nurses faces that were on duty, an afternoon without Torbjørn in the nursing home wouldn't be an entirely bad thing.

"Where do you want to go?" I said as we pulled out of the nursing home driveway. It was an exceptionally hot and sticky August day and large black thunderclouds were rolling in from the northwest. It looked like it would rain soon.

"I'm hungry. I haven't had a good square meal in weeks." He turned his head and looked at me and said, "Where does a young whippersnapper like you go to eat?"

I couldn't think of any place where I go to eat that would appeal to him. Then I said, "How about going to Ole's Bar? They've got great greasy hamburgers."

Torbjørn's eyes squinted. "You don't mean that Norsky outfit in south Minneapolis off Cedar Avenue? Is that dive still around?" I nodded my head.

"I haven't been there since, let's see, it must have been the late fifties. Does that old bastard Ole Myhre still own the joint?" I nodded my head again.

"Well, what in the hell are we waiting for boy? Let's go."

•

About twenty minutes later, I rolled Torbjørn into the dark and dank bar. I looked over to see Ole Myhre's mouth drop wide open and his face turn white.

Ole's Bar is not what you would call a run-of-the-mill, blue collar, neighborhood bar. It is far more than that. It is a Norwegian-American institution. It is a beacon of Norwegian-American pride where one can relax with cohorts after work and listen to some real Norwegian folk songs. The small, eighty-something-year old, two-story building with a cheap plastic stone front occupies a corner on Cedar Avenue in south Minneapolis. If you travel to northeast Minneapolis there seems to be a tavern or pub on almost every other intersections on all major streets. I've been told that the reason why there are so many drinking establishments there is because there were so many eastern and central European immigrants who settled in that area. Their traditions incorporated drinking into their daily life. If you travel to south Minneapolis, it was settled primarily by Norwegians, Swedes, and Germans. Their traditions—including the Lutheran Church—did not incorporate drinking into their daily life. That is why there are so few drinking establishments in the south Minneapolis neighborhoods. I guess you could call Ole's Bar a diamond in the rough. The décor of this place is dank, dingy, and twenty years out of date. Ole's smelled like a combination of a musty basement and week-old beer. For the most part the floors were sticky and you spent a minimal amount of time in the restrooms—if you had to use them at all. The bar is next to the front door. There were the usual suspects at the bar with a drink in their hands and a cigarette butt in their mouths. There were cheesy booths and some standing tables in the middle of the room. Toward the rear there was a small stage where local musicians performed, and if we were lucky, maybe a musician from the 'old country.' At the end of the room there's a small area for a pool table, restrooms, and a small kitchen, which you don't want to look into.

Legend had it that, thirty years ago, you could only enter the bar if you spoke Norwegian. They said there used to be a sign on the front door which stated something like: "If you don't speak Norwegian, then shove off!" My dad told me that if a fight broke out in the place and the police were called, then only the Norwegian-American police were let in to stop the fight. But, like most things, as time went on, immigration from Norway became only a trickle. Most of the old timers were dying off and English was accepted in the bar. Now, anyone could come into the bar, though I don't know why anyone but Norwegians or Norwegian-Americans would want to.

"Well now, as I live and breathe, I don't believe my eyes! Am I seeing a ghost or what? Is that Torbjørn 'the one-legged bastard' Ruud who has just risen from the dead?"

Torbjørn's eyes were beaming and a large grin enveloped his face. "The one and the same. How is the cheap bastard? Still charging too much for a brewsky?"

The old geezers caught up on thirty years of history while I ordered the beers. Torbjørn insisted on drinking good Norwegian beer and I knew there was no way I was going to talk him out of it. After about half an hour of catching up, Myhre went back to the bar and started working again. The bar was unusually crowded.

We plopped down on a sticky booth in a semi-quiet corner of the gloomy bar, both staring out into space and occasionally sipping on our beers. I was thinking of a subtle question that could steer him in the direction of continuing his story about what happened after Ida was killed. I was lucky, though, because out of the blue, Torbjørn said, "Do you remember, Jens, when I told you a few days ago how that bastard Mikkelsen killed my beloved Ida?"

I nodded my head and said, "Yes."

"Well, do you want to know what happened after that terrible night back in '34?"

I nodded, and said: "Of course!"

"Well, be a good boy and order us another beer and grab some peanuts on the way back. This may take awhile," he said.

As I walked toward the bar to order another round and grabbed a handful of peanuts from a nearby barrel, I glanced at the wall behind the bar counter. There were portraits of famous Norwegians and Norwegian-Americans. The top lone portrait was, of course, King Olav V. Now the Brits have their queen, the Catholics have their Pope, and the Italians have Frank Sinatra, but we have our beloved old King Olav V. The second tier of portraits consisted of Leif Erickson, the true discoverer of America, Thor Heyerdahl, the great explorer, and Vice President Walter Mondale. On the third tier there was Eric Severeid, Sonja Henie, Knute Rockne, Jim Arness, Peter Graves, and Jan Stenerud. As we sat down in a booth, I couldn't help but think that the infamous 'Wall of Fame' wasn't much, but that's all we had. I looked around the bar to see it filled with a mixture of city street department workers, just off their shift, guzzling down beers in their light blue uniforms and smoking non-filtered cigarettes; men and women in business attire sipping on beer and wine, winding down from a busy day at the office; and college professors and grad-school types from the nearby University of Minnesota and Augsburg College, wearing old sweaters and corduroy pants, quietly discussing metaphysics. It appeared that they all had something in common, *Noskdom*—everything Norwegian. To complete the scene, there was Norwegian folk music—always playing in the background—and most importantly, plenty of *Aass* and *Rigness* beer on tap.

As I sat down next to Torbjørn, I couldn't help noticing the old men sitting at the bar. They were all wearing baseball caps tilted a certain way, which must have been in style forty years ago. They all sat there, cross-legged, with a smoke in one hand and a drink in the other, discussing the important events of the day. One old geezer at the end of the bar just sat there with a blank stare. He didn't look at or talk to anyone. He looked as if he was a thousand miles away in another time and place. I didn't know if he was drinking to remember or if he was drinking to forget. I couldn't help but think that he was in an utter state of loneliness, a man whose life died many years ago, but the body just kept going through the motions.

After Torbjørn had eaten a few peanuts and washed them down with a few swigs of beer, he took a deep breath and said, "Well, let me see now, where was I? Oh yes... When I got home from work that night I saw that Ida wasn't home. I thought this a little strange because on Tuesday nights Odd would come home with me and Ida would cook dinner for us. I suspected she had to work late, so I decided that me and Odd should drive the flatbed Ford to the school and take her out to a fancy restaurant. When I drove within a few blocks of the school, I noticed a large crowd had gathered in the middle of the street. Now the moment I saw that crowd, I knew something was very wrong. I had seen this type of thing before, you know. I knew the street car that was stopped in the middle of the street hit somebody. I'll tell you this right now Jens, and I don't give a tinker's damn if you don't believe me," he was dead-on serious now, trying to speak quietly so none of the people in the bar could hear him. I looked at his eyes as he was talking and they were piercing right through me.

"Before me and Odd got out of the truck, I felt a heavy load on my heart that something horrible just had happened. I just couldn't explain it. I overheard a woman saying she saw the whole thing. She said a woman in a fast-moving car had just opened the door and jumped out. She had never in her life seen such a thing. She then said the second she jumped out, a street car moving the other direction hit her and dragged her on the tracks for at least a block until it stopped. I walked over to the police who had put a blanket over the body lying in the street. My heart was pumping faster and faster. I looked down at the blanket and saw it failed to cover up an outstretched hand. It was the hand of a woman. And on the wrist of that hand was a bracelet. It was the bracelet I had given Ida a few weeks earlier for her birthday."

As you can imagine, Torbjørn's face was red and those land-locked tears of his were flowing like Minnehaha Falls. He grabbed an old-fashioned handkerchief from his breast pocket and started to blow his nose. It made a real loud sound, and I looked around the bar to see if anyone had noticed. Myhre was busy washing beer glasses, and the usual suspects were too drowned in their own self pity to notice anything.

He stared right in my eyes and said, "Jens, can you imagine in your wildest dreams that you would ever come upon a situation where you see your wife dead, lying in the middle of the street?" He started to let out loud sobs now. We sat there for ten minutes, not saying a word. I had my head bowed down, not knowing what to say. I cursed myself for not being emotionally equipped to deal with the situation. He finally broke the silence and said, "You know, Jens, I can honestly say that a part of me—a big part of me—died that night along with Ida. A part of me just couldn't handle what had happened. I never wanted to feel the way I felt that night ever again. I truly wanted to die that night. I wanted to join Ida up in heaven. After that night I had no purpose, no drive, and no ambition. All of my dreams of having a wife and kids went down the toilet, just like that." He snapped his fingers and continued, "I can remember for the next few months I had no feelings whatsoever. I was like a zombie walking around, just going through the motions. I didn't want to talk to nobody and I hit the sauce pretty good every night. Most mornings I'd wake up not knowing where I was or where I had been the night before. I had my last talk with God that night. To hell with him. How could this all-powerful and loving God take away my beloved Ida? Can you tell me that? Can you tell me that, Jens?" I had to admit he had a point. Again, I was dumbfounded and didn't know what to say. We sat milking our beers for a few minutes, until Torbjørn sighed and said, "Oh, what the hell. I'm hungry. What's a guy supposed to do around here to get something to eat?" I walked over to Ole Myrhe and ordered two 'Viking' burgers with everything. I also picked up two more brewskis—I think more for myself to get through Torbjørn's emotional story—and sat back down at our table.

After we ate, I was dying to ask Torbjørn how he found out that Mikkelsen was driving the car. I finally worked up the nerve to ask him. He looked at me, and I thought he was just going to shut down and not say anything. Then he said, "Me and Odd heard through the grapevine that the car Ida jumped out of was Mikkelsen's. We still had some good friends who were connected in Mikkelsen's organization who said that he had had the hots for Ida. As you can imagine, when I heard about this, I wanted to get a gun and march right down to Mikkelsen's office and let him have it right between the eyes. Odd calmed me down a bit. He told me to be real smart about it and be patient and don't be such a hot head. Odd said we had to think of the perfect plan. We would kill him, of course, but we would do it and never get caught. Odd was the smart one, all right. He was the one who planned it all out, down to the last detail." Here we go again, I thought to myself. This story is too good to be true. Could he possibly be making this all up and making me the fool?

"You see, Jens Olav, Odd pounded it in my head that we had to be level-headed and wait for the perfect opportunity. And it came that next summer. Odd had many friends. He would sometimes scratch their backs, and they would sometimes scratch his, if you know what I mean. Anyway, Odd heard one day that Mikkelsen was getting greedy and wanted more of a piece of the Twin Cities. He had heard that this tough Irish gang in St. Paul was going on a bank-robbing spree all across the upper Midwest. You have to remember, Jens Olav, that this was during the Great Depression, and bank robberies were a dime a dozen. So,

Mikkelsen heard that this Irish outfit was robbing banks and stealing jewelry from safe deposit boxes and they even robbed a federal train with real gold bars. Mikkelsen's sources were telling him that this gang—the O'Brien brothers—were stashing their loot in some caves in St. Paul on the Mississippi. Now these O'Brien brothers were some tough customers, I tell you. They would rob banks in the afternoon, party all evening, watch the sun come up in the morning and start all over again. In the Twin Cities gangland territories in the 1930s, the Norwegian gangs controlled the Minneapolis side, and the Irish gangs controlled the St. Paul side. There was an unwritten truce between them. Mikkelsen, of course, was going to change all that. He was going to find the O'Brien brother's loot, steal it—supposedly while they were partying—and hide it on the Minneapolis side somewhere."

"When Odd heard about this, he thought it would be the perfect time to rub out Mikkelsen. Odd was going to tip off one of the O'Brien brothers to Mikkelsen's plan. He thought that surely the brothers would ambush Mikkelsen and his hoodlums. For an extra insurance policy, me and Odd were going to be there in the background, just to make sure that the O'Brien brothers finished the job, plus we might get the satisfaction of seeing Mikkelsen die a slow and painful death. If you know what I mean."

I sat there with my mouth wide open, thinking that, if he was making this all up, he must have a great imagination. Torbjørn took a long slow swig of beer and continued.

"Well, the day came, and we had planned the whole event to a T. Odd had tipped off Michael O'Brien that there was going to be some monkey business down at the caves that night and that he better beware. Me and Odd hid behind some rocks just outside the entrance to the cave in the late afternoon and waited until dark. Odd knew that Mikkelsen and his gang wouldn't come down into the cave until way past midnight. That was when he thought the O'Brien brothers would be good and drunk. Me and Odd were hiding there for hours, trying to swat off them damn mosquitoes. It was just about three a.m., and we were about to leave, and Odd was going to have some choice words with those so-called reliable sources, when we heard some rustling in the bushes just outside the cave. We both froze, and I could feel a tingle running up my spine. We could barely make out, by the faint light of the moon, some figures moving quietly about. I couldn't tell if it was Mikkelsen or some of the O'Brien brothers on patrol. It was a hot and sticky night, and all we could hear was the crickets chirping in the woods."

"We just sat there for a moment wondering what to do next. The shadows below were moving fast, real fast. We could see that there were at least ten men. The fact that they were so quiet told me that they must have been Mikkelsen. When the last shadow entered the cave it stumbled and fell. We could hear a few curse words whispered loudly followed by another man shushing him. I looked up at Odd, who had had a big smile on his face. The shadow had sworn in Norwegian. Later, we had found out that Mikkelsen had found out which of the O'Brien brothers was guarding the cave. Earlier in the day he had sent over a hooker to the tavern this guard frequented, who picked him up and took him to a brothel where they were busy all night. If ..."

"...you know what I mean," I interrupted, getting a little tired of hearing that phrase.

"You're goddamn right, if you know what I mean," he said, nodding his head. "A few minutes after the last Norwegian shadow entered the cave, all hell broke loose. There was a quick burst of a Tommy gun, then some shouting. After that, there was a great gun battle that seemed to last for at least twenty minutes. Then there was silence. Not a sound. We sat there for about ten minutes and wondered what we should do. Odd thought that the first gun barrage was from the O'Brien brothers ambushing them. Then he thought there would be some kind of gun battle, but the O'Brien's would surely win because they had the element of surprise. But no one came out of the cave. Did they just happen to all kill each other? We just couldn't tell. We waited another half hour. It would be daylight in another hour or two, so we had to act quickly. Me and Odd slowly made our way to the entrance of the cave. We had a flashlight in one hand and a revolver in the other. We kept our flashlights off and slowly felt our way in. The only sound we heard was a groaning coming from a corner of the cave. Confident that it was safe to turn our flashlights on, we made a quick sweep of the cave. The sight, Jens Olav, was indescribable. There were bloody bodies laying everywhere in heaps. The ground was awash with blood, and the walls were splattered with it. There were body parts and guts all over the place. Never had I ever seen such a blood bath. I recognized some of Mikkelsen's men, but Mikkelsen was nowhere to be found. Odd had turned his flashlight on the faces of the O'Brien brother's gang. Over in the corner was Michael, the leader of the gang, along with Billy, his younger brother. In all, we counted eleven dead on the Mikkelsen side and nine dead on the O'Brien side. But no Mikkelsen. Odd cursed and said it was just like Mikkelsen, the coward, to have his men do the dirty job while he was probably enjoying the company of a young hooker."

Torbjørn took another swig of his beer and looked up to the ceiling. He was thinking of how to put into words the next part of his story. "Just as my brother had muttered those words, we heard a faint voice coming from the corner of the cave. We quickly spun around and flashed our lights at a figure. Odd cocked his gun and yelled out 'Who's there?' We heard the faint voice say: 'Help... help... I've been shot. You must help me.' We both dashed over to the figure and sure enough, guess who it was?"

"Mikkelsen!" I blurted out.

"You're goddamn right it was Mikkelsen, Jens Olav. I see that you're paying attention. He was in a tough sort of way. But he looked like he could pull through. Odd thought that he must have been hiding behind his men when the firefight broke out and was using them as human shields. Anyway, he had taken a few bullets and was coughing up blood. When he saw that it was me and Odd, he had a great big smile on his face. I think he thought he was going to live now, because we were going to take him to the hospital. Then he has the balls to say: 'Oh look who's here. Well, if it isn't the Ruud brothers coming to save me. Please old friends, can you take me to a doctor, and fast?' He said it like we were all the best of buddies. I started to feel sorry for Mikkelsen, until I suddenly remembered seeing Ida lying in the middle of the street with a blanket over her. My feelings quickly changed. Odd asked, 'So what happened here tonight, Mikkelsen?' Mikkelsen looked at Odd strangely and lied, 'We were set up. We were going to have a meeting with the O'Brien brothers and carve up southern Minnesota into territories.'"

"Can you imagine, Jens Olav? This poor bastard is shot and dying and he's lying about some stupid meeting. Then Odd asked

Mikkelsen slyly... 'Oh? Or is it was because you wanted to steal all the loot the O'Brien's have hidden in this cave?' 'I don't know what you're talking about, Odd,' he said angrily. Then Odd said, 'I found out about your little plan and tipped off the O'Brien's on when you were coming to steal their loot.' 'What? You... tipped them off, you say? Why would you do a thing like that to your old friend, Odd?' The pain in his voice got worse. 'Why would you rat on your own kind?' said Mikkelsen. It was my turn now. 'So, Mikkelsen,' I said, 'since Ida is dead are you harassing any other ladies?' 'What are you talking about, Torbjørn?' he said."

"Then Odd said, 'Mikkelsen, we know all about what happened in the car that night last winter. We knew you had the hots for Ida and you were making the moves on her. We know you killed her!' 'I don't know what you're talking about, Odd!' says Mikkelsen. Then it hit him. Then he realized why Odd had tipped off the O'Brien's and how we planned all this. He got real scared and started to shake. He said he would make us his lieutenants and give us twenty-five percent of his entire take. He told us that in a few years we would be millionaires and control half the state. When we didn't say anything, he started to whine like a spoiled kid. He started crying and pleading with us to spare his life. It was really pathetic to see this bastard get reduced to a wailing pig."

"You know, Jens Olav, I thought I was really going to enjoy that day. I had planned in my head how it would feel to see Mikkelsen get his just rewards and die. But somehow, when it was happening, I didn't want any part of it. Then Odd pistol-whipped Mikkelsen in the face a few times and then handed me the gun. I drew the gun up to his head and my hand started to shake. I closed my eyes and started to sweat. After a few more moments, I finally said: 'I can't do it.'"

"By this time, Mikkelsen was screaming at the top of his lungs: 'I don't want to die. I don't want to die!' Odd said, 'Oh the hell with it. Give me the gun.' I handed it to him. He cocked it and put it to Mikkelsen's temple. Sheer terror swept over Mikkelsen's face. He closed his eyes and grimaced. Odd says, 'This one is for Ida.' He squeezed the trigger. Mikkelsen's head jerked back and blood and brains splattered everywhere. He cocked the gun a second time, pulled the trigger and said, 'And this one is for me.'"

Chapter XI

Torbjørn's story of his wife's death had a profound effect on me. I couldn't get the image out of my mind. To think the poor woman was dragged over one hundred yards! It was, to be sure, an unbelievable story, but I had no reason to think it wasn't true. His story reminded me so much of Dostoevsky's graphic scene in *Crime and Punishment* when the drunkard, retired government clerk Marmeladov, was crushed to death by a rich person's horse and carriage. Dostoevsky's vivid imagery was so realistic that I felt I was witnessing the entire event, as if I were there when it happened; much better than any movie could re-create.

I also couldn't get Torbjørn's description of Mikkelsen's death out of my mind, or of all the deaths that took place in that cave that night back in the 1934. I believed that would haunt me for the rest of my life, even if it was not true.

The rest of the week was filled with inspections of boring houses, trying to ignore my bosses' glares due to my recent low productivity, and visiting Torbjørn every evening at the nursing home. He hadn't talked much after he told me the disturbing story of Mikkelsen's death; however, last Wednesday, I found him in a curiously talkative mood again. I found him in his room, sitting in his wheelchair next to the ancient phonograph listening to my grandfather's old Norwegian records. He was listening to an energetic song with his arms gyrating back and forth like he was conducting an imaginary orchestra. I watched him conduct the song for a few moments and then acted like I had just walked into the room and said hello.

He looked up with a broad smile on his face and beaming eyes. A pleasant healthy color had resurfaced on his face, and he was attentive and energetic.

"Well, if it isn't Jens Olav Nilsen. How was work today?" Torbjørn said in Norwegian as he winked at me.

"Oh, fine. How are you feeling?" I asked.

"Couldn't be better, Jens Olav. I was just listening to your grandpa's old records." He stopped talking, looked up onto the ceiling and appeared to be thinking. He then said, "You know, I may have some old seventy-eight records tucked away in an old chest over there in the closet. Would you be so kind as to look there for me?" pointing his thumb at the small closet at the end of the room. I found a crusty old suitcase buried underneath a bunch of old clothes. I dragged it out into the room and opened it. It had a salty smell to it, like an old sea chest. In it, among other things, were neatly folded clothes. It appeared to be an old sailor's uniform. Under the clothes there was, indeed, a collection of old brown and red seventy-eight records. Next to these records was a framed picture. It was a portrait of an attractive woman that looked like it was taken in the 1930s. The woman looked so innocent and pure. All of a sudden, the hairs on my back stood up and a tingle shot through my spine. This was a portrait of Ida. Even though the photo was black and white and over fifty-five years old, Ida appeared so authentic and full of life. The photograph jumped out at me like I could touch it and feel the warmth of flesh and blood. I stood there petrified. I couldn't move. I visualized the last moments of her life and how agonizing and ghastly it must have been. What a waste.

"That's an awfully nice picture you have of Ida," I said to Torbjørn. He gave me a startled look. Then a slight smile formed on his face and he said in a soft voice, "Could you be so kind as to bring the photo over to me so that I can take a look at her again? It's been so long since I've last seen it. I've almost forgotten what she looked like."

I walked over to the wheelchair and handed him the photograph. He grabbed the portrait and started to stroke Ida's hair with his thumb. After a few moments he said, "This was the picture they took of her for the school's yearbook." He clutched the photograph and started to hug it with his head hanging down. After a few quiet and awkward moments, tears started running down his cheeks. After a few more moments, he asked me to set the portrait up on the nightstand, next to his bed.

We listened to the old and scratchy seventy-eight records from the old country. Torbjørn just sat near the window and gazed out over the horizon. After a few tunes, Torbjørn told me to turn off the record and close the door. I complied and sat down on the chair next to the bed. He slowly rolled his wheelchair near me and said to me in Norwegian, in a voice barely audible, "Do you remember my little story about how that bastard Mikkelsen bit the dust?"

I nodded as he wheeled himself over to the door and peeked out the small window. After he was satisfied that no one was spying on us in the hall, he rolled himself back to me and said, "Well, don't you want to know what happened to the O'Brien brothers' loot after Mikkelsen was gone?" I again nodded.

"Well, let me tell you." He sat back in his wheelchair, adjusted his body, trying to get comfortable and said, "Well, we knew we didn't have much time at the cave. It would be daylight in about an hour and we were so afraid we must have woken up the dead after that loud shoot-out." I nodded in agreement.

"Well, Odd drove our truck right up to the entrance of the cave. We spent the next hour or so carrying crates from the hiding place in the cave to the flatbed Ford. And let me tell you, Jens Olav, I almost broke my back lifting them things. By the time we were done, the sun was well up in the sky. Luckily, the cave was secluded on the Mississippi River bank and we didn't have any unexpected visitors. We tied an old worn cloth tarp over the crates and drove slowly to our house. We parked the truck in the small garage off the alley. We called the vegetable farm and told them we had gotten food poisoning and couldn't pick up any vegetables that day. We kept the loot in the garage until night. We didn't want to raise any suspicion, if you know what I mean. We had a nosy neighbor to the south, and we didn't want her to be poking her nose where it wasn't wanted." He stopped talking and looked at me, expecting some kind of a response from his statement.

I nodded my head and said, "There seems to be that kind of neighbor in every neighborhood." That seemed the response he was looking for because he nodded his head and continued.

"That night we started at about two a.m. and quietly carried all the crates from the truck into the basement. We kept an eye out for any lights being turned on by that nosy old lady Grøndahl who lived next door. We covered the basement windows with newspapers so we didn't have to worry about that old snoop starting up any trouble."

"Did you keep the loot down in the basement?" I asked. Torbjørn was a bit alarmed and told me not to talk so loudly. "If you hold your horses, Jens Olav, I'll tell you. Odd thought that the best place to hide the loot was under the front porch in the crawlspace. So that next day we spent punching open a larger entrance to the crawlspace with a sledge hammer. Then Odd thought of an ingenious way to disguise the entrance by moving the canning shelf over and putting a hinge on one section that would open by a secret latch so we could go into the crawlspace. After two days the loot was in its place."

"Then what happened?" I asked, barely able to contain my enthusiasm.

"For the next few weeks we acted like nothing had happened. The papers all said that there was a big gang shoot-out at the caves in St. Paul, and no one, as far as we could tell, lived to tell anything about the O'Brien's loot."

"So you were in the clear then?" I asked.

"Not so fast, boy. Like I said, we acted like normal, see, but we were both getting real edgy, if you know what I mean. We were afraid to be away from the house for more than a few hours at a time. We were afraid someone might find us out, you know, like put two and two together. We also were worried about common burglars in the neighborhood that might stumble upon it by chance.

"So Odd decided that we had to take the loot somewhere else. Some place safe, and far away. Some place where we could go every year or so and pick up some of it and live on that for awhile."

He paused for a second. It looked like he was having a hard time trying to decide if he should continue talking. He then looked me straight in the eyes and said, "Jens Olav, have you ever heard of Isle Royale?"

"The island off the north shore in Lake Superior?"

"That's the one. What do you know about that island?"

"Well, it's a small island belonging to Michigan and it's a national park."

"That's right. Well, Odd had this good old pal. This guy used to tell stories of when he used to work for the CCC on Isle Royale."

"The CCC?" I interrupted.

Torbjørn rolled his eyes in frustration and said, "You know—the Civilian Conservation Corps. That was part of Roosevelt's New Deal to keep America rolling. To keep out-of-work fellas busy doing public works projects and the like."

I nodded my head and felt a bit ashamed for not knowing that. Torbjørn continued. He was getting real worked up and excited.

"Well anyway, Chester... that was his name—Chester Solberg—said that a few years ago he was at some CCC camp on Isle Royale. They were building trails and the like around the island. Well, one Sunday afternoon, Chester and a pal of his went exploring and found the remnants of the old Island Mine. It was a copper mine from the 1870s. Anyway, the mine company had built this two-mile road from the mine down to Siskiwit Bay, see. They walked up from the bay and found the mine. The mine company had sunk a few shafts, but never found the mother load. They abandoned it a few years later. Chester said those mine shafts ran all over the place underground."

"Well, Odd got to thinking about those abandoned mine shafts. He thought that would be the best place to hide the loot. So, Odd and me went searching for Chester in all the old saloons around town. Sure enough, after the fifth joint, we found him, dead drunk in a gin joint on Washington Avenue. We sobered him up, took him for a bite to eat, and then Odd tells him a story about us needing to get some information about them old abandoned mines up on Isle Royale."

"What kind of story did you tell him?" I was more intrigued by the minute.

"Well, Odd cooked up this crazy scheme that he wanted to find a good place to hide some real hot guns and ammo. If he would take us to the old Island Mine and show us a good hiding place for the guns, then we would give him $1,000 for his troubles.

"Chester Solberg almost jumped out of his pants when he heard this. He asked when. Odd wanted him to go up to Duluth and rent an inconspicuous fishing boat and wait for Odd and me to come up in a few weeks. Odd then gave him $500 to rent a boat up in Duluth and lay low for awhile. He said if you can do that, stop drinking, and most of all keep your trap shut; there will be another $1,000 in on the deal."

"Did you really think you could trust this guy to keep his mouth shut?" I asked.

Torbjørn looked at me with his bright blue eyes and said, "No, not really. Deep down, Chester was a good man. He would give you the shirt off his back if you asked him. Odd thought that if he did help us find a good spot to hide the loot, then he would give Chester a couple more thousand. He didn't want Chester to know anything about the loot, though. That way, he couldn't possibly let slip anything about it."

"So we met up with Chester in Duluth a few weeks later. He found us an old fishing smack. There was only one hitch—the skipper of the boat had to come along with us. Chester told the skipper he wanted to rent the boat to take two gentlemen fishing to Isle Royale. The skipper of the boat, a Mr. Jones, said we could rent the boat, but he would have to come along and be the skipper. When Odd heard about this, he got real upset. He didn't want anything to do with this Skipper Jones character. It turned out that Chester had blown half of the money Odd gave him on alcohol. You see, Jens Olav, many poor folk, with no job and no family, back in them days took to the bottle. Alcohol was their family and lover. After awhile, they didn't need anything else. So, all Chester could afford for the rent was $250. That's how we got Skipper Jones and the SS Sturgeon."

"When we met Skipper Jones, a whole lot of bells and whistles went off in our heads. He was a shifty character who couldn't look you in the eye and always contradicted everything you said, even if you both knew you were right. He looked like a guy who gambled and drank by day and made secret whiskey runs to Port Arthur by night. When he met us I could see lug nuts churning in his brain. I could tell that he didn't think we were gentlemen by any stretch of the imagination and that he didn't think we were on any kind of fishing trip. I could tell he was going to be on his guard and that he was going to keep his ears perked up, if you know what I mean."

"It took about a day and a half to get to Isle Royale. We passed the Rock of Ages lighthouse on the southeast corner of the island and then ran up the island to Siskiwit Bay. Then, Chester told the old sea dog to anchor about two hundred yards off of Senter Point. Chester, Odd and me rowed to shore on a small skiff and we told the skipper to lay low for a couple of hours. We slowly rowed ashore and landed on Carnelian Beach. We could see the old skipper with a spyglass in hand watching us like a hawk. We knew he knew something just wasn't right."

"I asked Odd if it was a little strange that we were supposedly going on a fishing trip, but we didn't bring any fishing poles, tackle or nets with us. Chester starts to laugh, and then Odd gave him a death gaze and shakes his head. You see, Jens Olav, Chester got so excited about the trip that he forgot to bring any fishing equipment along with us. So, it took us a good hour to walk up the Island Mine Trail to the abandoned site. When we got there, it was pretty much all grown over with trees and weeds and there were even a few rusted-out steam engines and whatnot lying around. Chester knew where to go, though. In the outer area of the mine, near a small hill, Chester took off his backpack and grabbed a pickaxe and started hacking away at a bunch of fallen branches. 'I found this portal a couple weeks before we left the island for good, back in '31.' Chester said.

"A portal?" I asked. "What's that?"

Torbjørn gave me the same frustrated look he had given me previously and said, "A portal is an almost horizontal entrance to a mine. It connects to an adit. From there, there are the vertical shafts or winzes that go way down under the ground to get the copper, or coal, or whatever."

"Oh," I said.

"Well, anyway, Chester found the portal and he and Odd start walking into the small dark entrance with a large lantern that Odd had in his backpack. They both were carrying a lot of rope to get down the winzes. I could see the light from their lantern slowly fading into the mysterious adit."

"I was told to stand guard and let them know if anything was fishy. I didn't exactly know how I was supposed to do that, but I was hoping I wouldn't have to worry about it. I walked around a bit and watched the tall trees sway in the wind. It was making a sort of rustling sound that was nice to the ear. I sat down on a fallen tree and started to daydream about what I would do with my new-found wealth. Then I thought I heard the crackle of some twigs coming from the thick woods a few feet away. I jumped up and took out a small bowie knife I kept in a sheath on my belt. I instinctively yelled out: 'Who's there?' There was no answer, just the noise of the trees in the wind. I slowly walked around where the noise had come from. After a few minutes, I was satisfied that it must have been a small animal or something. I sat back on the stump. I waited for another hour, watching for light from the portal. I must have accidentally dozed off, because I remembered hearing Odd's voice saying 'Torbjørn, you fool, wake up!' I jumped up with a start, but didn't feel too bad when I saw Odd and Chester with great big grins on their faces. Then I heard Chester say, 'It's a great place to hide the stuff.'

'What stuff?' came a gruff voice from behind a tree. We all jumped back and turned to see Skipper Jones walking toward us and holding a large pistol, aimed at my face. 'I thought I told you to stay on the boat until we returned,' Odd said, his face red with anger. 'I do what I please, young man. Gentlemen going on a fishing trip,' he said mockingly. 'I didn't think so. How stupid of a man do you think I am? I knew the three of you were up to no good. What are you going to hide? Money? Whiskey? Maybe some guns, or maybe a body?'

'None of your goddamn business, old man,' Chester said with gritted teeth. 'Move along and get back to the boat.' 'Well, I'm making it my business, see,' said Skipper."

"Just then, I accidentally took a step backward and stepped on a twig. It cracked and made the skipper turn slightly toward me to see what was going on. Just as he turned, Chester threw the lantern he was holding. It hit Skipper square in the head and he was dazed for a moment. He fell to the ground and dropped his gun. Odd and Chester both pounced on him. Odd grabbed the gun and Chester grabbed the pickaxe lying nearby. Without a second of hesitation, he started bashing the ax against the skipper's head. First blood started to spray out, and then little pieces of his brains started oozing out. Odd had to grab the pickaxe away from Chester to stop the carnage. 'Enough!' Odd shouted. 'What the hell are you doing?'"

"Chester tried to compose himself and said, 'He gave me his word that he would stay on the boat. The bastard. This is what happens when you break your word to Chester Solberg, damn it!'"

"Odd and me just stared at each other. We couldn't believe what had just happened. Finally Odd blurts out, 'Great! Now what do we do?' Chester said, 'We throw this bastard's body down the mine shaft where nobody's going to find it. Then we sail the boat back to Duluth and sink it a few miles out of the port when it's dark out. Then we row in and sink the skiff and go our merry way. They're about twenty different men on the lakes who would like to see this bastard dead. No one will be the worse for it.'"

"Odd and me looked at each other as if to say, yeah sure, why not? That plan was just as good as anything we could cook up. We knew it was too late in the season to come back and bring the loot to the island this year. By next year, all of nature's critters would have taken care of the skipper's remains. So Odd picked up the skipper's arms and I grabbed his legs, and we slowly staggered our way through the portal and into the adit. After we had gone a few hundred feet we got to the entrance on the floor of the gloomy and cold winze. When we had him over the shaft, we swung him back and forth until we have enough momentum to throw him down it. We let him go and heard the body thumping back and forth making strange sounds like large watermelons hitting the floor and bones cracking. We heard a muffled echoed thud and then silence. Chester was right behind us, throwing down one of the backpacks, the skipper's various head parts and brains. We covered up the entrance to the portal and would have to wait until next summer to return."

"The next night we scuttled the SS Sturgeon a few miles off the port of Duluth and rowed the skiff into the harbor and sank it. We gave Chester another $500 to make it through the winter and by no means was he to hire another boat. Odd told him to lay low until next summer.

"So, Jens Olav, if you're counting, that makes a total of twenty-three people, if you include poor Ida, that has died because of this cursed loot."

He had finally finished his story. I just realized that the room had become completely dark. Where had the time gone? I just sat there in silence trying to take it all in. I could see that Torbjørn had been a bit worked up and was wondering if he had told too much to me. We sat there in silence for at least five minutes. I finally opened my mouth because I had to ask him a question I couldn't contain.

"If you don't mind me asking, just what was the loot?" I asked.

"Gold bars."

"How many?"

His face lit up and a smile cracked on his face. "Let me see here. I think there were about four gold bars in each crate. These gold bars were called 'London Good Delivery Bars' and each one of them weighed 400 Troy ounces."

"400 Troy ounces? How many pounds is that?"

"It's about twenty-seven pounds." He gave me a devilish grin and continued. "Do you know how much money a twenty-seven pound gold bar is worth?"

I shook my head, not having given it a great deal of thought in the past. "Well," Torbjørn said, "let's just say that, in today's prices, gold is going for $350 per ounce. How many ounces are there, Jens Olav, in a twenty-seven pound bar of gold?" He looked at me and didn't let me say anything. "432!" There are 432 ounces in one of those bars! That means that, in today's prices, a bar of London Good Delivery Bar is worth..."

"About $150,000!" I shouted.

"Shhh, keep it down, Jens Olav. Do you want to wake the dead?" he said in a loud whisper. He shuffled over to the window in the door again to see if any pesky spies were in the hallway. He shuffled back and in a quiet whisper said, "You're God damn right it's $150,000. And do you know how many crates with four bars a piece in them we had?

"How many?" I asked.

"Twenty!"

"Twenty crates!" I said. "At four a piece, that would mean a total of eighty bars at $150,000 a piece that would mean...."

"Twelve million dollars," Torbjørn said.

Chapter XII

I could see Torbjørn was getting extremely tired from his talk. He asked if we could take a break. I told him maybe he could resume his story tomorrow after a good night's sleep. He gave a polite smile and closed his eyes. Within minutes, he was fast asleep, snoring away. I felt that he would probably sleep for a good while, so I decided to go home and get some rest. My work was getting really backed up, and I had to go to the office tomorrow and try to catch up... somehow.

I got back to my apartment around ten p.m. and decided to wind down by watching some TV. I fell asleep on the couch in the living room and awoke with a start. It was broad daylight and I glanced at my wristwatch. It was 10:30 in the morning. I had fallen asleep in my clothes, but I didn't care. I took a long hot shower and got to work about an hour later. I worked for a good six hours, getting all my assignments in. I avoided Norm all afternoon. I didn't want to look up from my desk or even move out of my cubicle. I just slaved away at my computer. I wanted to get over to the nursing home to check on Torbjørn, but I could see Norm's light was still on in his office. I looked at my watch. Wow. He was still working away, past 7 o'clock. What a great partner this firm had. I was just about to start writing up my fifth appraisal when I saw Norm's light turn off. I heard him close his office door and skip down the aisle whistling some stupid tune. I quickly got my stuff together and ran out the door. I rushed over to the nursing home and prayed Torbjørn was doing all right. I just had a bad feeling about something.

When I got to Torbjørn's room I was shocked. He was sitting up in a wheel chair drinking orange juice from a straw. He saw me walk in and his face lit up immediately.

"Where the hell have you been? I thought you forgot about me," he said in Norwegian.

"Never. I just had to catch up on a bit of work at the office. How are you doing? You look good," I said.

"Ja. The nurse here gave me some medicine and I perked right up." He said as he pointed with his thumb to a young nurse whom we had never seen before.

"I thought you never take medicine," I said, trying to get a rise out of him. He smiled and said to the nurse in English, "Say miss, I've never seen you before. What's your name?" I groaned. He was up for a little mischief, for sure.

"Linda," she said, a bit startled.

"Are you married?"

"No," she said.

"Well this young man over here is single," he said as he pointed his thumb at me. "Maybe the two of you want to have coffee together, later on tonight?"

"Torbjørn!" I said. "You're embarrassing her," I said in Norwegian. The nurse's face turned red, and I told her that I thought the medication must be kicking in, big time. She gave me a nervous smile, wrapped a strand of hair behind her ear and walked out of the room. I gave Torbjørn a dirty look, and he smiled and winked back at me.

"What's up with speaking to the nurses in English?"

"I'm sorry, Jens Olav. I'm just feeling a little frisky tonight." He took a sip of his orange juice and set it on the table. "What difference does it make anyway? I don't think I've got much time before I move out to greener pastures. Sit down. Make yourself comfortable. I've got the rest of my story to tell you."

Torbjørn pointed at the small radio on his dresser and then to the door. The Twins baseball game was on, but I figured he wanted the radio off. I turned it off, closed the door, and sat down. He did his usual routine of wheeling himself over to the window next to the door and peering down the corridors. When he was satisfied, he said: "Do you remember where I left off from the other day, Jens Olav?"

"Okay," he continued, "So, it was too late in the season to take the loot out to Isle Royale that year. We had to sit on it at home for six months or so. If that don't drive you crazy, I don't know what would. We went through the motions all winter and waited for spring. Odd was planning. I asked him why we had to take all the loot with us, and why we had to hide it in such a desolate place. He told me that we didn't have to worry about anyone stealing it. He also told me we could go up there every year or two to check on it and take some bars if we needed them."

"Then Odd told me about his new plan. We weren't going to have that awful mess happen to us again. We would never let Chester hire another boat. We could trust nobody, see. So Odd wrote this letter home to Norway to our little brother, Stig. He said we had a great business opportunity for him and he had to come over this winter or next spring and help us out. We got a letter back from Stig saying he'd come but he had to bring his new bride and baby along with him. Odd didn't like that too much; he thought things would get too complicated. But what could he do?"

I thought to myself, Stig was Brett Ruud's grandfather, and the baby must have been Brett's father.

"So sure enough, come spring time," Torbjørn continued, "Stig, his wife, Agnes, and their baby came to Minneapolis. We told Stig all about the loot, and he got real excited. He said that when we got all that money we'd all have to go back to the old country and buy Mama and Papa a new house and boat.

When June finally came, we were ready. Odd wrote a letter to Chester that we required his service on the second week of that month. We had collected wood crates all winter and put a couple of bars of gold in each one. We loaded them up on the flatbed Ford and put a tarp over them. We set out early on a Saturday morning and told everyone, including Stig's young bride, that we were going to Kansas City to visit relatives for two weeks. By evening, we had met up with Chester at a roadside bar just outside of Duluth. Chester, of course, was a little tanked-up and was upset that he couldn't get a boat for us. There was something different about old Chester. I was beginning to dislike him. I couldn't put my finger on it. He was acting real cocky and he was drinking way too much for my taste."

"You know, Jens Olav, there's an old Viking saying: 'Confide in one, never in two. Tell three and the whole world knows.' Well, we should have known something was going on. Odd wanted to turn around and drive right back to Minneapolis, but we were tired of hiding the loot in our house and we had all of it in the truck, right outside the bar. He didn't want to create a scene and lose all that money. So, Odd said let's do it. When Chester staggered out of the saloon, helped by Stig, Odd pulled me aside and whispered in my ear to watch out for this guy, he's bad news."

"Odd drove off with Chester in his car to pick up the old fishing smack Odd had rented per our plan. Me and Stig got back in the truck and headed for Lake Superior. We drove to a small, secluded cove just a few miles north of Two Harbors. You know that small town about twenty miles north of Duluth?" I nodded, and he continued.

"We waited for about four hours and then finally, Odd and Chester come chugging along in a small fishing smack. It was a dark, moonless night. Not a breeze anywhere to be seen. The lake was as still as glass. Odd had told me to flash the truck lights a couple of times when he got within sight. Odd steered the smack towards us and cut the engine. He slowly and quietly drifted into the cove as far as he dared, not wanting to let the boat run aground. When he got about a hundred yards from the shore, he dropped the anchor. We then saw Chester crawl into a small rowboat, which was tied to the smack. We could see him grab two oars, and row into shore."

"I slowly backed up the Ford into the lake. Stig sat on the back and told me to stop when the water was about a foot from the bed. Chester rowed to the truck and Stig started handing him the crates. I could hear them huffing and puffing. Odd had me stamp 'Ammo' on the outside of all the crates so Chester wouldn't think any the better. When there were five crates on the rowboat, Stig told Chester to get out and get onto the truck. Chester stared at him for a good five seconds, and then gingerly got out. Stig then got into the rowboat. Chester and me watched as Stig slowly rowed out to the fishing smack. I could just see the outline of the smack. It was very dark. I could hear Odd and Stig talking in low tones. I couldn't make anything out, but I guessed Odd was telling Stig to watch out for Chester. When they had transferred the crates into the fish hold, we could hear the slight splashes of the oars rowing towards us. As the rowboat came up again, I could see the outline of Stig. Odd was a smart one all right. There was no way he was going to trust Chester out there in the fishing smack with half the loot. No way at all!"

"After two more trips, the loot was in the hold of the smack. Odd had told me that when all the loot was off, I was to hide the truck in some thick woods a few hundred yards from shore. When that was done, I waded into the ice-cold lake and Stig pulled me into the rowboat. He slowly rowed back to the smack. Within fifteen minutes, the engine was on, the rowboat was tied securely to the smack, and we were off to Isle Royale. It took us about a day and a half to get to the island. By six a.m. the second day, we set eyes on Isle Royale. We got to Siskiwit Bay and laid low until night. We were real fortunate, see, because there was nobody in sight to give us any trouble. At dusk we started moving the crates out of the fish hold and loading them into the row boat. We all kept our eyes on Chester and never left him alone with any of the crates. Odd had built a four-wheel wagon that was designed to hold about ten crates. So when we got the crates on the beach, we transferred them to this little wagon, and then the four of us pushed it the two and a half miles or so up the Island Mine Trail to the abandoned mine site. We hid the crates in some thick underbrush and repeated the process three times. Each trip took about three hours. We were still lucky—there was no sign of anybody around. We slept the rest of the day and tried to keep the blood-sucking mosquitoes at bay."

"The next day or so was spent with Odd and Chester going down into the mine and figuring out how to get the crates into the mine and find a good place to hide them while me and Stig guarded the loot. After the third day, we decided that the crates could be lowered by a pulley system down about 200 feet through the main shaft located about 200 yards from the horizontal portal we found last summer. Parts of the main vertical shaft were beginning to cave in and some of the support beams were buckling. There was no way a man could get through the narrow shaft, but miraculously we could lower the twenty crates, one at a time, down the shaft by a make-shift pulley system. Odd and Chester went down through the portal, and then climbed down the winze by a rope ladder to a drift, which is like a vertical shaft. Working their way toward the vertical shaft, they climbed down another winze to a drift which entered into a stope."

"What's a stope?" I asked.

"That's an excavated area in the mine where it was about two stories high. That's where the mined copper was removed and taken up the shaft to the surface. Me and Stig slowly lowered the crates about 200 feet to where Odd and Chester would retrieve them from the drift and carry them into the stope. This took all night and we decided to sleep in the stope with all the loot that next morning."

Suddenly, Torbjørn screamed, and clutched at his chest. His face turned red and he started to sweat. I immediately ran to the nurse's station. Nurse Thorson was there talking on the telephone. I interrupted her and told her of Torbjørn's condition. Within an hour I was sitting in the county hospital emergency room wondering if I'd ever see Torbjørn alive again.

•

The next morning I learned that Torbjørn had suffered a major heart attack and, due to his age and the damage to his heart, he wasn't expected to make it through the day. The nurse told me to prepare for his death. I decided to call Brett Ruud and Pastor Manders from the Norwegian *Mindekirken*. The church was a couple miles from the hospital and Pastor Buslett was the minister who led the outdoor service at Norway Day a few months ago. Brett wasn't home when I called, but, of course, Holly was there taking care of all the children. I told her of Torbjørn's condition, and she seemed sincerely upset. She told me that Brett was out of town on a fishing trip and she would let him know about Torbjørn the second he got back. Pastor Buslett said he would be over in the next hour or so to administer Torbjørn his last communion.

Three hours later, Pastor Buslett appeared and asked if I would like to participate in his last communion. I agreed, and we got permission from the ER nurse to go in. The pastor was getting ready to perform the ceremony, when suddenly Torbjørn's eyes opened. We were shocked. Torbjørn first focused on Pastor Buslett and had a questioning look on his face. Then he looked at me and a complete calmness came over him and he smiled. This relieved us both and the pastor started. After he had taken the sacrament, Torbjørn motioned with his head that he wanted to ask Pastor Buslett a question.

"Yes, Torbjørn, what is it?" the pastor asked in a caring voice.

Torbjørn opened his mouth and in a weak and raspy voice said, "Is it true, pastor, that all of my sins have been forgiven?"

"Yes, Torbjørn. If you truly believe that Jesus Christ is your Lord and Savior and the son of God, then yes, you are forgiven of all your sins."

"Will I then go to heaven, pastor?"

"Yes, Torbjørn, if you truly believe, yes."

A warm smile came over his face. He then asked, "Pastor, will I be reunited with my loved ones then? I mean, in heaven?"

"Yes Torbjørn."

"Will I see my beloved Ida then?" Pastor Buslett looked at me.

"Ida was his wife, pastor," I said.

Pastor Manders smiled and said, "Of course, you'll be reunited with your wife. You'll be reunited with your parents and siblings as well." Torbjørn just smiled and then closed his eyes.

•

The next day, Torbjørn's condition improved slightly. He was moved from the ER to the hospice ward. He was still unconscious and sleeping like a baby. I told myself that I wasn't going to leave the hospital until it was all over. I didn't know or care what day it was. That day I went down to the hospital cafeteria to get something to eat and then later on to get a late dinner. I sat in a chair next to Torbjørn for hours just looking at him and doing a lot of thinking. Why was I here? Why did I care so much about him? Was he the grandfather I never had? Or, was I here because maybe his crazy story could be true and if I played my cards right, I could be $12 million richer? After a few more hours of reflection, I came to the conclusion that it was a bit of all of those reasons.

The night had fallen again, and the nurse had made her rounds a few hours ago. Torbjørn had been sleeping peacefully for all that time, but all of a sudden I saw his face start to twitch. His eyes started to blink and then closed and he was moving his head. It reminded me of watching someone dreaming. It looked like he was talking to someone and then he would subtly nod his head. The whole thing was kind of creepy. It seemed like the temperature in the room went down about ten degrees. It was like an old, stale wind had penetrated the room, but a quick glance told me the window was shut and the door was halfway closed. I brushed it off, thinking it must have been the air conditioning that was blowing through an air vent.

Torbjørn's arms moved about and then he started moving his legs like he was walking. He started to mumble in Norwegian. I heard him say, "Odd, watch out Odd, he's got a gun." Then he gurgled some more and said, "the map, the map, where is the map?" He was quiet for a few moments and then it appeared someone was talking to him. He would nod a few times and then mumble some more. Then he was quiet again and appeared to fall back asleep.

After a few hours, I nodded off in the chair. Someone wakened me quite abruptly in a clear voice saying, "Wake up. Wake up, Jens Olav!" It was Torbjørn. I glanced at my watch and it was precisely three a.m. He looked alert and better than I'd seen him since the heart attack. There was something different though, I couldn't put my finger on it, but it was his eyes. The sparkle and the happiness in them were gone.

"Jens Olav, listen, I've got to finish my story. There's so little time, you know."

He sat up a bit and pointed to a paper cup of water with a straw in it. I grabbed the cup and brought it to his mouth. He took a few long sucks and thanked me with his eyes.

"As I told you before, we all slept in the stope of the mine with all the loot. Well, it appeared that our friend Chester had slipped some sleeping pills in our water supply. That means me, Odd, and Stig had slept a real long time. In fact, it was long enough for Chester to open a few of the crates and find out what was really going on. After all these years thinking about it, I believe his plan was to take a few of the crates for himself and then try to bury us alive."

"Well, that didn't happen, see. Odd was wise to his little games. He only drank a little bit of the water, guessing something was wrong with it. He woke up when he saw Chester attaching one of the crates to the pulley. 'Just what would you be doing there, Mr. Solberg?' Odd asked him. Of course, Chester had a surprised look on his face while Odd kicked me and Stig to wake up. 'Wake up, you fools, and look what I caught our trusted friend Chester doing.' We both got up, trying to take in what was going on."

"Then Chester pulled a pistol from his belt and said, 'Stand back, or I'll shoot you all.' Odd grabbed for the pistol he had had on his belt, but it was gone. 'What kind of fool do you take me for, Odd? Did you think you could pull a fast one on Chester? Did you think I was never going to take a look in them crates? I don't know why I shouldn't shoot the lot of you and let the critters eat you up like they did poor Skipper Jones.'"

"At that moment, out of pure anger, Odd lunged toward Chester. Chester, real cool, shot off three rounds at Odd, hitting him in the chest. The force blew him into the stack of crates. Well let me tell you, Jens Olav, Odd was a pretty big guy and him being blown into the stack of crates was enough for some of them to come tumbling down. The problem was that the crates, I guess about ten of them, came tumbling down on my left leg. There was a sharp cracking sound, and I could *feel* my leg bone snap. The pain was so intense, I couldn't believe it! I was pinned down and couldn't move. On top of that, Odd came falling down on top of me, pinning my arms. I couldn't think straight. All I could think of was to tell Stig to get the hell out of the mine and get some help. He immediately bolted down the drift toward the first winze. Chester heard me and fired at me. He pierced my ear and blood started pouring out. He said, 'I'll deal with you later, Torbjørn,' and then ran after Stig. I could hear distant footsteps. I thought Stig would be climbing up the first rope ladder. I was praying that somehow he could get out. I was breathing deeply and holding my hand to my ear to stop the bleeding, but I couldn't move with Odd on top of me and the crates pinning my throbbing leg. Even if Stig did get away, then surely Chester would come back to finish me off."

"You can't imagine, Jens Olav, the emotions running through me at that moment! My own brother, shot three times, lying on top of me, with his blood slowing trickling down on my face, stinging my eyes. I spit gobs of blood out of my mouth as I tried to wriggle free. But I couldn't. I was helpless. All I heard was a faint groaning sound coming from him. I knew it would be just a moment before he would die. I just lay there, waiting for old Chester to come back and finish his job."

"After about a minute, I heard two shots ring out and then I heard a blood-curdling scream. My heart started to pound heavier and heavier. Someone must have died, but whom? I could hear footsteps coming closer and closer. Oh, Jens Olav, it was terrible. What was I to do? Should I yell out? But, what if it's Chester? Then I figured if it was Stig, he would have yelled to me that Chester was dead. So I had to assume Chester was coming back. I closed my eyes and pretended I was dead. Odd's blood was all over my face by now."

"Then Chester walks into the stope with one hand on his pistol and the other holding a lantern. 'Well, well, well, what have we got here? Is it possible that I killed two birds with one stone?' he said smugly as I tried not to breathe so hard. He walked over to where Odd was lying on top of me. Odd was moaning just a bit. Chester bent down and felt his wrist for a pulse. 'Hum, this bastard's still alive,' he said and then raised the gun and shot Odd in the temple. We both jerked and then he looked at me. With all his might, he threw Odd off of me and bent down again to feel my pulse. I had just enough time to grab my bowie knife from around my waist and I stabbed him in the chest with every ounce of strength I had left in me. He lurched and tried to pull away, but his foot got caught on one of the fallen crates and he fell toward me. I stabbed him over and over again until my entire body was soaking in his blood. I pushed him over and shouted: 'Go to hell!'"

"So there I lay, pinned down by the crates, with my brother and Chester dead a few feet from me. I feared my other brother lay dead in the drift. I lay there for about an hour, trying to decide what to do next."

"What was that?" I asked, my head swimming with all the things he had told me.

"I could see the broken end of bone sticking out of the skin of my leg, and could see I couldn't get any leverage to shift the crates. Besides, every time I moved, pain shot through my lower leg like a bolt of lightning. And I guessed my foot was probably crushed beneath those damned crates of gold. So I used my bowie knife to cut clean through what skin and tissue still held my leg together. I was sure I was going to faint from the unbelievable pain, but somehow I kept at it until I was free."

"You've got to be kidding, Torbjørn! You cut off your own leg?"

"You're God damn right I cut it off. I then spilled the burning lantern oil on the stump. The pain was so great I passed out, but it stopped the bleeding. I can't begin to describe how painful that was! When I woke up, I wrapped the stump as good as I could and started crawling down the stope and into the drift. It took me a good day to climb up out of the mine and then I spent the next few days in the campsite, where we had food and good water."

At this point, Torbjorn's already bloodshot eyes were becoming wet and small tears started rolling down his wrinkled and aged cheeks. He took a few sobbing breaths and continued, "I did indeed find my brother Stig, dead, up in the drift, lying right where Chester had shot him. I wanted to give both my brothers proper burials, but my leg was hurting way too much and I'd be God damned if I was going to have the treasure kill me too. I then cursed God and everyone else I could think of for the deaths of my two brothers. The damn treasure wasn't worth their deaths, I tell you!"

"A day later I crawled down the Island Mine Trail and rowed to the fishing smack. The whole time, no one was there to see what happened. I set sail for Duluth and basically did the same thing we did to the other boat a year before. I sank the smack and rowed the small boat to shore and got some medical attention."

He stopped there and just looked at my reaction. I was beyond flabbergasted. How could anyone think up such a crazy story?

"So then what happened?" I asked.

Torbjørn's face was getting real pale now, and his voice was getting weaker. He appeared to be rushing things because he knew he didn't have much time. "What happened next is not important, Jens Olav. What is important is that you realize that the loot is cursed. What you have to realize is that the treasure, directly or indirectly, has killed twenty-six people, plus taken half my leg. I told you this story, because for over fifty years I've kept it a secret and I needed to get it out of me. When you came along I wanted to see if I could trust you. Because, I certainly don't trust anyone else."

"Anyway," he continued, "after I recuperated for awhile on the campsite, I hid the mine shaft entrance and the portal entrance with shrubs and branches. The location of the mine shaft and the portal is all marked out on a map of Isle Royale I have hidden somewhere. I want you to have it and do what you will with it. But I do ask that you keep all of this a secret and do not mention a word to anyone that the Ruud brothers had anything to do with it. Is that clear?"

I nodded.

"Lastly, Jens Olav, there are a couple of other things I want to say." He winced in pain and he lifted up his hand. His face was now extremely pale, as if the essence of life was vanishing. I grabbed his outstretched hand. It was cold and clammy. He squeezed mine, and continued. "I just want to say how wonderful it was for you to come into my lonely life. Since I met you, life was worth living again. You, Odd, and Ida were the most important things in my little, unimportant life. And I want to say that you have to start living your life and don't waste it away like I did for so many years. Don't have regrets on your deathbed like I have on mine."

He choked up again. His voice was barely audible. "Jens Olav, the gold don't mean shit. You, Odd, and especially Ida are what had meaning for me."

Then there was one final sparkle in his eyes, and I thought I saw just a hint of a smile. His grip on my hand loosened and then Torbjørn died. Tears ran down my cheeks, and the room got cold again. I could have sworn I heard someone come into the room, that I was not alone. I got up and turned the lights on and looked around the room. Torbjørn and I were the only ones there.

Chapter XIII

Later that morning, I drove home and told Brian that Torbjørn was dead. He offered his condolences and in the same breath told me that Nora was a bit worried that I had not talked to her in the past week and was wondering if anything was wrong. I cursed myself because I had totally forgotten about everything going on in my life, being so consumed by Torbjørn's illness. I quickly called Nora and told her about Torbjørn and asked if she would like to go out for dinner.

The next morning I called my boss and told him that an extremely close great uncle of mine had passed away and that I would be gone for a couple of days. I lied, but what the hell. How would he know, anyway? After a long and uncomfortable pause and an even longer uncomfortable sigh, he said okay.

With my boss out of the way, I decided to go to the *Mindekirken* and pay Pastor Buslett a visit. I told the pastor about the passing of Torbjørn and that I wanted to have a funeral for him. Pastor Buslett just nodded his head and said it was a very Christian thing to do. I said it was the least I could do for him.

Next, I drove over to the nursing home. My sister had left me a message informing me that Brett had called the nursing home and asked if he could pick up Torbjorn's suitcase later today. I knew if Brett was interested in that suitcase then he must think there's something of value in it. As I got to Torbjorn's floor, I didn't want the nurse on duty see me poking around his room. I was relieved to see no one had cleaned out his things yet. I walked over to the closet and got the old suitcase out. I opened it and was bombarded by the same musty air I had smelled the first time I went into it. There was the same old sailor's uniform and knickknacks from around the world that I guess a sailor would have collected. There was a carved whale bone, a piece of coral, some paper money from China and South Africa, a pocket watch and the like. For some reason I felt uneasy. I walked over to the door to see if anyone was coming. The coast was clear, so I closed the door and walked back to the suitcase. My heart started to pound. I didn't know if I felt guilty looking through some dead man's belongings or if I was nervous about finding the thing I was really looking for. I took out every item. The only things that intrigued me were an old log book and a photo album. Nothing, absolutely nothing. What was I thinking anyway? It was a complete hoax. It was just a story to keep a fool like me entertained. I walked around the room and started looking through drawers, the night stand, anything. A few more minutes produced nothing. I glanced out the window and saw the street below. My heart sank when I looked out and saw Brett get out of his red pick-up truck. He was here. What would he think if he saw me here? He would know something was up.

I started to panic, but took a few deep breaths. 'Think, Jens, think!' I walked over to the door and cracked it open. No one coming. I had one last chance to find it. I walked over to the chest and started to feel around the inside edges. Nothing. My headed started to pound and sweat was running down my forehead. I started to put all the items back into the suitcase when I accidentally dropped the pocket watch. It bounced. The bottom was hollow. I pounded with my fist on the bottom of the chest. Yes, it was definitely hollow. I picked up the suitcase and swung it upside down. The false bottom fell out as well as an aged, waterlogged map. It was folded and had some Norwegian words written in pencil on it. Bingo!

I quickly put the false bottom and the rest of Torbjørn's things back into the suitcase and threw it into the closet. I grabbed the old map, the log book and the photo album and ran out the door. I glanced down the hall and cringed. He was standing at the nurse's station, undoubtedly asking the nurse where Torbjørn's room was. He had his face turned toward the nurse, so I don't think he saw me. I dashed into the next room. I could hear him walking down the corridor with the nurse, who was chatting about Torbjørn. I could feel my heart pounding faster. I had to make a run for it. I peeked out the door and saw the nurse walking back to the station. I knew he was in the next room. I glanced at the old lady who was lying in the bed. She had been staring at me the entire time with a quizzical look on her face. She looked vaguely familiar. I waved at her and was about to leave when she said, "Young man, have you seen my mother?"

"I'm afraid I haven't, ma'am." I ran out the door and into the waiting elevator.

•

I decided to drive to my favorite spot in town, Nicollet Island, and look at the items I'd collected in Torbjørn's room. I had taken Torbjørn and Nora to see the wonderful view of St. Anthony Falls many times. I sat at a picnic table and was happy to see no one was around. After all, it was Monday afternoon and most people were still at work. It was another beautiful summer day with a dark blue sky and puffy little white clouds. I could hear the powerful roar of the waterfall.

I decided I would look at the map last. I opened the logbook and looked through it. It was a typical nautical logbook, with dates and places in it, longitude and latitude markings and the like. Someday I wanted to look at it closely so I could track Torbjørn's journeys, but not now, I was too excited and moved on. I then grabbed the photo album and found that much more interesting. The first page was full of very old black and white photos of a house and farm that must have been from Norway. There was also a photo of a family posing in strict late-19th century poses. This must have been Torbjørn's family. There were five little ones, so I couldn't figure out which one was Torbjørn. The next few pages were the ones that most intrigued me. They were photos of Torbjørn, Odd, and most of all, Ida. I recognized her from the portrait on the nightstand in Torbjørn's room. There were also photos of the vegetable stand, the little O & T Grocery store and even the flatbed Ford. All of Torbjørn's stories were coming to life and flashing before me now. The photos corroborated some of his stories, anyway. I saw a photo of Torbjørn and, I assumed, Odd. He was a big, rough sort of fellow who had intelligent eyes and big working hands. I can see why Odd made all the decisions and was the leader. I turned the page and saw a photo of Ida and Torbjørn overlooking what appeared to be the Badlands in South Dakota. They were holding hands and smiling at each other. They looked genuinely happy, so young, and most of all, so alive.

As I continued to look at the photos, music came into my head. I imagined Tommy Dorsey playing a melancholy song in the background. I imagined that somehow I was transformed and I was there with Torbjørn, Odd and Ida, the instant they were taken. I hate to admit it, but I was getting a little too emotional about it. I felt like I knew these people so well, that they were my friends, and now, sadly, they were all gone.

I looked around to see if anyone was close. A teenage couple walked hand and hand a few hundred yards away admiring the falls. I carefully unfolded the map, so as to not tear the old frayed paper. It was a large U.S. Department of Commerce nautical chart of Isle Royale dating from the 1920s. The island was cut in half with the northern section on the bottom and the southern on the top. It had water depths around the coast of the island and even topographical elevations. I turned my attention to Siskiwit Bay in the bottom half of the map. In pencil was a line running from the southern tip of the island called 'The Head,' then running through Houghton Point Passage and ending with an X just off Senter Point. Senter Point—that sounded familiar. Then, on land, the pencil mark went up the Island Mine Trail to an icon that had a shovel crossed with a pickax. It read, 'Island Mine (Abandoned).' My heart began to pound and sweat again started to pour off my face. I turned the map around and on the back was more writing in Norwegian and a diagram. Then it hit me; it was a diagram of the mineshaft! I started to read the old and faded writing, when I heard a bunch of yelling and screaming. I looked up and saw a Minneapolis school bus unloading about fifty elementary school kids. They must have been on a field trip to the falls. I collected all my stuff on the picnic table and left.

•

Two days later we had the funeral at the *Mindekirken*. The only attendees were my immediate family, Nora, Brian, Paige, and a few brave souls from the nursing home who were not afraid of being yelled at by the ghost of Torbjørn. The one person I noticed who was not there was Brett Ruud. After the burial, Torbjørn was supposedly resting in peace. I should have felt good about the funeral, but I was tense and uptight. I needed to be alone. I needed to take a good long walk on the Mississippi Parkway and think.

I felt such a loss with Torbjørn gone. Somehow, I felt like I lost another grandfather. I got out of my car and started walking south toward the University of Minnesota's West Bank campus. I walked a few blocks and looked down at my sore feet. I forgot that I was wearing my dress shoes from the funeral. As I continued to walk, I said to myself, 'Is that it now? Torbjørn's dead.' Was I going to go back and start devoting my whole life to work again? But something in my heart told me no... no! Don't let them win. I felt the presence of my great grandfather. I told myself that map must be true and would show me where the treasure was hidden in the abandoned mine. I promised Grandpa Jens that somehow I was going to Isle Royale. I would find that damn treasure, and prove to everyone that Torbjørn's life meant something.

I drove immediately to my favorite map store in downtown Minneapolis. I'd always had a love affair with maps, and have an extensive map library in my den. I was looking for any map that had to do with Isle Royale, in particular, and Lake Superior in general. I found a really nice U.S. National Oceanic and Atmospheric Administration map and a nice U.S. Department of the Interior Geological Survey topographic map of Isle Royale. I also picked up a NOAA map of Lake Superior.

After that, I drove to the Minneapolis Public Library—thank God they had late hours—and tried to find everything I could on Isle Royale. About an hour later, I checked out seven books and drove home. I set up my makeshift research center on a worn table in my den. For the next three hours I learned a lot about Isle Royale. This 45-mile-long archipelago of an island, situated in the northwestern portion of Lake Superior, was formed more than 10,000 years ago. Its maximum width is about nine miles and it has an area of about 850 square miles. Through the years the island had many nicknames like 'the rock,' 'the copper island,' and the 'floating island.' The Ojibwa called it 'Minong' meaning 'a good place to live.' Native Americans started to mine copper on the island about 4,000 years ago. The French claimed the island in 1671 and named it. The Americans acquired it in 1783, and it was defined as a Chippewa Territory until 1843. Congress made the island a national park in 1931, and in 1940, Franklin D. Roosevelt officially established it as a park. The island was used for mining copper, but the copper was of low quality, and the extraction was too expensive because it was so remote. Logging and commercial fishing also proved unsuccessful. By the early 1900s, resorts and private summer cottages sprang up.

Okay, enough of the history lesson. What I really needed to know was that there were more than 160 miles of hiking trails and the park opened every year in mid-April and closed on October 31st. The busy tourist season was from mid-July until the third week of August, and least crowded times were April and May, and mid-September to October. It's hard to get to the island. There are only a few passenger ships that depart from ports in Michigan or from Grand Marais on the Minnesota north shore. Once you get there, you have to obtain a camping permit from ranger stations in either Windigo in the southwest or Rock Harbor on the northeast. There are no roads. There are about thirty-six campgrounds and groups of seven to ten people can get reservations. Smaller groups can get campsites on a first-come, first-serve basis. This could be tricky.

I unfolded my new Isle Royale map to find out how close some of the campsites were to the abandoned mine. I found Island Mine Campground about a half mile north of the mine. I thought that would be the best place for my center of operations, but I didn't like the fact it was so close to the mine. I didn't want nosy campers poking around. The maximum stay at that campground was three days. I found two other campgrounds; Siskiwit Bay on the beach about four miles to the mine; and Hay Bay, which was about four miles by water from the mine. The longest one could stay in those was also three days. That didn't give me much time. Maybe I could stay in Island Mine for three days, then move to Siskiwit Bay for three days, and then if need be, back to Island Mine.

Torbjørn was correct about the mine. The copper mine was opened in 1873 and three shafts were sunk. It only lasted for about two years. I guess there were low yields, shaky economic times and skittish investors. John J. Senter, who was a mining prospector, help build a stone powder house which was later used by the Island Mine Company. This building was right on Siskiwit

Bay. The mining company built a wide gravel road to the mine, which was encouraging, knowing that some of the trails in national parks can be hard to traverse. The only question was what condition the trail was in now. The other interesting bit was that, in the 1930s, there was a CCC (Civilian Conservation Corps) camp in an open area a few miles southwest of Siskiwit Bay. Torbjørn had been right about that, too.

The most troubling information was that the National Park Service prohibited taking any property from their parks. The U.S. Attorney's office and the Department of the Interior lawyers would deal with the violators to the fullest extent of the law. The way I saw it, Torbjørn's treasure wasn't put there for people to see. Hell, it wasn't even a park when Odd and Torbjørn hid it there. If someone was clever enough to snatch the treasure, then they deserved to keep it. Certain plans now were formulating in my head.

Chapter XIV

I got up and stretched my legs. It had been a long day. The funeral seemed like days ago. I went into the kitchen and got a can of beer. I walked around the apartment some more. I was antsy and not a bit tired, so I decided to take a walk around Lake Harriet. It was only a three-mile walk and it was just across the street from my apartment.

The wind was cool and dry. I loved the city at this time of night. It was so quiet and still. 'Okay Jens,' I said to myself. 'Think. Think of a plan. So it's illegal to just go to the island and take the gold. So that meant I'd have to be secretive. I'll have to watch out for all those park rangers.'

Next, I had to get there. Then it hit me. For the past few years, Brian and I have been chartering a sailboat up on Lake Superior. A friend of my father's was a part owner of a small marina on Madeline Island, the largest island of the Apostles. In high school, I worked as a laborer at the marina during the summer. I had chartered sailboats and went on expeditions in and around all of the twenty-two Apostle Islands. After I met Brian, and we became roommates, I took him along on these excursions. I guess Brian told Paige about the great time he had and she wanted to experience the fun. When Nora and I started getting more serious, Paige hinted around that maybe the four of us could go on one of these notorious weekenders. Why not plan a little sailing expedition to Isle Royale? It wouldn't arouse suspicion if two couples were innocently poking around the inlets and bays of Isle Royale, would it? We would be minding our own business and no one would be the wiser. I knew the marina master pretty well and already knew which sailboat would be the best to charter.

Now, the next question I had was, when? We had to go when the park was open, so I had to go when there were the smallest crowds. That meant April, May, September or October.

Well, I knew that it would still be cold in April and the bugs hatch in May, and it could be too cold in October. That meant that September would be the best month to go. Better make it the last half of September, though. Better to be a bit cold than to have a bunch of nosy people about.

Okay, now, the big question. Could I convince Brian, Nora, and Paige to come along on this little voyage? Could I trust them? What about Paige? Could the two of us get along without tearing out each other's hair? I was sure her idea of roughing it was having to stay at a motor lodge. She couldn't stand two weeks on a tiny boat or in a small and damp tent. Could she? As I was pondering this difficult question I noticed a crack of light rising from the eastern horizon. Could it be? I glanced at my watch. It was 5:30 a.m. God, I'd been up all night!

•

Nora, Brian and Paige were surprised when I invited them all out for drinks on Wednesday night. I'm not usually an instigator, but I needed to reveal my plan to them. I chose the pub where we usually met on Friday for happy hour. I chose it because of the great beer selection, and, man, did I need a beer or two while trying to pitch this crazy scheme. I got there fifteen minutes early and found a nice booth far from the bar and the speakers, where we could converse. I had ordered a beer from Estonia and started sipping it when Paige came over and sat down. The next five minutes seemed like an hour. We were both very ill at ease and were really searching for things to say. Thank God Nora came walking in and saved the day. She laid into me, though, about why tonight of all nights did I have to get everyone together. She said she had a tough day tomorrow and had to get up extra early. I tried to brush it off by telling a few jokes, but I wasn't succeeding. Brian came about five minutes later. He ordered a drink for everyone, celebrating the fact that I finally took the initiative to ask them to go out for a drink. Nora ordered the same drink as Paige, and Brian ordered two Guinness beers.

"So Nilsen, what's the story? Why have you assembled us all here?' Brian asked. I took a deep breath, and then said to myself, what the hell, here goes.

"You know guys... I was thinking. Well, I mean, I was wondering if ..."

"Yes, Jens? What are you trying to say?" Nora interrupted.

"Well, before I start, you all have to promise me that you'll keep what I'm about to say in the strictest confidence." I looked around the table for a reaction. Paige just rolled her eyes, but Nora and Brian appeared intrigued. They all nodded their heads, and I took a long gulp and finished my beer and continued. "You, see, in the few months that I knew Torbjørn, we got to be really close. He started to tell me this outrageous story."

"What was it about?" Brian asked.

"Well, he told me how he was born in Norway, joined the merchant marine at sixteen, sailed around the world and then ended up in Minneapolis in the late 1920s.

"Fascinating," Paige interjected.

"Yes, Paige, I'm sure to you it's just another boring immigrant's tale, except for a couple of things."

"Don't leave us in suspense Jens," Nora said. "Out with it."

"He happened to fall in the company of some gangsters and had a shoot-out with another gang. After the shoot-out, he and his brother came into possession of some loot."

"Loot? What do you mean, loot?" Paige asked.

"You know, money... treasure. Actually, it consisted of boxes of gold bars." Now that got the attention of everybody. A waiter came by, and gave Brian and me our Guinness' and we ordered two red wines for the women. When the waiter walked away I heard Nora say, "Do you believe Torbjørn was telling you the truth?"

"I don't know. I've checked a few things out that seem to confirm his story, but I'm not really sure."

"Do you know when this shoot-out happened? Did it happen in Minneapolis?" Brian asked.

"I think it was St. Paul and I think it had to be about 1934," I said.

"You should check out the old newspaper database at the St. Paul Library to see if there's a story about it," Brian said.

"Where is the treasure... I mean, where are the gold bars now? Nora asked.

"Torbjørn said that it's all hidden in an abandoned mine on Isle Royale, up on Lake Superior."

"Don't tell me," Paige interjected again, "This old, bizarre man tells you, a complete stranger, that he has buried treasure on some island on Lake Superior, and we're supposed to believe this? How many gold bars are we talking about here?"

I looked straight in the eyes of Paige and said nonchalantly, "Eighty."

"Eighty!" Brian said. "How much does a gold bar weigh?"

"Torbjørn said that they were London Good Delivery Bars and each one of them weighed 400 Troy ounces or about twenty-seven pounds," I said.

"What is the price for an ounce of gold going for nowadays?" Nora asked.

"Last time I checked it was $350 per ounce," I said.

"Per ounce!" Paige demanded.

"Per ounce," I said mockingly.

"That means it's worth a lot of money, Jens, doesn't it?" Nora said. I smiled and hesitated a bit for the effect. "Yes, Nora, it's a little bit of money. In today's prices it's about 12 million dollars."

There was complete silence at the table. Everyone had dazed looks on their faces. The waiter brought the wine for the women, and we all started sipping our drinks as I poured out my heart and told them my story from when I met Torbjørn all the way to his death. As I was telling my little story, I was observing the reactions of my friends. Nora and Brian seemed to be quite excited. Paige on the other hand, needed convincing.

"What's the plan then, Nilsen?" Brian asked. "I know you. I bet you've already checked into everything about the island, haven't you?"

I told them about my little investigation of the island and about all the rules of the Park Service. I told them about my plan to sail there on the *Peer Gynt,* the old, reliable sailboat that Brian and I usually charter. I also explained about the campgrounds on the island. I had to do more research about the Island Mine and about how one goes about exploring old and dangerous ones. I could tell that Nora and Brian were hooked. They were just as eager, if not more than I, to go on this little expedition.

"But what if it's all untrue?" Paige went on. "What if Torbjørn just made up the story of the gold to prove his life wasn't all a mistake?" Wow, I thought, Paige certainly has a way with words.

"So what if the gold's not in the mine? Just the adventure is enough, isn't it?" I paused, trying to keep my voice casual, "Oh, yeah. Torbjørn told me the treasure is cursed."

"How so?" Brian inquired.

"I guess because so many people have died who have been associated with it."

"Do you believe him?" Nora asked.

"No, not really."

"Well... let me think about it," I heard Paige say. Just then, The Romantics' song, *What I like about You* came over the speakers and many people in the pub rushed down to the dance floor. Nora yelled out, "Why don't we all dance?"

Brian stood up and said, "That's a great idea." So the four of us got up and ran over to the dance floor where we set up in a circle and started dancing wildly.

•

Near the end of August I was planning the adventure of a lifetime. I had to buckle down at work and get my production up. Hell, I was broke and I needed money to finance the trip. We had to think about chartering the *Peer Gynt*, and buying food and supplies for at least two weeks. We also had to figure out how we were going to find and get into the abandoned mine, as well as how to bring the gold up and how to get it back to the boat. Brian and I enrolled in a sailing navigation class at a local community college. The course specialized in night sailing. I knew if Einar Tviet, the marina master, was going to let us sail the *Peer Gynt* to Isle Royale, then I had to get certified to sail at night.

We all bought good hiking boots and started to break them in. I bought a good durable backpack—with my credit card, of course—and filled it with about 100 pounds of weights—about the same as four gold bars—and walked around Lake Harriet every morning and evening. I wanted to break in the boots and get into shape by carrying heavy loads in the backpack. At eighty bars, that would mean that Brian and I could carry three or four gold bars at a time and Nora and Paige could carry one or two. It would take us about seven trips walking the two and a half miles from the mine to the beach. I figured it would take us about an hour to walk from the mine to the beach and another hour to walk back. So that meant seven trips at two hours each or about fourteen hours just to transport the gold. Then I had to figure out how to get the gold on the skiff and then onto the *Peer Gynt*.

Time was of the essence. I wanted to get to Isle Royale this season. I didn't want to wait over the cold, long winter. After coordinating everyone's work and personal schedule, I determined that the best time for us to go was the first week of October. It would be cold, not to mention the possibility of early winter storms that the inland sea is known for. But it was also the least frequented time of the year for campers and hikers. I didn't want people around, and we had to steer clear of the rangers. We could bring along a lot of warm clothing and we didn't have to worry about those dreaded bugs.

I kept myself busy with work and planning for the trip for the next two weeks. I came home one night and was blown away by what came in the mail. It was a letter addressed to me with no return address. It was written in a surprisingly readable hand:

July 30, 1987
Dear Jens Olav,

By the time you read this letter I will have departed from this world and hopefully joined Ida in the next. I just wanted to thank you again so much for coming into my life. I do not think you will truly ever understand how much it has meant to me. I know my health is getting worse and I have had some bad chest pains for the last few weeks. I just thought I had better write down some important details about the gold if my ticker goes pretty soon or I may have forgotten to tell you some of the important things about the island and the gold.

First of all, and I do not know how to tell you this any plainer, don't go after the gold! It's cursed and it's bad luck. It's meant to be in the ground in that abandoned mine forever! Too many people have died who are some way connected with the gold.

Now that's said, I know you, Jens Olav. You are just like me when I was your age. You are going for the gold, aren't you? Well, my advice is this, don't tell too many people, only the ones you trust, and watch out for them too. Gold does a funny thing to a person. It's like a disease. I know, it's made me crazy ever since we dropped off the gold in the mine.

I want to warn you about the mine. It's dangerous in there. Parts of the shaft could have caved in, or water could have filled in some of the shafts during the years. You also have to watch out for poisonous gasses. I urge you to read up on old mines and be cautious and prepared. I forgot to tell you that it rained a few days we were there putting the gold in the mine. Some of the shafts, especially the vertical shaft, filled up with water. I'm just saying that some of the shafts, drifts, and stopes might have filled in with water, and you may need scuba gear to get to the gold. I just don't know.

The last thing I want to tell you, Jens Olav, is that if you are so lucky as to get the gold and get it off the island and you or any of your companions aren't dead, then I want you to contact a Mr. Oskar Sæther who lives in Bay Ridge, Brooklyn, New York. He's kind of a shady character, but he can exchange gold for gold, if you know what I mean. I knew his father quite well back in the bad old days and his son has followed in his dad's footsteps, if you know what I mean. You'll maybe get eighty cents on the dollar, but it's still a lot of money.

Well, this is it, Jens Olav. I'm giving this sealed letter to that old battle-axe Thorson. I told her to mail it a week or two after I'm gone. If you are reading this, then she truly fulfilled my last wish. Good luck, Jens Olav.

Your Friend,

Torbjørn

Chapter XV

The next week went fairly quickly. Brian and I were busy studying for the navigational class exam and we were hiking around the lake every day with our full backpacks. I neglected my work and my quality and turn-around time was suffering. My work problem came to a head on Wednesday afternoon. When I arrived at the office, I noticed a handwritten note from Norm to see him when I get back in the office. Great. Now what? I walked up to his office door and saw him behind his messy desk talking on the telephone. He motioned for me to come in and sit in the chair next to his desk. I gingerly strolled over to the chair and sat. Norm appeared to be talking to some mortgage company, trying to explain in an obsequious way why some appraisal assignments were late. He was really sucking up to the person on the other end of the line. I guess the customer is always right.

Finally, Norm hung up. He looked up at me from his desk and studied my face, trying to make a sincere smile. He failed. I could tell he was processing thoughts on where to begin our little talk. I knew it wasn't going to be pleasant.

"So Jens... how are things going for you?"

I studied his face this time, wondering where he was going with this conversation and paused a bit. "Fine. How are things going with you?" I asked.

By the baffled look on his face, I think he was disappointed. I don't think that was the answer he was looking for. He shifted his puffy body and tried a different tack. "Are things going well on the home front? Are your parents well?" he asked.

"Yes, thank you."

This time a sigh, "All right, let's get to the point, shall we? Why has your appraisal production gone down in the past few months? Are you ill? Do you have some sort of injury or something?" Norm asked.

"No," I said.

Another unsuccessful stab at making a sincere smile. "Okay then, is there something in your personal life that is causing this staggering lack of production?" I didn't say a word. I could tell he had a lot more questions, so I let him continue. "I've got to tell you, Jens, that I've been getting some complaints from clients about late appraisals and poor time management. Our appraisal review department has found some rather common and quite stupid mistakes on some of your work as well. You used to be one of our shining stars. We could count on you to get the job done day or night and even on weekends." He took another deep breath and said again, "What's wrong with you, Jens?"

I just sat there, staring at him not knowing what to say. I hated myself for that. I could never spew out my innermost thoughts. I had to think really hard. I knew I would have something clever to say five minutes after I left his office. For the moment, though, my mind was blank. What I really wanted to say is that I hated this job, and you can stuff the production numbers and turn-around times. For that matter, you can stop counting on me day and night and weekends too.

"I... I know I've been slacking off a bit. I... I think it's because of the death of that... uncle I told you about. I promise, I'll buckle down and get my production up."

He again smiled and said, "Good Jens. I'm glad we had this little talk."

•

After work, I decided I was going to pay a visit to the library again and get all the information I could on copper mines, especially copper mines from the 1870s. I also wanted to get any information I could on the dangers of abandoned mines. I was particularly concerned about poisonous gas and cave-ins. I also worried about the possibility that a portion of the mine could be flooded. Brian and I were scuba certified a few years ago when we started going to the Caribbean on winter break. The tricky part was learning how to scuba dive in abandoned mines. I knew the water would be extremely cold, the shaft would be extremely dark, and there could be cave-ins or other obstructions in the shafts. I found some good information and checked out a few pertinent books.

I got back to my apartment at about nine p.m. I had to get in another practice walk around Lake Harriet before I turned in for the evening. I put on my boots and my weighted backpack and walked out the door. It took me about an hour to walk around the lake. As I was walking into my apartment building, I saw something that made the hair on my back stand up. Parked right in front of the building was the same large red pickup truck that I had seen outside of Torbjørn's nursing home just a few weeks ago.

I quickly ran upstairs to my apartment. As I walked through the door, I realized I still had my heavy backpack on, so I began to take it off. Brian and Brett were standing in the living room, and they were both staring at me.

Brett smiled at me and was processing the information that was presented to him. Brian said, "Jens, this is Brett Ruud. I guess he's Torbjørn's nephew."

"We've met," Brett said. Then he looked me up and down and said, "Are you going camping anytime soon?"

I was thunderstruck. I didn't know what to say. I shot a panicked look at Brian. He noticed my level of concern and shot back to me a look like 'I don't know what's going on here.' I hadn't told Brian about Brett. It had slipped my mind.

"Is there anything I can help you with, Brett?" I finally got out. The tension in the room was as thick as a triple lane highway. Brian was noticing the utter contempt between the two of us. Brett was giving me this hard ass-look like he was saying, 'do you want a piece of me?' He had an obnoxious smirk about him that was nauseating.

"I was just wondering if you knew where some of Uncle Torbjørn's things are? I guess the nursing home must have misplaced them."

Uncle Torbjørn? Is that what he said? This is the guy who's only seen him once in the past five years, never talked to him or cared about him and now he has the audacity to call him Uncle Torbjørn? We had another stare-down contest and then I said, "No I haven't seen any of his things. I'm surprised you even know what his things are. How many times in the past five years have you seen him at the nursing home? Oh, and by the way, we missed you at the funeral, too."

I could see his cheeks turning red. He was trying to contain his anger. His face settled down a bit and he said, "Okay, I probably deserved that. I admit that I haven't been the best nephew, but he was still my uncle." The tension in the room calmed a bit. Brian went into the kitchen and brought out three beers. Brett continued, "If I can just take a little of your time, Jens. Just a few minutes... please?"

Brett and I sat down on opposing chairs as Brian gave us beers and excused himself. I could tell he didn't want any part of this. I was prepared to hear any kind of self-pitying story of how the system did him in—strange, that sounded kind of familiar.

We both took a couple sips of beer and tried to settle down. My heart was pounding wildly. As he started to talk, many thoughts bombarded my brain. Like, how did he find where I lived so quickly? What was he doing here? What was his game? I knew I had to be on my toes. He was planning something.

"Did Torbjørn talk about my grandfather Stig at all?" I took a breath and carefully thought of a response that would be both correct and vague. "He mentioned that he came over from Norway with his wife and son..."

"Did he also tell you that he died the same year he came over?"

"Umm... well, let me think. He may have said something about it. Why?"

"No particular reason. It's just I never got a straight answer from my mother—or Torbjørn—as a matter of fact."

"Did you grow up around here?" I asked trying to change the subject.

"I grew up in a couple of places in northern Minnesota. My dad had a drinking problem and split on us when I was about five years old. I never saw him after that. I got word that he committed suicide about ten years ago. My mom and me kind of moved around from family member to family member until she got a job at the Itasca County courthouse." How lovely, I thought. So this guy did have it rough. I guess it passes from generation to generation. I was getting a little sucked in by his story. Man, these Ruuds could spin a yarn. Brett continued, "So I guess I mostly grew up in Grand Rapids. That's where I went to high school."

"Is that where you met Holly?" I asked. He smiled and looked at me.

"Yes. She was a cheerleader and the most popular girl in school. I was on the hockey team and pretty good... I guess. We were even king and queen at our senior homecoming. Those were the good old days... but then things changed. I got a full scholarship at the University and there was even talk of the North Stars drafting me. I wanted to break up with Holly because I knew I would be moving down to the Cities in the fall. She wanted to move down with me, but she was enrolled to go to the technical college in Hibbing. It got kind of scary; she followed me all over that summer and accused me of having affairs behind her back. She told me she would never give me up. What could I do? Then I got the news that she was pregnant. She told everybody in town that the baby was mine. I got mad and got really loaded at a local bar. When I drove home I got into a big car accident. I lost my chance at the scholarship and the NHL. We got married, and I got a job at the paper factory."

A slight variation from the story I heard from Holly, I thought to myself. I guess there are always two sides to a story. Why was he telling me this? Did he think I cared? Was he trying to get me to sympathize with him? He had a lot of work ahead of him.

"I guess you're wondering why I'm telling my life story to you." Bingo. "You see Jens, I guess it's because I had a chance to make it big time. I was going to be someone. I know you think I'm some kind of uneducated hick from the sticks. But I had the potential to be an NHL star. Holly ruined it for me," he said.

"Oh come on, Brett. You could have kept Mr. Happy in your pants. I don't think she had a gun to your head when the two of you were in bed." I couldn't believe I just said that to almost a complete stranger, but he really pissed me off.

"I was a young kid. I'm sure you would have done the same thing in high school. She told me she had protection. She lied to me. I made a couple of mistakes. If I hadn't slept with her that one night and if I hadn't had that accident, my whole life would have been completely different. Just two frickin' mistakes when I was eighteen years old and now I'm paying for it for my entire life!"

He was right. If I would have ever had the opportunity to have my homecoming queen in bed, I would have probably done the same thing.

"Brett, why did you really come to see me?" I asked.

"I don't really know. I guess I just wanted to see if Uncle Torbjørn said anything about me. I was wondering if he left anything for me," he said.

Okay, I thought to myself. Here it comes. "Didn't you get all of his belongings after he died?" I asked.

"Yes, but when I opened his old suitcase, I found a part of the suitcase under the regular chest—kind of a secret part on the bottom. It was empty. But some dust had been recently disturbed. It looked like something was removed recently."

My heart sank. He was a smart one. He knew something was going on. We both knew that I have something that he thinks is rightfully his. I was scared. I knew he saw it in my face.

Chapter XVI

I had a difficult time trying to fall asleep that night. I couldn't get out of my mind that Brett Rudd had been in my apartment, snooping around. I was sure he hadn't seen the map—I had hidden it away. Still, he knew I was hiding something from him—or did he? How smart was this guy? I got out of bed and walked into the den. It was 3:00 a.m. I liked being awake when the whole town was asleep. I turned off all the lights, sat down in my reading chair and gazed out at Lake Harriet. The moonbeams were skipping back and forth on the water. Everything was so still and so very peaceful. I was just about dozing off in the chair when I was jolted awake by the ringing of the phone. It was 3:30 a.m. Who the hell was calling at this hour?

"Hello?" I said.

"Hello? Jens? Is that you?" It was the faint voice of a very upset and distraught woman. She sounded like she had been crying and the voice seemed vaguely familiar.

"Nora?" I asked. "Is that you?"

"Nora?" The voice said on the phone. "No, it's Holly. Holly Ruud."

"Can... can I help you Holly?"

"I'm sorry to call you so late... but I'm in trouble and need some help."

"Go on, what's wrong?" I asked.

"Well... it's Brett. He's gone crazy. He came home tonight really drunk and started tearing up the place. He smashed out all of the living room windows and he pushed me around," she said.

"Why was he so upset?" I asked.

"I don't know. But I think it has something to do with the death of Uncle Torbjørn, or what Uncle Torbjørn did or didn't leave. He's been driving down to the nursing home every day and asking a lot of questions about Torbjørn and you," she said.

"Me!" I said a bit too excitedly. "Why would he be talking about me?"

"I don't really know. It's just that Brett has been acting really strange for the past couple of days. I'm so scared he might hurt the children. I sent them up to their grandma's place in Grand Rapids. Well, when Brett came home tonight, he was drunk again. He wanted to know everything you said to me when you came to visit. You know, it was about a month ago or so," she said.

I said, "Yes," and cursed myself again for going there in the first place.

"Well, when I told him the things you said, he wanted to know if you asked anything else, like if we had any belongings of Torbjørn at our house. When I told him you didn't ask such a question he got mad and started pushing me around and hitting me." There were a few sobs and I could hear her blowing her nose. "I'm used to him pushing me around, but this time it got really out of hand. When he had to go to the bathroom, I ran out the door and never looked back. I could hear him yelling for me, but he was too drunk and I heard him trip and fall and swear a lot. So now I'm at a pay phone at some truck stop and I don't know where to go or who to turn to," she said.

"Can't you call the police? It's against the law for him to hit you like that."

"If I call the police, then they'll take him away, and the children and I wouldn't have any money coming in or, worse yet, the county will put my kids in foster care and I'll never see them again. No, I can't do that," she said.

I sighed and cursed myself again for getting involved with these people. "Where are you specifically? I'll come and pick you up." I couldn't believe what I just heard myself say, but she needed help. I just couldn't let her stay there all night. I picked her up about an hour and a half later. She looked awful, and I offered to take her to an emergency room to look over the bruises. She told me that she would get out of the car right now and go home to Brett before she would go see a doctor. I thought that would be the worst thing to do, so I drove her back to my apartment.

She took a shower and, it being around breakfast time, I made her something to eat. Brian was a bit surprised to see this strange woman in my robe come out of the bathroom. I explained everything to him. He got so upset about the assault and battery that he offered to be her lawyer for free. She declined. He did want to have her talk to someone in his law firm that specialized in spousal abuse. She said she would think about it. Brian said he would call her in a few hours and then left for work.

"Don't you have to go to work too, Jens?" she asked.

"Yes, but I can't leave you here alone," I said.

"Why?"

"Because Brett knows where I live and I bet this will be one of the first places he'll look for you."

"I'm sorry I'm so much trouble for you. Why don't I just go back home? I'll have to face him sooner or later anyway," she said.

"I think it's best not to do that yet. Listen, I called my girlfriend while you were in the shower, and she agreed to let you stay at her apartment until we can figure out what to do next. I know Brett doesn't know where she lives." Well, at least I hoped he didn't. I didn't want to get Nora involved in any of this, but I felt I was indirectly responsible for the situation and I had to think of some way to get her out of it safely.

"Would that be Nora? The person you thought I was when I called you last night?" she asked. I nodded my head.

"She must be really lucky to have a nice boyfriend like you," she said. We drove over to Nora and Paige's duplex about twenty minutes later. Nora was waiting at the door and helped Holly in. I think she was a little surprised to see Holly wearing some of my sweat clothes, which I had given her since her clothes were too dirty and bloody to wear. Nora told me to go to work and she would take care of Holly. I knew Nora wanted to get into this type of law and Holly would be in good hands. As I left her place, I drove around the block a few times just to make sure there wasn't a big red pickup truck lurking around. After I was satisfied, I drove to work. I tried to write up as many appraisals as I could. I wanted to get Brett and Holly out of my mind for the moment. I had so many other things to worry about. I had to take that damned sailing exam this week and I still had to figure out the basic logistics of the trip. Now, not only did I have to worry about Brett snooping around, there was Holly.

I called Nora at lunch. There was no answer. Good. At least Nora told her not to answer the phone. I left a kind of coded message that, if Holly was there, she could give me a call. A few minutes later, she did call and told me everything was all right. Nora had gone into her office for a few hours and would be back soon. I told her to lay low and not to answer the phone or the door unless she was sure it was Nora, Brian or I.

I polished off a few more appraisals in the afternoon. I could tell by the look on Norm's face that he was pleased by my production that day. I rushed over to Nora's place, only to find everything in fine shape. Nora and Paige had finally convinced Holly to go to Lutheran Social Services and spend the night there. They would help her out.

Nora, Holly, and I got into my car and drove off to the Lutheran Social Services building a few miles away. As we stopped at the second stop sign, a large red pickup truck came rushing down at us and blocked the front of the car. Brett got out of the pickup and started waving a baseball bat.

"Get out of the God damn car!" he yelled. "Get out of the God damn car or I'll smash in every one of your windows. Do you hear me?" Holly and Nora started screaming, and I could feel my heart racing. What the hell was I going to do? I looked into his angry, bloodshot eyes. He was a madman willing to destroy anything in his path. I wondered how so much hate could be in one man. Holly rolled down her window and started yelling at him. I got out of the car and told him to calm down.

"Why should I listen to you, asshole? What have you done to my wife? Were you screwing her last night?"

"Shut up and put the bat down. You're already in a lot of trouble. Don't make it any worse. We have witnesses here," I said in an unsuccessful authoritarian tone.

"Screw you, college boy. I knew you were no good the second I laid eyes on you. Just let me have my wife and then I'll go on my merry way. Do you understand?"

That statement riled up Nora. She got out of the car and informed Brett that she was a lawyer and was going to see him go to prison for a long time for assault and battery. Brett told her to go to hell. Nora had diverted his attention long enough for me to take a running start at him. I don't know where it came from, but his last statement so incensed me that I tackled him. He fell, and his head slammed into the side of his truck. The bat rolled out of his fist. Nora picked it up and threw it across the street.

"Is he all right?" Nora said.

"I don't know," I said, as Brett rolled around in the street rubbing his head. He looked up at me and I could see the hate and anger in his eyes. He then sat up and said, "You bastard! You'll pay for this, asshole!"

"Let's get out of here," Nora said. We got back in the car and sped off. I was trying to settle down from all the excitement and almost missed the turn onto Lyndale Avenue. After driving a few blocks, I glanced in my rear view mirror and saw Brett's red pickup truck getting bigger and bigger. I turned around and saw him catching up to us. He must have been going sixty.

Suddenly, there was a loud bang, and my car jolted forward and the women gasped. Brett had rammed the front of his truck into my rear bumper. I slammed the accelerator and I watched as my speedometer needle ran up toward fifty miles per hour. I weaved in and out of traffic with Brett right on my tail.

"Jens! Slow down! We'll all get killed!" I heard Nora say.

"What do you want me to do? This guy is crazy!" I took a sharp turn on an entrance ramp to I-94. I could hear the squeal of Brett's tires as he followed me. We were now weaving back and forth between the lanes, reaching speeds of up to ninety mph. I was hoping to see a state patrol car or even a police car, but no such luck.

"Jens, watch out!" yelled Nora. I had been watching Brett in my rearview mirror and didn't realize I was coming up behind a slow-moving semi. I had to slam on my brakes to avoid hitting him. My car slid to the left, and I almost lost control and smashed into the median. We were lucky. I decided I would head to the Minneapolis Police headquarters. I crossed over a few lanes at high speed to a downtown exit. Brett was following right behind me.

Then a miracle happened. A few blocks ahead of us was a maroon Minnesota State Trooper cruiser with its lights flashing on the side of the freeway. He had stopped someone. I pushed down on the accelerator again and drove up right behind the trooper and slammed on my brakes. The trooper immediately jumped when he heard my tires squeal, and he turned around and started yelling at me. I jumped out of the car and told him about Brett and how he was chasing us. The trooper drew his service revolver and told me to lie down on the ground with my hands on my head. I obeyed. I wasn't in the mood to get shot. Nora got out of the car next and tried to explain the situation. I guess she wasn't as intimidating to the trooper as I, because he listened to her story. Brett had already driven by and kept on going.

We drove to the closest police station and filed a complaint. It didn't take much to convince the police to issue a warrant for the arrest of Brett when they saw the fresh bruises all over Holly's body.

•

Lying in bed that night, I reviewed the events of the day. I thought about the assault with the baseball bat, the wild and curiously invigorating car chase, and my wrestling with Brett. I couldn't believe it really happened. These were the kind of things that only took place in books or movies. For the first time in my life I actually did something so interesting that someone would want to read about it. I couldn't believe how dangerous the whole car chase was and how close we came to death. I couldn't help think how thrilling and invigorating the entire experience was. I actually felt alive again.

•

The next couple of weeks were uneventful. I was busy with work and preparing for the trip. Brian and I both passed the night navigation test and were certified. I heard Brett was arrested that night and was spending the next few weeks in jail. Holly went to Grand Rapids to stay with her mother and kids. Everything was going smoothly, except for Nora. She seemed distant. I had only seen her once in the past two weeks and she said she was busy preparing for a trial. When the beginning of the third week came and she said she was too busy to see me during the weekend I knew something was up.

"Nora? What's going on? Why don't you want to see me?" I asked her.

I heard her sigh and then say, "I don't know Jens. It's just... I don't know if I'm cut out for this crazy adventure of yours. I'm beginning to have reservations about the whole thing. I think Torbjørn's story is a little far-fetched, and that incident with that bizarre Brett guy. I don't think I've got it in me to go on with this trip."

I felt like a stack of bricks had just landed on my chest. I kind of expected this from the glamour girl, Paige, but Nora? I had to think fast. She had to come on the trip with us. It was all planned and there wasn't room for any mishaps or screw-ups. What was I going to do?

Chapter XVII

It was a week until liberation day—the day I would make my ascension from my mundane life and breathe the sweet fresh air of adventure and excitement. Everything was going according to plan except for Nora. I decided to leave her alone for awhile and let her sort things out. I knew the car chase had spooked her. I hoped maybe after a week or two she would decide to come with us. I also found out Brett was in jail for a month, so we wouldn't have to worry about him again at least until we came back. I also heard from Brian that Paige was beginning to have cold feet too. Brian even suggested maybe we postpone our little trip until next summer. I got annoyed. I was surprised though, to see Brian's reaction when I tried to rationally explain to him why right now would be the best time to go on the trip. In fact, he looked a little frightened.

I was trying to stay on the positive side. I told myself that we only really needed two people for the trip. If Brian were to bug out, then I would ask Mickey or even my brother, Karl, or my sister, Sigrid. There was no getting around it. I was bound and determined to go to Isle Royale in a week, period.

•

Monday and Tuesday flew by. I was extremely busy trying to complete all of my appraisal assignments by Friday. Norm had laughed and thought I was joking when I asked him if I could take a vacation for two weeks. When he realized I was serious, he pointed out to me that it was against the company's policy to take more than a week of vacation at one time. I knew that I had to think of a really good reason for taking two weeks of vacation in a row that my boss would approve of. Then it hit me. I knew that Norm was an evangelical Christian. I told him that my church was building a mission down in Central America and I needed two weeks to help build the church and school. He thought about it for awhile and then said yes. He said I could only have this two week vacation once, since it was for such a good cause. I felt bad about lying to him, but it was the only way I could get the time off.

I tried to get a hold of Nora several times on Thursday. I was getting nervous because I hadn't heard from her and it was almost crunch time. I left three messages, but still no answer. I thought she would have the courtesy to let me know one way or another. When I got back to my apartment after work, I saw a note from Brian saying Nora wanted me to come over to her place for a talk. Oh my God, I thought to myself. That didn't look good. I rang Nora's doorbell, expecting the little talk had to do with cooling off the relationship and maybe we could become the dreaded, 'friends.' It wouldn't have been the first time that had happened to me.

She let me in. She was dressed in jeans and a sweater. I could smell food from the kitchen and the dining room table was set for two. Great, I thought. What is this, the last supper? Nora asked me to sit down at the table. I could hear French music playing on the stereo. She served me one of her favorite French dishes, though I can't recall its name. I think it was duck, but I didn't want to ask any stupid questions.

After dinner we sat on the living room couch and sipped French wine. Nora looked at me for a few moments and said, "Are you really going forward on this thing?"

"Of course I'm going through with it," I said.

"Aren't you the least bit afraid of sailing on the open lake, the danger of going into an abandoned mine and... what about that Brett guy?"

"What about him? He's in jail now and he didn't make bail. He'll be there for a few weeks. We don't have to worry about him."

"What happens if a storm comes up on the lake or if we get stuck or fall in the mine shaft? Have you planned for all of those things, too?" she asked.

"I've got it all planned out. First, we'll have a radio on the boat that we can keep in constant contact with the coast guard. Second, we have radar and Loran positioning linked up with satellites so we'll always know where we are."

"That's great, Jens. And I know you and Brian are experienced sailors." She sighed and continued, "It's just the thought of us out on the open lake and it's such a small boat—that's scary. And you guys may have to scuba dive in an abandoned mine shaft, that's really dangerous. And did you ever think of the ramifications if we get caught taking property from a national park? It's illegal, Jens. I'm going to be a lawyer. I don't want to jeopardize my career for this. Do you think that's fair?"

I looked at her and my heart sank. Everything she said was true. I should have thought of all of those things before I had made all of my plans. I was just blinded by the thought of actually finding gold in that abandoned mine. I didn't have a response to her questions. I opened my mouth, and my argument came gushing out. I started off telling her that all my life I have been basically sitting in the audience of the play of life. I told that if I didn't go on this trip, then I would probably end up dying of boredom.

When I was done, she looked at me straight in the eyes and said, "Yes, I'll do it. I'll go. For you, Jens, I'll go."

I was overjoyed, but I could see by her eyes she really didn't want to. She was, indeed, doing it for me. She also looked as if she was going to regret her decision.

Nora slid down the couch, right next to me, set her wine glass on the coffee table and bent over and kissed me. I felt a charge run up and down my body and gave her a passionate kiss back. She then hugged me and I think I heard her whisper under her breath, "Oh, Jens..." We both got up and slowly walked into her bedroom. I sat down on her bed as she went over and put on the song *Chariot,* by Petula Clark. She then walked over to the door, closed it and turned off the lights. The next few hours were heaven, and then we fell asleep in each other's arms.

•

I woke up anxious. There were too many thoughts bouncing around in my cranium. I tried repeatedly to fall back asleep, but I couldn't. I looked at Nora sleeping next to me. She looked so beautiful and peaceful. I loved watching her sleep and listening to her gentle breathing. I couldn't help but think how fortunate I was to have her in my life. And now she was going to accompany me on my first true adventure. I looked at the clock on her nightstand. It was 3:30 a.m. I was wide awake. I decided to write Nora a letter and tell her that I had to get back to my place and pack and that I'd pick her up tomorrow at 12:00 p.m. sharp. I gave her a little kiss on her forehead and left.

I drove around her block a few times just to be safe and see if anyone was following me. I did the same when I got to my apartment. I tried to be as quiet as possible, so as not to disturb Brian and Paige. I kind of lied in the letter I wrote to Nora. I was already packed. In fact, I had packed everything two days ago. I had made numerous lists and had checked and double-checked them. I made sure I had covered every contingency and included all equipment necessary for the voyage. I had planned every meal for every day down to the snacks. I felt I was extremely prepared. But I didn't want to get too confident.

After what seemed like an eternity, seven a.m. finally came, and I decided to get to the office early and finish up all of my assignments and loose ends. Brian and I decided that we would leave our apartment at one p.m. sharp, which would get us to Bayfield and on the ferry to Madeline Island by five p.m. I worked until 11:30 a.m. and then went to pick up Nora. After I picked Nora up, I drove around the block a few times, just to make sure no one was following us. I knew Brett was still in jail, but he had a bad habit of showing up at the wrong time.

The four of us finally got to my apartment about 1:30. I was a little upset that it took Paige an extra half hour to get there, but I guess it really didn't matter. We needed to get to Madeline Island by the time the last ferry ran. We all went over for the last time what to bring on the trip and tried not to forget anything. We set off, driving Brian's dad's new Chevy Suburban. It was as large as a tank and could carry all of our gear for the trip. In fact, we had already packed it full of everything we needed the previous night.

•

A couple of hours later, we found ourselves descending a large hill on the freeway and seeing the skyline of Duluth and the expanse of Lake Superior. The car windshield was consumed by the dazzling blue from the lake. We saw in the distance the aerial lift bridge, the dreary industrial buildings with their hefty smokestacks, and the massive rusty railroad bridges. Every time I drive down that hill and see the lake I get goose bumps. It is the largest freshwater lake in the world, smack dab in the middle of the North American continent. I don't know why I get so excited. It is like seeing an old, dear friend. It's like a part of my soul. There is something about the size, the beauty, the power, and the mystery of the lake that intrigues me.

I knew I had a natural inclination to love this lake and water in general. It was in my ancestry. When I see the lake I think of my Great Grandfather Jens, sailing his schooner, the *Valkyrie*, in the 1870s. I imagine him standing at the helm with a pipe in his mouth sailing through a fierce storm. The ship would be bobbing like a cork and waves would be splashing on deck, but there would be Grandpa Jens, steady as ever, lashed to a mast, and braving the storm.

Since we were all getting hungry, the four of us decided to have lunch at one of those trendy Canal Park restaurants, right down on the harbor near the aerial lift bridge.

•

A couple of hours later, we found ourselves in the quaint little town of Bayfield, Wisconsin. It is a touristy little town known for its New England style architecture, and small marinas that dot the coastline islands. By four o'clock we were driving onto the ferry to cross over to Madeline Island. We all got out of the Suburban and walked over to the passenger deck on the ferry. I surveyed the looming island. It's about fourteen miles long, and about three miles wide; the same size as the Island of Manhattan, but Madeline only had a year round population of about 180 people. The island has had a varied and interesting history. It was first occupied by Native Americans over 3,000 years ago. The Chippewa settled in the southern portion of the island near the present day village of La Pointe. However, they abruptly moved back to the mainland after a few generations, telling stories about the island being haunted by spirits. The first Europeans on the island were the French explorers Radisson and Des Groseillers in 1659. By 1663 Father Claude Allouez founded a mission called *La Pointe du Saint Esprits*. The French built a fort and the Northwest

Fur Company and American Fur Company were established by 1834. Also, by the mid-century, lumbering, commercial fishing, and rock quarrying concerns existed on the island. By the beginning of the twentieth century there were large hotels and resorts as well as private cottages. It is essentially a tourist spot with many expensive summer homes. But I still like the flavor of the island. Sure there are new condos being built, and a golf course and yacht club, but if you travel just a few miles out of the La Pointe area, it still feels like a pristine wilderness.

The ferry landed in La Pointe and the sun was shooting gold and crimson light over the horizon. La Pointe is basically one street running north to south. There are a spattering of small shops, a few restaurants and bars, a couple of hotels, a church, and some seasonal cabins. We drove about a mile south to the marina on the southwest point. The place hadn't changed much since I had been there a few years ago. The marina used to be part-owned by a friend of my dad's, but when he died, his partner quickly sold it to the first available investor. One stipulation of the sale, however, was that the charter master and his wife would have a job and a place to live at the marina for as long as they lived. Interested investors couldn't buy the marina unless they agreed to those terms, which they did. They found out it was a blessing in disguise, because the charter master kept the place in perfect condition.

I banged a few times on the marina master's office door. After a few moments, I heard some mumbling and cursing. Then a fat, crooked finger slowly parted a curtain behind the front window. I was startled to see a bloodshot eye peering at me. Then the front door swung wide open and a short, stout man who appeared to be in his late seventies, with huge hands and a bald head, wearing a tattered pair of old, dirty blue jean overalls, smiled at me. "Øj, Øj, Øj! As I live and breathe! If I'm not in the presence of a ghost!"

I really wasn't surprised at this outburst. In fact, I expected it. This little old marina master was an old and trusted friend of my father.

"Nora, Brian, Paige, may I introduce you to Mr. Einar Tviet? He's the marina master here, and I used to work for him when I was in high school and college."

"Nice to meet you, Mr. Tviet," Brian said as they shook hands.

"Oh, please call me Einar. It's a pleasure to meet you young folks. Won't you come in?" We followed Einar through the back door of the office and into a small room that was used as a living and dining room as well as a kitchen. "Please, will you be so kind, sit." He pointed to a small couch and some dining room chairs that had seen better days. A worn blanket was spread over the couch. He turned and yelled through yet another door in the back. I knew the rear was where the bedroom and tiny bathroom was.

"Wenche Tviet! We have company. Get your butt out here. Have I got a surprise for you!" We heard a weak voice that sounded like she had just woken up saying, "I'm coming. I'm coming, old man. Keep your britches on." A round little old lady, wearing a house coat, shuffled into the room. She had a scarf on her head and looked like a peasant woman who had just gotten off the boat. She put on a thick pair of glasses which made her bright blue eyes larger. She walked up to Nora and Paige, eying them up and down and then she walked over to me.

"Mercy me. I don't believe it. Herr Halverson has risen from the grave. Uff da!" By this time, Nora and the others were in a state of confusion. Wenche Tveit walked over to the small kitchen area and poured cups of coffee and served us sugar cookies (which always seemed to be on hand for company).

I explained to Brian and Nora that my dad's friend owned the marina and how the Tviet's worked for him. Einar and Wenche interrupted me many times to embellish about how nice my dad and his friend had been to them.

"What's this business about Jens being from the grave?" Nora asked.

"Oh that," said Wenche. She slowly got up and walked over to the coffee table. She opened a side door to the table and grabbed an old, thick photo album. She waddled back to her chair and plopped down. She opened the album and started to page through it, muttering to herself the entire time. I looked up at Einar and he smiled at me and gave me a wink. Nora saw this and appeared to get more agitated. Finally, Wenche stopped thumbing through the photo album and said, "Here we go, this is it." She carefully removed one of the photos and gave it to Nora. She studied the photo, and after about ten seconds said, "So? It's a black and white photo of you Jens, on board some old ship. What's the big idea?" Wenche, Einar and I started to laugh. Nora's face turned red, and I could tell we were reaching her boundaries of playing a joke on her.

"Turn the photograph around, child, and see the date it was developed," Wenche said in a motherly tone. Nora slowly turned the photo around and read, "July 30, 1877." She gave a look of disbelief and said, "How could this be?"

Wenche now had a serious look on her face and said, "That's not a picture of Jens Olav Nilsen, my dear. That's a picture of his great grandfather, Jens Halverson, taken on July 30, 1877. And he was just about the same age as Jens is now."

Nora's said something to the effect that the hair on the back of her neck just stood up. She again studied the photo and finally said, "But Jens, he looks just like you."

An hour later, Einar walked out to the sailboat that I had been chartering from him for the past ten years. It was a fifteen-year-old, forty-one-foot sloop called the *Peer Gynt*. It was Einar's baby. He cherished that sailboat. The owner, who had passed away a few years ago, had willed it to him.

"Here she is. Isn't she a beauty," Einar said, more of a statement than a question. He jumped on board with the agility of a panther and pranced around the deck as if he were fifty years younger. He smiled and said to Nora, "I just can't help myself. Every time I get on this boat, I feel so alive and young again, it's like magic."

Brian said he thought the sailboat was beautiful and very well maintained. Einar was beaming with delight and started to show me all of the sailboat's idiosyncrasies—which I already knew—and went over which radio band I needed to be on to communicate with him. I wasn't too pleased to see a questioning look on his face. I think he was surprised to see us taking the *Peer Gynt* out so late in the season. I could also tell he was uneasy about us sailing to Isle Royale.

"Have you sailed there before?" Einar gingerly asked me.

"Ah ... no, but Brian and I did take a night navigation course offered by the coast guard and we are newly certified to sail at night," was my feeble reply. He turned away and I could hear him muttering something—like the classroom is nothing like the real thing—to himself.

"Well, have a good time, watch the weather, and don't have too much fun," he said as he stepped off the boat and started shuffling off to his next project. We all waved good-bye and thanked him.

"Einar and his wife are so sweet. You didn't tell me you knew such charming people up here," Nora said, as I walked down the ladder to the main deck to get everything ship shape for the sailing trip.

We loaded the gear onto the *Peer Gynt*, saving the scuba equipment and digging paraphernalia for nightfall. I didn't want Einar to get more suspicious. Brian and Paige said they were hungry, and Nora and I agreed. We walked a few blocks to the main street and went to our favorite café. It had burned down a few years ago and I guess the owners couldn't afford to build a new one, so they basically built the new café around the remaining portions of the original building and added a semi-truck trailer with decking all around. There was a huge tarp suspended over the entire café that gave it a *Gilligan's Island* feel. The place was bubbling over with character and panache, with tree stump chairs, rope railings, old sailboat masts and spars used as poles to hold up the tent, and countless small plaques giving pieces of advice or common sense sayings such as 'Sorry, we're open,' and the like. It appeared to me that the café was built from the remnants of a shipwreck that had washed up on shore.

We sat down at a round table under a thatched umbrella. There was a folk singer playing an old Great Lakes sailing song in the corner next to the bar. We ordered beers and wine and started to take in the atmosphere. Our food came a half hour later—service was not a high priority—and enjoyed our dinner. As the evening progressed, the café became packed with all the weekend vacationers. It got so smoky and loud that we couldn't even hear the music anymore. We paid our bill and walked along the lake back to the marina in complete darkness and could feel the cool breeze running off the lake.

After, we quietly (and hopefully inconspicuously) transferred the scuba gear and other paraphernalia onto the sailboat, Brian and I went up to the cockpit, cracked open a few beers and lit a couple of cheap cigars. We gazed up at the unbelievable display of stars, took a few sips of beer and puffed on our cigars. The women came up a few minutes later with glasses of red wine, and the four of us talked for an hour.

"What's the name of the sailboat again?" Nora asked.

"The *Peer Gynt*," I said, taking a last drag of a cigar.

"*Peer Gynt*. Let me see," she said. "Isn't that the name of a play by Ibsen?"

"Ja, you betcha," I said. "You know, it's about that Norwegian dreamer, *Peer Gynt,* who wanders around the world trying to find himself." I added, smiling.

"Too bad this isn't your boat, Jens. I think that name fits you perfectly," Nora said.

"How so?" I asked.

"Because Jens, to me, you're that Norwegian dreamer trying to find yourself."

Chapter XVIII

Again, I couldn't sleep that night. My mind was running endlessly, like a ghastly song, going over all the things that could go wrong on this little trip. One thing that kept creeping into my mind was Brett Ruud. He had a propensity for showing up at the wrong time. I had this uneasy feeling that I hadn't seen the last of him. Hopefully he would stay in the slammer for awhile. As the designated skipper, I (and Nora) got the rear berth, which was a double berth and afforded a small degree of privacy. Paige and Brian got the fore v-berth with some privacy but only half the room.

I woke up for the tenth time and looked at my wrist watch. It was 4:00 a.m. and I wasn't the least bit tired. I got dressed and walked over to the men's locker room and took a long, hot shower. I knew it was going to be a while before my next one. I shaved and dressed and decided to drive around—just to be on the safe side. I drove around the tiny village of La Pointe and became satisfied that there was no evidence of Brett.

When I returned to the *Peer Gynt*, I was surprised to see that everyone was up and taking showers. Perhaps I wasn't the only one anxious about this little undertaking. By 8:30 a.m. we had eaten at a quiet restaurant near the marina, listened to the Coast Guard weather broadcast, and found ourselves slowly motoring out of the marina. We waved good-bye to Einar and Wenche Tviet as we passed by the charter master's office. Wenche was waving with a handkerchief and had that concerned motherly look on her face. Einar still had a look of worry on his face. We slowly weaved our way out of the marina and headed for the North Channel between Madeline and Basswood Islands.

My plan was to sail up the North Channel the length of Madeline Island and split between Stockton and Oak Islands, and sail past Manitou Island and Otter Island and anchor and spend the night at the southern portion of Devil's Island. That is the northernmost island of the entire Apostle Islands chain. I figured it would be the best place to start the overnight sail to Isle Royale.

The weather was behaving nicely with a slight breeze running up the channel allowing us to sail long pleasant tacks. It was a bright, clear day with just a hint of a chill in the air. I asked Brian to take the helm as I walked down the ladder to the main cabin. The *Peer Gynt* was an older boat and had probably seen better days. But she was responsive to the helm and she was built like a battleship. The cockpit was in the middle-rear portion of the boat with a rear berth at the stern. The main cabin with the galley, mess and navigation desk was forward of the cockpit and accessible via a small staircase.

Forward of the main cabin was the fore v-berth. The sailboat was ideal for two couples because it had two separate berths with the main cabin in between. The boat also had two heads, which was very nice.

After we had sailed for a few hours and were settled in, I happened to see, off my port bow, an old two-masted schooner heading our way about a mile off. It was an ancient schooner that was now used for tourist excursions around the Apostle Islands. As it came closer, I could see the deck packed with tourists listening to an amplified voice explaining the history of the particular island they just passed.

It took a few hours of hard sailing up the North Channel and by lunch time we found ourselves turning due north, running up between Stockton and Oak Islands. Paige and Nora served sandwiches, chips and beer. Brian and I were cooking spaghetti and meatballs for dinner. It was Brian's only specialty. Well, at least he had a specialty.

As the four of us sat lazily in the cockpit and observed the copper-colored islands and the bright, clear sunshine, Paige asked, "So Nora, if and when we do find the gold, what are you going to do with it?"

"Well, I really haven't given it that much thought. What will you do with your portion of the money, Paige?"

"I would move to New York City again and possibly buy a penthouse, and then, oh, yes, I would have to have something in L.A., maybe Malibu."

Apostle Islands Map

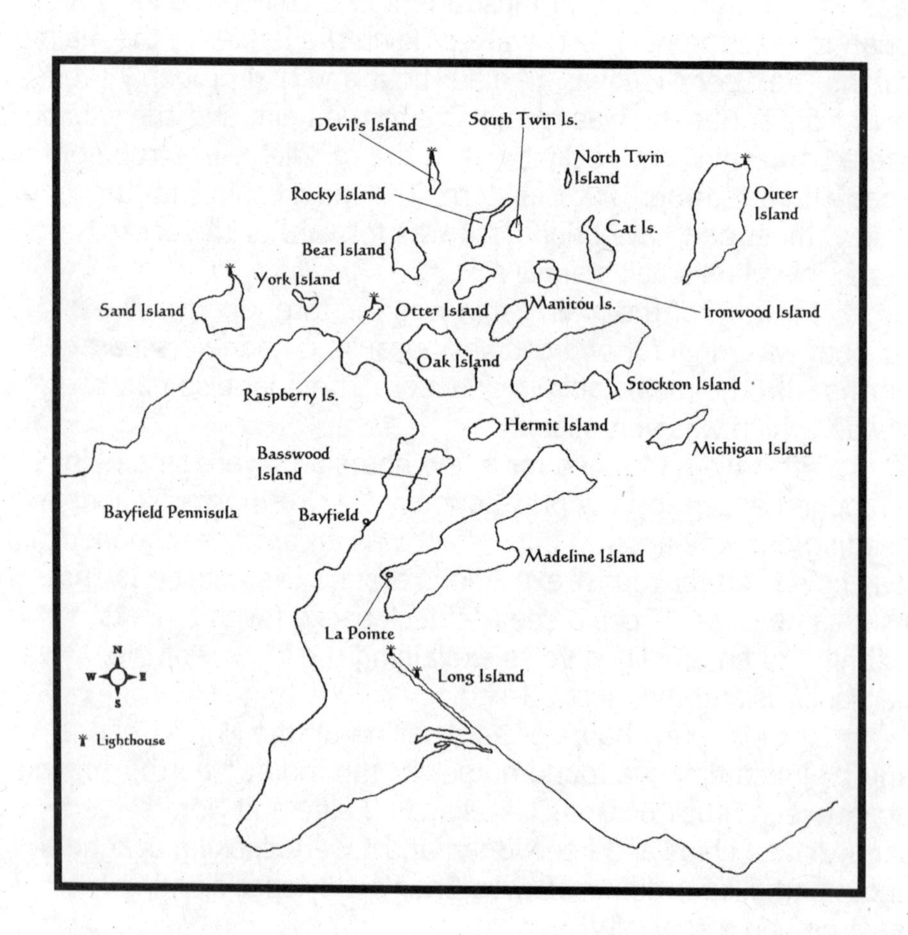

"What would you do with your life though, Paige?" Brian inquired as we all watched a commercial fishing boat sail by us with a huge flock of seagulls following it.

"Oh, boy, that's a tough one. Maybe I'd start up my modeling career again or maybe take acting lessons or something. What would you do Brian?" Paige asked perhaps feeling a bit embarrassed about her dreams and wanting to turn the spotlight over to someone else.

"I don't know. I would probably start my own law firm so I could take really interesting cases."

"Where would you live?" asked Paige. Brian took a swig of beer and said, "Maybe I'd live on Lake of the Isles Parkway or the Edina Country Club area."

"Oh," was Paige's reply.

"Where would you live, Nora?" I asked, thinking that this conversation was getting really interesting. I also thought about all the marriages that split up after people won millions of dollars in the lottery. They had so much money and could do anything they wanted, which often wasn't the thing their spouses wanted to do.

Nora said, "I'd probably find a nice house in south Minneapolis."

"That's it?" interjected Paige.

"Well, maybe I'd get an apartment in Paris to spend a few months a year."

"Now you're talking," Paige said, and added, "What would you do for a living?"

"I'd continue my plans to get a law degree and then I would work for legal aid, or battered women."

"You would do that even if you had enough money that you never had to work again in your life?" Paige asked with a startled look on her face.

"I'd just get bored if I didn't work. What would the point be if you didn't do something fulfilling in your life?"

"I can think of a lot of things in life I could do that are fulfilling that don't include work," replied Paige.

The tension between them was getting thick. Paige was missing Nora's point. Brian could feel it too, and he turned to me and asked, "So Nilsen, what would you do with your share of the treasure?"

"The first thing I would do is quit my job. I would march into my boss's office and tell him that I'm moving on. Then I think I'd go back to the university and take some classes I'm really interested in."

"What classes are those?" Nora inquired.

"I'd like to take history and literature, and then maybe some marine archeology."

"Marine archeology, what the hell is that?" Paige demanded.

"It's the study of shipwrecks and stuff, right?" Brian said as he looked at me.

I nodded my head as I heard Nora ask me, "Where would you live, Jens, if you had all of that money?"

"I think I would buy just an average size house in St. Louis Park."

"You'd live in St. Louis Park even though you could afford to live anywhere?" Paige asked, disbelief on her face.

"Why would I want to live in a place with a bunch of snobs? I'd prefer to live modestly with people with whom I grew up. I guess the biggest thing is having the security and the freedom to do anything you want."

"What about living on Lake Superior, Jens?" Nora asked.

"Oh yeah, that's right. I'd have a nice cabin on Lake Superior, too, and even a small place on the ocean in Sørlandet, Norway, near where my Great Grandfather Jens was born."

As the afternoon progressed, I was surprised by our advancement. After a leeward tack, I steered the *Peer Gynt* straight for the dock on the southern coast of Devil's Island. I figured we would get there in about twenty minutes, way ahead of schedule. This tiny speck of an island is the northernmost tip of the state of Wisconsin. It's just over a mile long and about a half mile wide. The Native Americans called it the 'Evil Spirit Island,' because of the sea caves on the northeastern part of the island that were cut out of the sandstone after thousands of years of winter storms. They are said to hold magical powers, and the images of the light bouncing off the cave walls is spectacular. When there's a storm brewing, strange noises are said to come from deep within the grotto. There's a lighthouse on the island that was built in 1898. This lighthouse is the most important on Lake Superior because approximately ten to twelve miles due north of the island are the shipping lanes to the Duluth/Superior harbor. In 1978, the lighthouse was automated and there was no need for the five-man Coast Guard unit. In the summer months, there is a park ranger on the island that gives tours of the lighthouse and makes sure nothing gets destroyed by the visitors.

We tied the *Peer Gynt* to the 175-foot-long dock on the south shore provided for visitors by the park service. There was an old boathouse on the beach as well and a narrow road built by the Coast Guard leading to the lighthouse. Nora, Paige and Brian immediately jumped onto the dock to stretch their legs. I quickly scanned the horizon before I jumped onto the dock; thankfully, there wasn't a boat in sight. I had attached binoculars to the helm in the cockpit and periodically scanned the horizon for boat activity throughout the day. For the most part there were only a few sailboats and small commercial fishing boats; nothing to worry about.

We walked up the narrow road and ended up at the lighthouse about a mile north. The automated lighthouse was unsightly; like a bad science fiction rocket ship from the 1930s. The park ranger had moved back to the mainland a few weeks ago, and we appeared to be the only ones on the island. We walked around the old lighthouse keeper's houses and gazed out upon the vast, blue, liquid plain of the open lake. Looking to the northwest, I saw the looming coastline of Minnesota's north shore, forty to fifty miles away. As I gently turned my head northeast I knew that some ninety-five miles away, invisible to the naked eye, lay Isle Royale. I could hear that enchanted isle calling me.

As we walked back to the *Peer Gynt*, Paige asked about the infamous caves on the windward side of the island. I don't know how he did it, but using all of his persuasive solicitor's skills, Brian talked me into taking the skiff with all four of us on board, over to the caves. I was apprehensive about leaving the sailboat alone, but there wasn't anyone in sight. There was only an hour of daylight left, so we hurried. A few of the caves extend some seventy to eighty feet into the island. The skiff is small enough to maneuver in and out of most of the caves. We were fortunate the wind was calm and we could navigate with ease inside the caverns. There was one particular cave that was large enough that we could actually get out of the skiff and climb around the grotto. I enjoyed looking deeply into the crystal translucent water to observe the fascinating rock configurations. I also enjoyed watching the never-ending dance of light shimmering off the blue-green water into a halo effect on the ceiling of the cave. Periodically, when the intensity of the wind elevated, we heard mysterious howling noises bouncing around in the chasm.

We enjoyed exploring the caves and completely forgot about the time. Our stomachs were telling us that it was past dinner time; time to gather up the troops and make our spaghetti and meatball feast back on the sailboat. We finally gathered back into the skiff and I pull-started the small Evinrude outboard motor. We slowly made our way back to the *Peer Gynt*.

My heart sank as we headed toward the dock. Scanning the reddish, sun setting horizon, I thought I saw the hint of white sails looming far out in the distance. I quickly tied the skiff lines to the Peer Gynt, jumped on board and grabbed my binoculars, which were wrapped around the destroyer-type helm in the cockpit. I scanned the horizon and thought I saw some sails, but then the next instant they were gone.

"What's wrong Jens?" Nora cried out from the skiff.

"I don't know. I thought I saw a sailboat off in the horizon," I said as I point in the general direction where I was just looking.

"So what?" was Brian's reply. "What's so strange about a sailboat out there? I'm sure there many sailboats out there somewhere, Jens. Don't be so frickin' paranoid. No one is following us. Relax, Nilsen."

After I had settled down a bit, Brian and I decided to make dinner. It took about an hour to make and consume the spaghetti and meatball feast. After we cleaned the galley, I suggested that everyone go to bed. We all needed sleep and we would leave first thing in the morning.

After an hour or so, I heard Nora starting to breathe heavily; I couldn't sleep so I quietly walked out of the aft cabin and into the main cabin. I grabbed a sweatshirt and a blanket and opened the hatch to the cockpit. I was met by the brilliant illumination of thousands of lights populating the heavens. What a sight! Living in the city, one tends to forget about nature's wonderful display. I made out the Little Dipper immediately and then looked upon the North Star. I was overwhelmed by the sky's lovely presentation, but eventually turned my attention to the vast dark horizon, wondering if there were any other mysterious sailboats out on the lake.

A few hours passed and I could slowly feel myself falling asleep. My eyelids were heavy, and I started to jerk my head back when I would catch myself dozing off. The lake was calm, and the stars and moon illuminated the water. I could faintly hear the water lapping up on the sailboats and dock. It was so peaceful... so peaceful.

The next thing I knew I awoke with a jump. I was a bit disoriented until I realized I was in the cockpit of the *Peer Gynt*. I looked at the eastern horizon and saw that the sun was beginning to make its daily appearance. My body was shaking uncontrollably and I realized I was freezing. This was, after all, the first week of October and the temperature was probably in the forties. I needed to go down into the cabin, put on another layer of clothes and turn on the small onboard heater. I grabbed my binoculars and surveyed the horizon. The morning was becoming lighter by the second, but I could see no boats or sails anywhere.

We ate a quick breakfast and within an hour untied our mooring lines and gently pushed off the dock. I started the motor and we glided around the island and onto the open lake. It was a crisp, clear day with massive, white puffy clouds rolling extremely high in the sky. The wind had picked up a bit from the northeast, and we raised the jib and main sails in due time and found ourselves moving quite nicely on a starboard tack.

I asked Brian to take the helm, and I went down into the main cabin. I walked to the navigation station on the rear port side of the cabin across from the galley. This was my domain. The station consisted of an angled chart table and a built-in cushioned bench. I had plenty of room for my nautical charts of the lake and its various islands, as well as my navigation tools that I used for plotting and position finding. These tools consisted of an overlay plotter, parallel rulers, dividers, drawing compass, course protractor, and course plotter. Einar Tviet had taught me many years ago how to plot and position-find a sailboat. He said that was how they used to do it in the old days. He would say: 'What would happen if your battery went dead?' or if 'them fancy machines go wrong?' Just above the station, mounted on the wall, were important instruments like a compass, Loran receiver, wind and speed direction, a depth finder, a small radar screen, and the two-way radio. There was also a radio with a cassette player that was installed just below the built-in bookshelf. This shelf was where I kept my nautical books. These were *The Annapolis Book of Seamanship*, *The Yachting Book of Coastwise Navigation*, and the Lake Superior bible, Bonnie Dahl's *The Superior Way, A Cruising Guide to Lake Superior*. I sat on the bench, turned on the radio, and tuned to the National Oceanic and Atmospheric Agency (NOAA) Weather Service frequency. This service has weather buoys scattered throughout the lake gathering important information such as wind direction, wind velocity and the height of the waves. It is essential to listen to the forecast every few hours to keep a handle on this lake's peculiar personality. I was satisfied the lake would be behaving for the next twenty-four hours. It appeared to be smooth sailing all the way to Isle Royale. I turned on the radar to see if there was any activity in the area. I saw Devil's Island and a few of the other Apostle Islands and a rather large blip heading east and running fast. I turned off the radar and went back to the cockpit. I grabbed my binoculars and surveyed the horizon. Nothing. I took the helm again and tried to relax.

Our objective was to sail the ninety-five miles to the ranger station at Windigo on the southwestern part of Isle Royale. We had to register our sailboat there and inform the park ranger of our campsites and how long we intended to stay. I was hoping, with the help of the brisk southeast wind, that we could take long tacks, cutting into the wind as much as possible. I estimated our arrival at Windigo at about 4:00 a.m., so we would likely have to wait in Washington Harbor until the ranger station opened at 8:00 a.m.

We had been sailing a good hour when I sighted something large bearing down on us from the northwest. It had a great plume of smoke rising from a smoke stack. I grabbed my trusty binoculars for a better view. It was a large saltwater ship. We were crossing the major shipping channels now, and I was thankful there was no fog to worry about. It was amazing how fast and large these commercial saltwater ships are. As it came closer, I could see she was running low in the water, which meant she had a full load of cargo on board. It passed a little less than a mile in front of us and I could see crewmen lazily hanging on the railings and waving at us.

We returned the wave as Nora asked me, "Where is that ship from?" I took my binoculars and tried to see if there was a flag flying from the rear mast or an insignia on the smoke stack to identifying the shipping company. There was a flag with a red background and a blue and white cross. It was the Norwegian flag! This must be good luck. As we sailed closer to each other, I could barely make out the name of the ship that was painted on the fore portside. It read *Kristianfjord*. It looked to be a newer saltwater cargo ship, about 600 feet in length. I waved again and yelled out at the top of my lungs, "*Hvorden ha du det! Alt for Norge!*"

I doubt anyone on that cargo ship heard me, but it got me excited. I was in a good mood again. It was a bright, sunny day with moderate but effective winds. We were moving at a good clip and for the time-being, I forgot all about that mystery sailboat. I asked Nora to take the helm and steer right at seventy degrees, pointing to the arrow in the compass on top of the helm. I went down into the main cabin and turned on the radio to a Duluth oldies station that played old pop hits from the 60s and 70s. I returned to the cockpit and relaxed on one of the cushions. Brian grabbed a couple of beers from a cooler he had tucked into the corner and handed me one. I nodded, opened the can and took a large, long swallow. Never mind it was eight a.m., we were on an adventure of a lifetime, and I was going to enjoy it.

As I sat there in the cockpit, I looked out on the endless, blue horizon again and I could make out yet another large blob coming—out of the east this time. Because of the black colossal hull and white superstructure, it appeared to be a laker. It looked to be on a collision course with us, so I decided I better take the helm. It rang its loud and obnoxious horn, just to let us know who had the right of way. I didn't want to get too close, but it was a real rush to see the enormous object up close. It was a newer laker, riding high and empty. It was like a large building with tall walls of steel moving past us at a good clip. The main hull had to be at least fifty feet high and then there were another five stories on top of it to the bridge deck. The name of the ship was the *Walter J. McCarthy*, Buffalo, New York. I asked Brian to take the helm for a second as I quickly dashed down the ladder to the main cabin to fetch Einar Tviet's copy of the *Know Your Ships*. It is a yearly publication used for quick identification of the larger lakers and other ships on the Great Lakes. I ran back up to the cockpit and looked up *Walter J. McCarthy* and said to anyone interested, "It's a laker from the American Steamship Company, built in 1977."

"How big is it?" Paige asked as she craned her head staring up at the massive structure moving in front of her and waving back to the sailors on the nearby railings.

I looked in the book and read out loud, "It holds 60,000 tons of iron ore or taconite pellets, is 105 feet wide, and sits in the water 56 feet when fully loaded."

"But how long is it, Nilsen?" Brian asked.

"Oh that," I said, trying to egg them on. "It's only 1,000 feet long."

Chapter XIX

Just like everything in life, the enormous ship soon passed us by. All of our stomachs got a jolt and the *Peer Gynt* bobbed up and down like a cork when the wake of the gigantic ship passed through. We tacked to the port side and Brian continued at the helm. The laker slowly disappeared into the blue abyss of the west.

By lunch time, we had sailed for about seven hours. Periodically, I went down to the navigation station and checked our progress on the Loran. This computerized gadget's real name is LOng RAange Navigation. When a Loran receiver measures the difference in transmission time between a master station and a secondary station and our sailboat, somehow, don't ask me how, I can find out the location of the *Peer Gynt* within 300 feet or so. After finding our location, I was a little concerned. We weren't as far as I'd hoped. The winds had dissipated, and we had lost speed. I immediately decided to take down the jib sail and replace it with a larger one, and raise the spinnaker sail. That's the large balloon type sail that you see in the extreme forward part of the sailboat in front of the jib; the more sail area, the faster you go. Our speed increased, and I relaxed.

Nora had just taken the helm, and we were on a port tack. I surveyed the horizon again and was happy not to see a sail or ship in sight. I walked down into the main cabin and saw Brian looking at me with questioning eyes. I had promised him a while back that I would teach him plotting and position finding on the charts. It wouldn't do any good on the open waters, but once at Isle Royale, I would need to plot a course to the ranger station at Windigo and then to Siskiwit Bay. Brian was an eager and quick learner. He caught on quickly, mastering the plotting of a course, dead reckoning, and the like. I couldn't think of anything this guy couldn't do if he put his mind to it.

At dinner, Paige and Nora made sandwiches and a vegetable dish. We ate in the cockpit while Brian manned the helm. We washed down our food with water and pop. The wind had subsided again and I worried. I wanted to get in a few more miles before dark; to make sure we were clearly out of the shipping lanes before nightfall.

At six p.m., after I entered another Loran position into the log book, I took the helm. The crew appeared to be tired from being out in the sun all day. I told them they should go down into the cabin and go to bed. I wanted them to be rested and ready tomorrow when we got to the island. Brian said he'd try to take a nap for a few hours and come back up and keep me company.

At about 6:30, I found myself alone at the helm watching the sun slowly sink into the western sky. The sunset was splendid. I was reminded of the Jules Verne book called *The Green Ray*. In the book it claims that if you look carefully at the setting sun just before it sinks below the horizon, you can see a green ray momentarily emanating before complete darkness takes over. Somehow—I don't known why—I have always enjoyed this time of the evening most. Or right before night becomes daylight in the morning—although I'm rarely up at that time of day. There's something about the transition between day and night or night and day that intrigues me. Like the transition between life and death, or youth and adulthood, or middle age and elderly. I guess you don't notice it, it just happens, and before you know it, it's dark. Pitch dark and you wonder where the light went.

As darkness enveloped the *Peer Gynt*, I found myself dozing. I yawned a few times and immediately slapped my cheeks with my open hand to perk myself up. I heard a very strange noise coming from the port stern. I turned around and felt a tingling sensation running down my spine. A large sailing ship was coming up from behind, and it was only a few yards from our sailboat! It was an old-fashioned, two-masted schooner with a long slender white hull that had to be more than 100 feet long. It was moving much faster than the *Peer Gynt,* and it appeared to be floating on air as it glided by.

There was something unusual about the ship, though. It was ghostly and had a musty and sodden odor to it. I couldn't see a soul on board, save for a lonely dark figure at the helm in the rear of the deck. As the ship glided by, I got a better look at the young man at the helm. He wore a full beard and was smoking an old-fashioned pipe. He had a sailor's hat and was wearing an ancient peacoat. He took his pipe out of his mouth with his free hand and waved at me. He looked vaguely familiar. "'Tis a grand evening to be sailing, don't you think?" he said in Norwegian. I didn't have any time to respond before I heard him say, "You be careful out there and don't rush into anything rashly. It will be more dangerous than you think, Jens." He smiled and waved again as the stern of the schooner passed by me. I glanced at the name of the ship painted on the stern. It read *Valkyrie*. The next moment the ship vanished and the sky became dark as the sun completely set except for a momentary flash of green flickering over the horizon.

My first inclination was to yell down to my crew mates and tell them what had just transpired. But did I want to wake them? Secondly, did I really want to tell them I saw my great grandfather sailing by on his schooner, and worse yet, talking to me? They would think I'm nuts. Come to think of it, I was wondering, myself! Was I dreaming? I must have been. That's it. I was dozing off and dreamed the whole thing... right? Perhaps I would just keep this little incident to myself.

•

A few hours later, I was wide awake and adjusting the sails. I put the helm on automatic pilot and took down the spinnaker and put on a smaller jib sail. I didn't want to get caught in a sudden squall with too many sails up. A gentle breeze was slowly shifting to the northwest and the *Peer Gynt* was picking up speed. The moon was rising out of the east like a huge spotlight reflecting on the colossal lake. Sitting back at the helm, I wondered how many mariners throughout the ages gazed upon the moon to keep themselves company late at night. I was feeling good now. It's hard to explain, but after the initial shock of seeing—or imagining—my Great Grandfather Jens and the *Valkyrie*, it began to have a calming effect on me, as though he was watching out for me. I was enjoying this voyage at the moment and wanted to be alone in my thoughts. The stars were out glimmering brightly. I thought of my grandfather's Norwegian record with the song *Sjømannen og Stjernen— The Sailor and the Star*. I started humming the tune to myself thinking about all the time my great grandfather spent at the helm of his ship staring at the same stars. What had he been wondering about late at night? Calm seas? Could he get his cargo into port on time? I wonder what he liked to do? Did he like literature? Music? Did he ever think about his future kids, grandkids, or even his great grandkids? I doubted it. Somehow, even though he died forty-two years ago as an extremely old man, I felt very close to him. I sensed him standing next to me guiding me through this great lake journey adventure.

Another hour passed, and I was still wide awake. I kept a constant eye on the compass, taking nice long tacks. Periodically, I turned on the automatic pilot and went down into the main cabin to check the radar and Loran positions.

Just then the door to the main hatch opened and Nora came up. She saw me and smiled. As she walked over to where I was sitting, I couldn't help but enjoy the vision of beauty before me. She had been sleeping for the past few hours, but looking at her you wouldn't have known it. She had a profound beauty, not striking in the glamorous Hollywood sense, but in a down-to-earth, authentic sense. The more I got to know her, the more beautiful she became. It was her allure and personality that was as pleasing as her good looks. She wore faded blue jeans, white tennis shoes, and a pull over hooded sweatshirt. Her light golden hair was pulled back in a ponytail, reflecting the light of the shimmering moon. She sat down next to me and gave me a heart-filled hug.

"What was it Mark Twain said about Lake Superior?" she asked me as I put my arm around her and we snuggled.

"What was that?" I asked.

"Didn't he say that the coldest winter he ever experienced was a summer on Lake Superior?" Nora asked.

"That must have been it," I said as I smiled at her.

"It's so cold out, Jens. How can you stand it?"

"I don't know, it isn't that bad. I remember the story my Uncle Olav told me years ago about the time when my Great Grandfather Jens was caught in a freezing ice pack on a sailing ship in the middle of the Baltic Sea," I said.

"What happened?" she asked.

"Well, as I remember it, my grandfather had picked up some coal from a town in northern Sweden and was bringing it down to Copenhagen when a fierce storm erupted. Brutal winds forced the sailing ship into a dangerous, roaming pack of ice. Grandpa Jens watched in horror as the dreadful ice smashed down on the ancient wood ship. All hands—including my grandfather—thought they were doomed and it was just a matter of time before the ship would sink. Just then, the winds dramatically shifted, sails were set, and the ship barely avoided disaster."

"Wow, what a story." Nora said and then, smiling, added: "Are there any roaming ice packs on this part of the lake?" We sat there, just the two of us for another hour or so taking in the sheer beauty of a midnight voyage on the lake. We didn't say much. We had fortunately gotten to that part of our relationship where it was all right to be quiet with each other and not feel uncomfortable during long pauses in conversation. What I really wanted to do, was to get down on my knees and thank her for being who she was, being my girlfriend and coming along on this crazy voyage, and tell her how much I loved her, but I thought it was too corny and it would ruin the moment.

Brian and Paige appeared about a half hour later. Brian asked if we wanted any freshly brewed coffee. Nora accepted, and I declined. When the two of them came up onto the cockpit with wisps of steam rising from their coffee cups, they were all yawns and shivers, trying to bundle up against the harsh October night. Somehow I felt that Paige was uncomfortable.

"God, it's cold out here," Paige said. She appeared to be in one of her famously bad moods. Brian had once indicated to me to watch out when she's in one of these moods—it can get really dicey. Then, out of the blue, I said in Norwegian, "*Ja det er kald i kevld.*"

"What!" Paige said.

I said, "Oh, I just agreed with you and said it was cold tonight."

"Oh. Well why didn't you just say that in English?"

Brian rumbled out, "Paige!" like he couldn't believe her rude tone.

Paige was staring at me now—baiting me—daring me for a reply. I knew this had been on her mind for awhile. She probably thought she found the right time and avenue to voice her issues.

It was the age-old question every immigrant group faced when they came to America. Do you immediately conform to the new society's culture and throw away your ancestor's, or do you cling to the 'old county' culture and be alienated by the new? In the Norwegian-American community, this question was much more relevant to my grandparent's generation than mine. By my generation, the American culture had won hook, line and sinker. I know I'm a minority by clinging to some of my ancestral past. Hell, how many in my generation can speak their ancestor's foreign language? Not many.

In the past, I used to shirk conflict. Now, Paige had laid out a frontal assault, attacking my way of thinking and my philosophy. I wasn't going to be a wallflower anymore like I had been with my boss, Norm. I glared at Paige and then I started to speak slowly, choosing my words carefully. "Yes, Paige, throughout the history of America when various waves of new immigrants came to our country, they were always confronted with the question of whether to keep their ancestral homeland beliefs or give it all up and assimilate into American culture. The Norwegian-American historian, Odd S. Lovoll, wrote a wonderful book called *Cultural Pluralism versus Assimilation: The Views of Waldermar Ager*. Have you ever read it, Paige?"

I got a sarcastic smile and a shake of her head as she blurted out, "I can't say I've had the pleasure."

I continued, "Well, in the book, Mr. Lovoll brilliantly points out that many advocates of sustaining a Norwegian culture in America had no problem living in America, speaking the English language, working hard and having their children attend public school, side by side with the rest of America. They also thought that it was important to experience and sustain their Norwegian identity and retain the traditions and language of the old country." I glanced over to Paige—she didn't look too impressed. I went on, "I think you have to agree there is a subculture in the Black community or Jewish community and even the Irish community in America." I looked over at Brian and saw him nod. "These people are all American, it's just they have an extra flavor to their culture instead of belonging to a large, bland American community. I can remember when I was young and would watch my favorite TV shows. All of the families or characters in the shows had names from the Commonwealth." I smiled and glanced over at Brian. "It was the Andersons, Cleavers, Bradys, Bunkers, Howells, Rockfords."

"Jeffersons," Nora interjected as we all laughed.

"The Professor," Brian said as more snickers went out.

"Yes, well you get the point. When I was growing up I thought you had to have a Commonwealth name to be a real, true blue, American."

"Boo hoo, cry me a river," Paige replied. "I think we all have to get over it and move on, Jens. America is for Americans. If you don't like that, then you must be unpatriotic. I don't know why you just don't move back to Norway."

"Because I'm not Norwegian," I said.

"Right, you're American," she said as her voice intensified.

"No, I'm a Norwegian-American," I replied. Paige was just about to bring in the reinforcements and start off on a new verbal onslaught when we all heard Nora say, "Look guys, over there," she pointed off the starboard side, "There's a light flashing." A thin fog had formed, as the eastern sky began to brighten, and we could see a faint light flashing in the distance.

"Is it a ship Jens?" Brian asked.

"No, the light is white, not green or red. And the light is stationary. It's not moving."

"Could it be land then?" Nora asked.

"It has to be," I said. I turned the ship on a new tack and headed for the light. Our hearts all started to beat a little faster in anticipation of what was before us. The flashing light grew brighter and bigger. The light fog was burning off, and we saw where the flashing light was emanating from: a large white lighthouse with a black top. It had to be the Rock of Ages Lighthouse on a small island at the extreme southwestern portion of Isle Royale. As we passed the outskirts of the lighthouse, it stood up like a bright beacon of hope pointing us in the direction of adventure and riches.

Chapter XX

As the sun intensified in the east, shooting light beams through the crystal clear water, the *Peer Gynt* slowly cruised past the towering Rock of Ages Lighthouse. The lighthouse was built in 1908, and the flashing Fresnel lens of light on top is 117 feet above the surface of the lake. The light can be observed up to twenty-five miles away. I read once that the lighthouse got its name from mariners who were so happy to see the guiding light warning them of the dangerous rocks and shoals surrounding the entrance to Washington Harbor. There are numerous shipwrecks populating the bottom of the lake in and around the Rock of Ages Lighthouse, like the *Cumberland* that sank in 1877 and the *George M. Cox* that sank in 1933 after the lighthouse was constructed. I guess that ship's luck must have run out after seeing the lighthouse, and I wonder how it came to rest in Davy Jones' locker.

Our heated discussion was forgotten and filed away for another time. I could sense electricity streaming through everyone in the cockpit. I think the crew was surprised by my navigational skills and that I had found the island with little difficulty. I grabbed my binoculars and scrutinized Isle Royale. It looked like a hazy prehistoric serpent peacefully slumbering in the distance. The infamous morning fog was burning off, and I could see the fall trees bursting out of the sunrise. There wasn't a boat anywhere to be seen. I was relieved.

In my research of the island, I had found three approaches to Washington Harbor. I read it was a difficult task to navigate through the tricky shoals and deadly submerged rocks that were sprinkled about the bay. I decided to take the middle approach, which meant sailing on the north side of Washington Island, which sits at the entrance of Washington Harbor like the mythical dog *Garm*, guarding the entrance to *Nivlheim*—the Norse hell. We took down the jib and mainsail and motored pass the small island.

Gliding between the tiny Thompson and Grace Islands proved to be thorny because of the treacherous shoals lying in wait to scrape the hull of our sailboat. Once we passed through this hazardous area, we found ourselves in the protected entrance of Washington Harbor. Fifteen minutes and three and a half miles further, we moored on the huge two hundred foot long Windigo Dock. At the turn of the century, there was a large lodge in this area, now there is a small general store, a gift shop, and a smattering of small park ranger buildings. Looking around, I noticed all of the trees had turned color, and there were heaps of red and orange leaves spread over every inch of the harbor, except for the sand and rocks at the beach head. I had a sense that there was something mysterious and magical about this island.

We tied the *Peer Gynt* to the dock and immediately filed off and stretched our legs. It was a relief for us landlubbers to finally get on solid ground again. As I started walking toward the small ranger station to register our boat, I got the dizzy sensation that I was rocking back and forth, still on the water.

The park ranger was sitting at a small desk inside the office. It was 8:00 a.m. and the office had just opened. He was a tiny man with beady little eyes and a beak-like nose. His ranger uniform was impeccable, from his little name tag that read "Ranger Stevenson," to his polished shoes, to his service revolver strapped around his waist. His receding hairline was combed straight back and he wore thick black-framed glasses with an athletic strap. I could read his face like a book. He glanced up at me, appraising what type of person I was and if I was going to be trouble. He started off by telling me we could only stay a maximum of three days at a particular campsite, however, being this late in the season, he didn't think that would be a problem. Then he went into the rules and regulations about how to take care of all the trash, where you could have a fire at the campgrounds, and to be aware of the weather. After I wrote down the number of our party and where we were planning to stay, I detected a certain level of unease and curiosity about him. I think he couldn't understand why we were at the island so late into the season.

"So how long will you be staying around Siskiwit Bay then... ah... Mr...?"

"Johnson."

"Yes... Mr. Johnson. How long do you intend to stay at that location?" he asked.

I looked at him, trying to be as casual and cool as possible. "I don't know. Maybe a few days or so. Why do you ask?" I said.

"I don't know. Just curious, I guess." He looked up at me with those beady little eyes, trying to look right through me. He shot me a glance as if to say—okay, come on, tell me the real reason you're here. He finally said, "You know, the island will be shutting down for the season in a few weeks and it can get mighty cold this time of year, especially at night. We just don't get your kind of people this late in the season, that's all," he said.

"I know it can get cold. I guess we just don't like big crowds when we're on the island." Now I cursed myself for saying that, because the second I said it, he stopped what he was writing in the registration book and fixed those bird-like eyes at me again. He didn't say anything, he was just thinking loudly. In fact, looking at his face, it didn't take a rocket scientist to figure out what he was thinking.

As I was leaving he said, "You know that drugs and alcohol are illegal in the park." I nodded and he continued, "And loud music and parties are not tolerated, especially at night." I nodded again and then he had to add, "There is a ranger patrol cabin not far from the Siskiwit Bay Campground, so we will be keeping an eye out. Have a nice day."

Nora, Brian and Paige had decided to go into the Visitor Center next to the registration office while I had my meeting with the park ranger. They got a quick history of the island and saw some historical artifacts. When I met up with them, they were at the small general store up a small hill, buying candy and supplies. They had showers available in the back of the store to anyone who wanted to pay for it, and we all obliged. There's nothing like taking a hot shower after two days on a boat.

After we bought sufficient provisions to get us through our little adventure, we shoved off from the Windigo dock and headed back onto the open lake. I turned around to get a last glimpse of Windigo and I saw Ranger Stevenson on the dock. The *Peer Gynt* was motoring away too quickly so I couldn't make out exactly what he was doing on the dock. He appeared to be holding something in his hands and it was up towards his face like a binoculars or a camera. That guy gave me the creeps. Somehow I knew I'd be seeing him again.

After we navigated through the tricky narrows of Washington Harbor and traversed Washington Island, I gave Nora the helm so I could go down into the main cabin and listen to the weather forecast and write down the necessary information in the ship's log. The weather report was favorable, but you could never be too sure. We had more than twenty miles of open lake sailing ahead of us without any safe harbors or bays to run to if inclement weather should arise.

In half an hour, the sailboat was heading south-southwest, around Cumberland Point. I pointed out to Nora the buoy marking the Cumberland Reef and told her to maneuver well clear of it. She acknowledged and slightly turned the steel destroyer-type steering wheel to take us out over the open lake. It was hard to keep my eyes off of her with her still damp hair waving in the wind. I loved to look at her hands. They were so well proportioned and confident holding on to the helm. I could tell she really enjoyed taking control of the sailboat, trying to keep a straight bearing from the compass, and watching the tell tales—those little pieces of rope attached to the sails indicating the maximum efficiency of sailing into the wind.

We were now heading in a southeasterly direction and would pass by The Head, the southernmost part of the island, in a few hours. I figured we'd get to Siskiwit Bay by dinner time, so he had a full day of hard sailing ahead of us. The wind was picking up and we started to heel over from our starboard tack. This got the attention of Paige, who was putting away the new supplies. We heard a few bumps in the main cabin and then saw Paige stick her head out of the main hatch door and say, "Hey, what's the big idea? Can't you straighten out the boat so I can put the rest of the groceries away?"

"What do you think you're sailing on, Paige, the *Queen Elizabeth II*?" Brian said as Nora and I laughed.

"Ha, ha. Very funny, McGinnis. Why don't you get your little butt down here and help me?" I had never seen someone jump so quickly after an order was issued. Nora and I smiled at each other and when Brian had gone below, Nora quietly mentioned, "I guess it's just a question of time before they get married."

By mid-afternoon, we'd eaten sandwiches for lunch and were munching on some delicious Bayfield apples. Paige had the helm, and we were passing by McCormick Reef. I looked behind me at the island and saw Feldtmann Ridge, a small group of tree-covered hills running inland a mile or so from the coast. I saw the old fire lookout tower on top of the ridge and wondered if it was still being used.

Nora pointed to the point where the island appeared to end, about five miles northeast of us and said, "Is that where we go to get into Siskiwit Bay, Jens?"

"Yes," I said, "That's Houghton Point, and there are some buoys about a half mile north of the point called Houghton Point Passage. There are underwater rocks and shoals throughout the entrance so we have to be extremely careful not to scrape the bottom of Einar Tweit's boat or he'll have my ass." As I said this, I pointed my finger at the end of the point for more dramatic effect.

I felt good about this sailing experience. I was glad we decided to sail to Isle Royale instead of taking a power boat. I thought of my Great Grandfather Jens and the age old tradition of sailing. Sailing was nice and slow, and moved at its own pace.

I decided that I had better take the helm when we got to Houghton Point Passage. I figured if the sailboat was going to get scraped by submerged rocks, then I should be the person responsible for it. Houghton Point is like a peninsula jetting out at a northeast angle some five miles from the middle southern portion of the island. At the end of the point, there is a series of small islands, rocks, and shoals that extend out in a narrow band for another eight miles. About a half a mile from the point is a passage identified by four buoys. I decided to take down the sails and motor through the passage. I wanted to take it slow and have the motor's advantage of maneuverability through the hazardous passage.

After we passed uneventfully through the passage, we motored the remaining six miles through the large open bay to the Siskiwit dock near the campsite. The word Siskiwit is an Indian word meaning a large species of lake trout. The name is quite popular on the island; the seven-mile-long lake not too far from the bay is Siskiwit Lake; the Siskiwit Islands make up part of the Houghton Point peninsula; there's the Siskiwit River and Falls, and even Mount Siskiwit in the Greenstone Ridge in the center of the island.

As we motored closer to the 170-foot-long concrete dock jetting out onto the lake, with a rock breakwater extending in front of it, we saw that the crystal clear lake water had turned to a reddish copper. We learned later this is caused by water deposits from the Big Siskiwit River which empties out into the bay not far away. I was a bit relieved there were no sailboats in the vicinity; however, there was a small park ranger boat tied up near the front of the dock. This was to be expected. We had to clandestinely operate around the park rangers snooping in and around the island.

By the time we docked and settled in, the golden sun was setting. Brian and Paige were going to camp at one of the many campsites so Nora and I would have the sailboat to ourselves.

Island Mine Detail Map

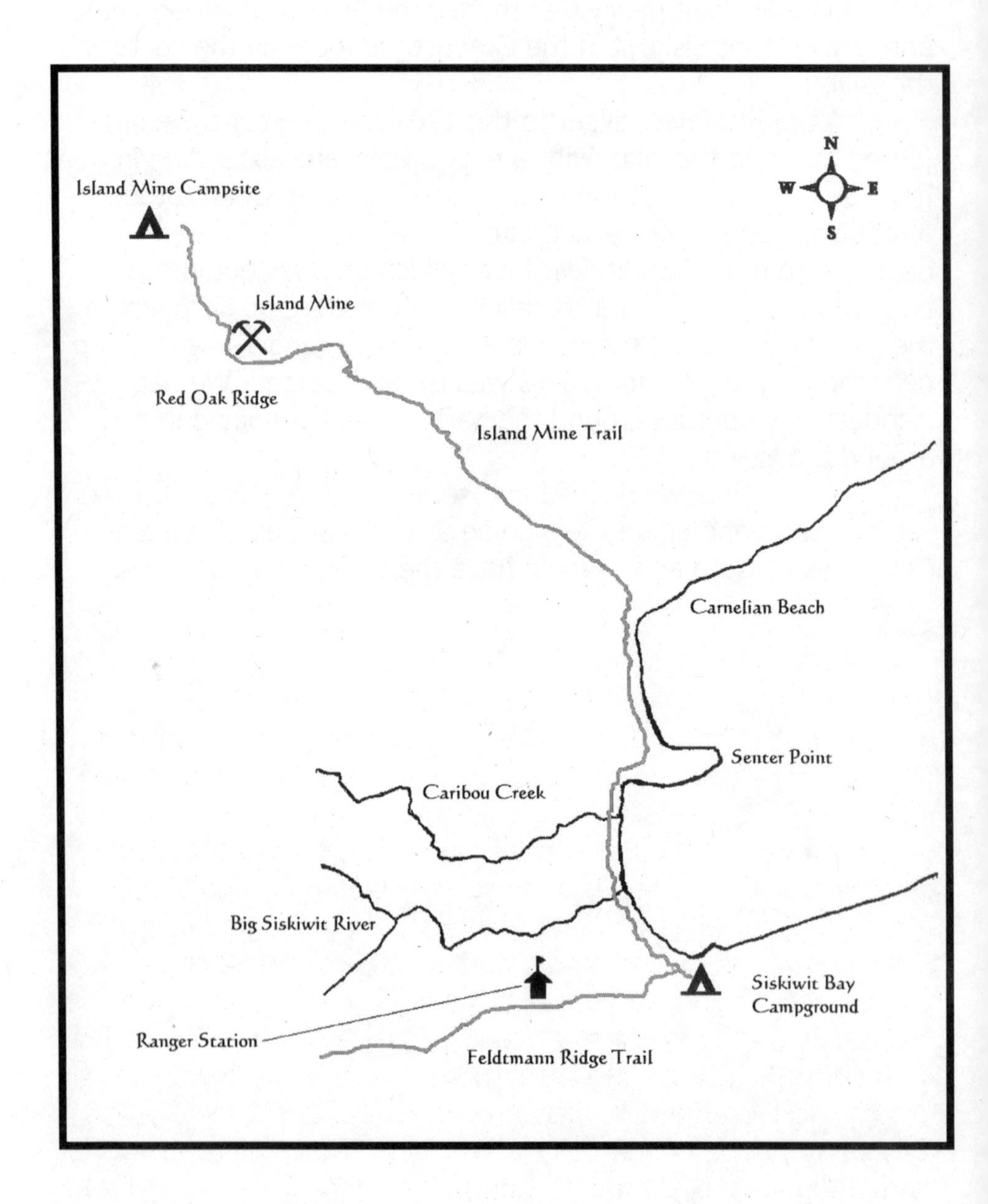

Chapter XXI

I had a hard time sleeping that night. I couldn't wait to get on the island and do some reconnaissance. After dinner, I pounded down a few beers to calm myself down. It didn't. Earlier, I went up on the deck and saw Nora sprawled out on the foredeck writing in a notebook, so I didn't want to disturb her. She was wearing a stocking cap with a large blanket covering her entire body. It was cold and there were just a few shimmers of light glowing far off on the western horizon. I looked out onto the big, beautiful island and in the approaching darkness saw the trees, with their glorious red, bronze and orange leaves weaving back and forth in the breeze and sounding something like a symphony. Some had fallen to the ground and it looked like a wonderful kaleidoscope.

•

A few hours later, out on the deck, it was pitch black, except for the light on the mast—required to be on at night when moored at the park—and the wonderful stars. The moon was making its appearance in the far eastern sky. Nora was fast asleep in the rear cabin while I was warmly dressed and sipping my third beer of the evening, wide awake and thinking about where I would explore in the morning. I knew I had to keep my eye out for park rangers and I wanted to see where that park ranger patrol cabin was. I wanted to know if there was a ranger permanently stationed there or if they just stayed there from time to time. I also had to find out if there was anybody staying at any of the nearby campsites. From my vantage, I could see Siskiwit Bay campground and even—with my binoculars—Malone Bay campground on the other side of the bay. When we hiked up to the abandon Island Mine tomorrow, I would also have to check out the Island Mine campgrounds about a half a mile farther on the trail. The only concern I had—when it came to campgrounds—was the secluded Hay Bay campground. This was about four miles from the dock just inside Hay Bay. I couldn't see any boats because of Point Hay, which is a small peninsula and completely hides the site. There are no hiking trails to this campground; it is only accessible by boat, so I made a mental note to periodically check it out with the skiff.

•

Early the next morning, donning hiking boots and backpack, I set out for the park ranger patrol cabin. The sun was just rising, and Nora was still fast asleep on the sailboat. The ground was saturated with dew and it was cold. I stepped off the *Peer Gynt* and onto the dock and walked past the park ranger patrol boat. As I strolled by Brian and Paige's tent on the first campsite, it was quiet and I thought I heard Brian snoring.

I made my way up the trail a few hundred yards and found myself at the junction of the Feldtmann Ridge and Island Mine Trails. I decided to take the Feldtmann Trail and hiked up the steep pathway. I could tell it was going to be a bright, cool, crackerjack of an autumn day. The wind picked up a bit, and I heard the trees wrestling in the wind, with an occasional colorful leaf spiraling to the ground. When I had gone about a quarter of a mile, sure enough, there was the typical small, brown national park cabin, with moss growing on the green roof shingles, sitting next to a grove of trees. There were narrow streams of smoke rising out of the chimney and a light shone through the front window. I walked up to make a closer inspection. I took two steps, when suddenly the door opened and a woman park ranger was staring at me.

"Howdy stranger," she said, as she gave me an appraising eye, "Did you come in on that sailboat last night?" She was a short, squat woman with short black hair and big round glasses. She looked at home here on the island and appeared to be tough as nails. I also noticed that she was sporting her service revolver in her holster and a badge that read: Ranger Harvey.

"Ah, yes we did. We came in around six p.m. How about you?" I asked, to see if I could get any information out of her.

"Oh, I came in about an hour before you. I check out most of the campgrounds, spend a night or two, if needed, and then I go on my merry way. It's not too busy this time of year, you know. The cold weather scares off the hikers and the potential lake storms scare off the boaters."

"Oh, really?" I asked.

"How many are in your party, and how long do you intend to stay on the island?" she asked. I explained our prearranged cover story. We wanted to be consistent with our plans no matter who we told them to. She appeared to be satisfied and I could tell by the look on her face that she thought they sounded plausible.

"Okay then, if you're still around in a few days, I'll probably see you again." She closed the door, and I turned around and headed back to the *Peer Gynt*. By the time I got back to the sailboat, everyone was up and eating breakfast.

"Where the hell have you been, Nilsen?" Brian asked with pancake stuffed in his mouth. I explained to them about my meeting with the park ranger and where the patrol cabin was. Brian wanted to know if I had found any campers. I told him no. By eight a.m., I was leading our group on our first expeditionary adventure. The first mile and a half, we found ourselves walking on the copper colored sand of the Island Mine Trail, enjoying the sun's sparkling reflection off Siskiwit Bay. After we crossed over the Big Siskiwit River footbridge and another smaller creek footbridge, we passed Senter Point, where there was the foundation of the old storehouse. Built in the 1870s, it was reduced to a remnant of its original size. I can still remember Torbjørn's weak and feeble voice talking about this point on the night of his death. The trail then turned into the old road that was built for wagons to haul supplies up to the mine and copper on the way back. Surprisingly, it was in pretty good shape and was a relatively easy and level hike for a mile or so. Then the trail started to gain elevation and we found ourselves climbing up the Red Oak ridge. The woods thickened, and the trees changed from birch, spruce and fir near the water to sugar maples and red oaks in the higher elevations.

As we hiked the remaining mile to the abandoned Island Mine, I picked up the pace, filled with anticipation. We jogged the last few hundred yards to a simple park sign that read "Island Mine." We looked around, expecting something totally different than what we were looking at. The woods had totally enveloped the area.

"This is it?" Paige said in an upset voice.

"It's got to be," said Brian, "Look at the sign."

"Jens, is this really the place?" Nora asked with an incredulous voice.

"Like Brian said, it has to be," I said and tried to clear my mind of what I had thought the abandoned mine site would look like. I walked off the trail a bit and stumbled on some large, rusted iron machinery that may have once been a steam engine. At the same time, Nora found old abandoned machinery a few yards away.

I pulled Torbjørn's map from my backpack and sat down on a stump of a fallen tree. I was hoping no one noticed my hands shaking as I carefully unfolded the fifty-some-year-old map. I was nervous because I wanted to convince everyone that I was competent and in control. I wanted to let everyone know that this little expedition of mine was well planned, that I knew what I was doing. I turned the map around a few times to get my bearings. I suddenly remembered that Torbjørn had drawn a detailed diagram of the abandoned mine entrance in the corner of the map. I turned it around and studied the diagram closely.

"Well Jens?" Paige snapped impatiently, "Can you find the entrance to the shaft?"

"Give the guy some time, Paige," Brian almost scolded. Paige glared at him.

"If I can find a reference point on the map, I can get a start on finding that portal," I said, thinking out loud.

"What's a portal again?" Nora asked.

"It's a horizontal entrance to a mine shaft," I said. "So we should look back over there." I pointed back into the woods. "The hill starts over there and maybe we can find the entrance. But remember, it's been covered up for more than fifty years, so it's going to be tricky to find." We spent the better part of an hour walking back and forth in the woods surveying every inch of the site. We did find two vertical shafts that were fenced off by the park service with a subtle sign: DANGER! DO NOT ENTER! I looked down over one of the shafts and wondered if this was the shaft where Torbjørn and Odd used their makeshift hoist to lower down the gold bars. I felt a mysterious hint of air emanating out of the shaft and wondered why the hell anyone in their right mind would take a chance and go down into the mine. Debris from old logs and rocks had been used by someone in an attempt to plug up the shaft many years ago, and Mother Nature's vegetative undergrowth covered the rest. I turned on my flashlight and concluded that there was no way anyone, not even tiny Paige, could fit into the shaft.

I could sense my friends were getting frustrated. There were some wisecracks shot back and forth. I had to somehow divert their attention and get them busy doing something else.

"You know, I think somebody ought to check out the Island Mine campground to see if there's anyone there," I said. There was an uncomfortable ten second pause, broken by Brian saying, "Jens, you're right. Paige and I will mosey on up to the campground and check it out."

"Great. It's about a quarter of a mile up the trail. Nora and I will continue to look for the portal," I said. Brian and Paige started walking up the trail as Paige shot Brian her ever-so-familiar glare. Nora and I watched the two of them. I knew Paige was talking about me—but I couldn't let that get to me.

As the tension subsided, I sat down on the same stump to examine Torbjørn's map again while Nora went on searching for the entrance. I tried to get into Torbjørn's head and figure how he would show the best way to find the entrance to the mine. According to my calculations, the entrance to the portal he identified was at this site. For a second, the thought that he had made this all up shot through my brain. Could it be? No way. I walked back and forth where I thought the diagram showed the portal to be. Every time was a failure. Every time I came up empty.

After an hour I was began to wonder why Brian and Paige had not returned, when I heard Nora say, "Oh Jens. I think you want to see this." I ran over to where she was standing. It was in a very secluded spot that I had gone over time and time again. "What is it?" I asked. Nora had a questioning look on her face and said, "Do you see those trees and undergrowth there?" pointing to a spot that I had seen a few times before.

"Yes, what about them?"

"Well, something just doesn't seem right," she scratched her forehead, deeply thinking, and quickly and automatically wisped some of her hair behind her ear as she wrinkled her slightly freckled nose—I loved that about her—and continued, "I mean look at all the trees and how they are shooting up horizontally over there, but over here, they are at an angle."

"Yeah, so?

"Well, it seems to me those trees at an angle are much younger and grew later than the rest of the trees."

"Like fifty years ago?" I asked.

"You got it," she said. We both ran over to the angled trees. I got out my pack shovel and began to clear out the underbrush and small trees. As Nora and I were clearing, I could feel a hint of a musty air softly flowing out of the ground. This was it! We'd found it! Fifteen minutes later we had cleared away enough area for me to crawl into the small entrance. I grabbed my flashlight and told Nora to stay behind. When I snaked my way through the entrance, I felt an immediate chill and turned on my flashlight. I stood up and was bombarded by the site of an old, musty, cobweb-infested adit. I saw the old timber support logs holding up the ceiling and sides of the adit every twenty feet. Some of the support logs were seriously cracked and a few had fallen down. I took a few steps and heard a cracking sound and looked down. I had only stepped on a twig, but it had really jolted me. The air was so damp and foul, like walking down into an ancient, smelly farm cellar. I got another sense there were worse things in here than the creepy crawlers and cobwebs. I felt there was someone or something watching me. I quickly panned my flashlight around the adit. The flashlight wasn't powerful enough to see the end of the shaft. For some reason, I felt I wasn't alone. I wondered how many dead men's souls were in this abandoned mine. I felt the place was haunted. I gathered up what little guts I had and took a few more steps. I remembered Torbjørn warning me to watch my footing because of the unexpected winzes or vertical shafts in the adit. They were boarded up, but the wood would be weak. I didn't want to fall into one of the winzes and die that way. I figured I better wait until Brian got back and we could explore the mine together. As I was leaving the adit and snaking through the portal, I thought I heard an eerie voice bellowing deep inside the mine.

When I got out, I saw that Brian and Paige had returned from their scouting trip. I thought since Nora was standing next to them they would be all smiles because we had found the entrance to the mine. The expression on all of their faces was one of concern and I knew something was wrong.

"What is it?" I asked.

Brian replied, "There're some people staying at the Island Mine campground."

Chapter XXII

"Did you see any of them?" I asked.

"No. There were just four small tents, and it looked like they had a big fire last night," said Brian. I could see by everyone's faces that the emotional highs and lows of this adventure were taking a toll. I was thinking of a plausible explanation why there would be these campers out here so late and that we had nothing to worry about.

"Four small tents mean there has to be between four to eight campers," I said. "I think we have to treat it the same way we did with the mysterious sailboat we saw off of Devil's Island. We'll have to play it cool and keep our eyes out for them." Changing the subject, I continued, "I think we should hike back to the *Peer Gynt*, eat an early dinner and go to bed. That way we can get up at sunrise and explore the mine." It looked like everyone was in agreement, so we hiked back to the sailboat, after we had sufficiently hid the newfound entrance to the mine. When we climbed on the dock, the ranger patrol boat was gone and the park ranger had indeed gone on her merry way.

•

At the crack of dawn the next morning, we all marched to the abandoned mine. The temperature was mild for this time of year—in the low forties. I glanced back at Paige and had to chuckle to myself because she was overdressed, with a down winter coat, stocking hat and mittens.

Our first task was to clear away a substantial amount of underbrush around the portal area so we could get ourselves and equipment easily into the adit. After that was completed, I positioned Nora behind a clump of trees a few hundred yards from the Island Mine campground and Paige about a quarter of a mile south of us on the Island Mine Trail to watch for any activity coming up from Siskiwit Bay. Communication would be by walkie-talkies I bought at an Army surplus store. Paige started to complain how bored she would be hiding in the woods. Brian asked her if she wanted to take his place and go down into the mine. That shut her up, and Nora offered her a couple of good books to read to kill the time. We decided we would check in with each other every hour, just to be on the safe side. I knew the walkie-talkies probably weren't going to function properly underground, but we needed to somehow stay in touch with each other.

Brian and I began the mine exploration at about 10:30 a.m. We wore backpacks full of rope, water, emergency first aid kit, a collapsible shovel and pick ax, saw, compass, power candy bars, flashlights, old miner's hats with a light bulb in the front—also from the Army surplus store—and Torbjørn's map in a watertight baggy. It might seem silly, but we also had a couple of World War II era gas masks that I also bought, just in case there was deadly gas trapped in the mineshafts. How we would find out about the deadly gas in time to put on the gas masks was beyond me, but I thought I could at least take the precaution.

Entering the dark, cold and musty abandoned mine, we tried our best to conceal the portal behind us with shrubs and branches. Slowly we began to weave our way through a maze of rotted fallen support timbers, clumps of rock, ancient discarded metal wheels from mine cars, and the mine car tracks. The air seemed to get mustier and cooler. The copper and red walls and ceilings were damp and appeared to glow when we pointed our flashlights at them. The ground was littered with ancient debris and there were puddles sprinkled about the audit.

"Don't step in any puddles," I said, "and don't touch any of the support timbers. They're all probably rotten to the core and could collapse at any moment."

"Great, Jens, that's comforting to know. What about the puddles?"

"Those seemingly shallow puddles could turn out to be deep winzes."

"What are winzes?" Brian asked.

"They're vertical shafts. Pay attention to any old boards you see on the floor. They could be covering up the winzes, and if you step on one, it might break and you could fall hundreds of feet to your untimely death," I said.

"Wonderful," Brian said, shaking his head and then blurted out under his breath, "Why are we here and doing this, again?"

I stopped, turned around and said, "For the twelve million dollars, man."

"Yeah, well, that would do it," he answered.

We cautiously continued down the adit for another forty feet, shining our flashlights and miner's hat lights all over the ground. There was a bone-chilling, almost haunting draft emanating from the bellows of the mine. The thought of all the dead souls lying about crept into my mind and gave me the willies. What were particularly disturbing were the mystifying sounds that came from deep within the earth. It was almost like someone was taunting us, daring us to explore deeper into the abyss.

"Stop... look!" I said excitedly, pointing to the ground where there were rotting boards. I took out Torbjørn's map and tried to figure out our location. "This has got to be the first winze. Be careful and walk around the edge of the boards." Cautiously, we walked around the aged lumber and proceeded onward. After another fifty feet of maneuvering around the adit's debris, we came upon the second winze. We were fortunate because, ten feet past that winze, was a major cave in with rock and timber blocking the adit. I drew in a deep breath and took off my backpack. According to Torbjørn's map, this is where we had to go straight down about eighty feet. Brian picked up a rock from the ground and dropped it into the mysterious hole. It seemed like an eternity before we heard it hit the bottom. Brian whistled as I got out the hundred foot rope ladder from my backpack and tied it securely to some massive boulders. I dropped the ladder over the side, and it seemed like another eternity until we heard it hit the bottom. Brian looked at me with a broad smile and said, "Be my guest, stud."

Our plan was for me to go first; then, using a rope, Brian would lower the supplies, then he would climb down the ladder. I slowly straddled the wobbly rope ladder and began to descend into the darkness. At about fifty feet, I stopped and rested, got out my flashlight and pointed it downward, trying to see the bottom. I thought I heard the end of the ladder hit the floor, but there was a possibility that the winze was deeper than a hundred feet, and I hated to think what would happen if I took the hundred and first step.

"Can you see anything, Nilsen?" I heard Brian yell down.

"I think so. I think I have about another thirty feet to go," I yelled back up to him.

"Be careful, Jens, I don't want to have to go down and rescue you." Now he was the one with the sarcastic voice. I got my courage up and began to descend again. I counted about thirty more steps and thought I was just about at the bottom when I heard a large screeching noise and the fluttering of wings. A huge mass of black objects began flying all around my head. I was so startled I lost my footing and fell off the rope ladder. Luckily, I was only a foot from the ground. I fell onto my back and raised my arms over my face to shield it from the critters. Twenty seconds later, the noise subsided and I decided I must have disturbed a bunch of sleeping bats. Then it was Brian's turn to do all the yelling when my new friends flew by him.

I dropped my flashlight in the fall, and my miner's hat had fallen off. I found myself in complete darkness. I began to cautiously feel around the ground for them when I came across something and picked it up. It was very light, hard and kind of hollow. My imagination went wild and I dropped it. I heard a clattering noise. A few more moments of fumbling around and I finally felt the long plastic handle of the flashlight. I picked it up and turned it on. I flashed it on the thing I had just picked up, my body froze and I felt the hairs on my back stand up. There was the gruesome toothy smile of a human skull staring right at me. I let out a screech and I heard Brian yelled down, "What's going on?"

I took a few deep breaths and said, "I'm okay."

"What's down there?" Brian asked.

"Oh, I think I found the skull of Torbjørn's brother, Stig."

"Stig?"

"Yes, Stig. You know, Brett Ruud's grandfather."

"Cool."

Ten minutes later, the supplies and Brian were down the second level adit. We paid our respects to Mr. Stig Ruud and continued to explore this subterranean world. The air seemed heavier now, and very stale. I kept my gas mask in easy reach, just in case. Advancing thirty-five feet, we came onto another winze. This hole was about six feet in diameter. I pointed the flashlight down to see it was full of water. Brian and I stepped cautiously around it and continued on. I felt my heart rate increase dramatically as I glanced down periodically at Torjørn's map to see our progress. Sweat started running down my forehead as we approached the drift where Torbjørn's map indicated the gold was. It was just about thirty feet ahead...

'Is this it?' I thought to myself. Was I going to find the treasure? Where were all the bad guys, the pirates, the phantoms guarding the treasure so no one could take it? This was way too easy. I heard Brian say, "Where do we go now?" Ahead was a massive cave-in with copper-colored rocks, old timber logs, and worn out mine carts completely blocking the adit. It was a dead end. My mouth opened in disbelief. "It can't be! No, not here!" I looked again at the map. I went back to the winze we had descended and paced off the steps again. According to my calculations, the cave-in had occurred just a measly twenty feet before where the gold was buried.

•

That night Brian and Paige stayed on the *Peer Gynt* by themselves. Nora and I camped at one of the enclosed shelters on the Siskiwit Bay campground. At this point the four of us needed separation and space. The drama and friction between Paige and me was getting a bit ridiculous. The two of us had come to verbal blows over the cave-in issue. She demanded to know why I simply hadn't anticipated any cave-in problems and why I hadn't brought the necessary tools to take care of them. She was also 'bored to tears' over why she had to sit so long in the 'dreadful' woods, on guard duty.

In a last feeble attempt, I convinced Brian we should carry our scuba gear into the mine that night and, first thing tomorrow, explore the flooded winze. Maybe it led to the drift from another direction. At least I convinced Brian of that. I noticed Nora was feeling sorry for me, and maybe thinking that some of the negative things I had said about myself in the past were true. Paige was her usual self—snippy, arrogant and condescending.

For security reasons, we moved the *Peer Gynt* about a mile north of the Siskiwit Dock and laid anchor about a quarter of a mile off the sandy, red Carnelian Beach. People could easily snoop around the sailboat when it was moored on the dock and we all felt it was one less thing to worry about.

Later that evening Nora and I built a fire at the campground and ate a quiet dinner. After a few hours of writing in her journal she went to bed. I was restless and wide awake and sat down near the campfire. My heart rate increased as I went over the unfortunate events of the day. I watched as the last flicker of light in the smoldering ashes went out. I looked out over the bay, deep in thought. I saw the white light on the mast of the *Peer Gynt* off in the distance and all of the magnificent stars populating the night sky. The weather was unbelievably mild for early October. There was a warm breeze off the lake and the temperature must have been in the low fifties. Off in the distance, I could hear the faint calling of a loon. It sounded so beautiful, but also so forlorn.

I heard a sudden noise from just within the woods and it snapped me out of my thoughts. I don't know if it was an animal or perhaps a branch falling off a tree, but I felt a chill running down my spine. I instinctively said: "Who's there?" and waited for a response. Nothing. I got up and walked over to the shelter and peeked in. Nora was peacefully sleeping. I grabbed a flashlight, turned it on and stared looking into the woods. Nothing. I sat down near the fire pit and looked over at the *Peer Gynt*.

As I sat back down near the fire pit, I had a feeling. The gold was in the mine, hidden in that drift, and the flooded winze was the key to getting there. I suddenly yawned and I became extremely tired.

Chapter XXIII

The next morning, Nora and I hiked to the beach to meet up with Brian and Paige. We watched as they slowly made their way onto the *Peer Gynt's* skiff, started the tiny Evinrude, and pushed off toward the beach. The fog had moved in sometime late last night like an ominous specter. As the skiff neared, we could see they were engaged in some kind of heated discussion. I could only imagine who she was complaining about. As we all hiked back to the Island Mine, the tension was so thick, I felt like I could practically touch it. No words were said though, as I was waiting for Paige to make a full frontal verbal assault about my poor planning and incompetent execution of this adventure. But thankfully, it never came.

Just as we were walking off the trail onto the Island Mine site, I just about jumped out of my skin when we saw the park ranger we had met at the Windigo station. There were three other rangers with Mr. Stevenson and they appeared to be inspecting the partially covered main mine shaft. He looked over at us and said in a surprised voice, "What are you people doing here so early in the morning?"

We were stunned. I stood there with my mouth open, and Mr. Stevenson noticed my reaction and examined me with his beady little eyes. He shot a look at us like he had just caught us red-handed doing something. 'Think, Jens, think,' I said to myself.

"We've decided to camp at the Island Mine campground for a few days and thought we'd get an early jump on things," Brian mustered, putting his think-on-your-feet lawyer skills into action.

"Do you have a permit for staying there?" asked the inquisitive ranger. I reached back to my back pocket and produced my wallet, remembering I put our campground itinerary in it. I opened the folded paper and handed it to him. Mr. Stevenson grabbed the paper and started to scan it. He disappointedly groaned a few times and handed me back the paper and said, "What are you doing around these abandon mines? They can be extremely dangerous. Every week or so we like to hike around these parts to make sure nothing is damaged and make sure no one has fallen into them."

"We're just doing a little exploring, Mr. Stevenson, and admiring the beauty of the island," Nora said in her most charming voice.

"Well... be careful and enjoy your stay," Mr. Stevenson mumbled as the rangers started to walk down the path toward Siskiwit Bay. We stood there dumfounded for a full minute. We were all mortified.

"Now what do we do?" asked Paige.

"Let's go back to the boat and regroup," Brian replied. We waited an hour or so at the abandon mine site and then headed back to the boat. We decided that since we told the ranger we were going to stay at the Island Mine campground, we had better get our tents and set up camp there. So we spent the better half of the afternoon hiking up the trail and pitching our tents. It was a gamble, but we moored the *Peer Gynt* in Hay Bay, locked her good and tight, and then hid the skiff in some underbrush on Siskiwit Bay.

The Island Mine campground consisted of four smaller campsites to the north of the main trail with one outhouse and a larger group campsite to the south of the trail that also had an outhouse. The larger group site was already occupied—that was the campsite that Brian and Paige had discovered the other day when we found the portal to the abandoned mine. We thought it best to occupy campsite number four—the most northern and farthest site from the group campsite. When evening came, we built a fire from wood we collected from nearby and cooked a hearty meal of camper's stew. About six p.m. we could hear distant voices from the group campsite. For the most past, they sounded young and we could hear laughter and singing. By nine p.m. they were quiet.

•

The next morning, we got up at the crack of dawn and hiked the quarter of a mile to the abandoned mine. We had all agreed that we would give this thing one last shot. This time Nora

Diagram of the Island Mine

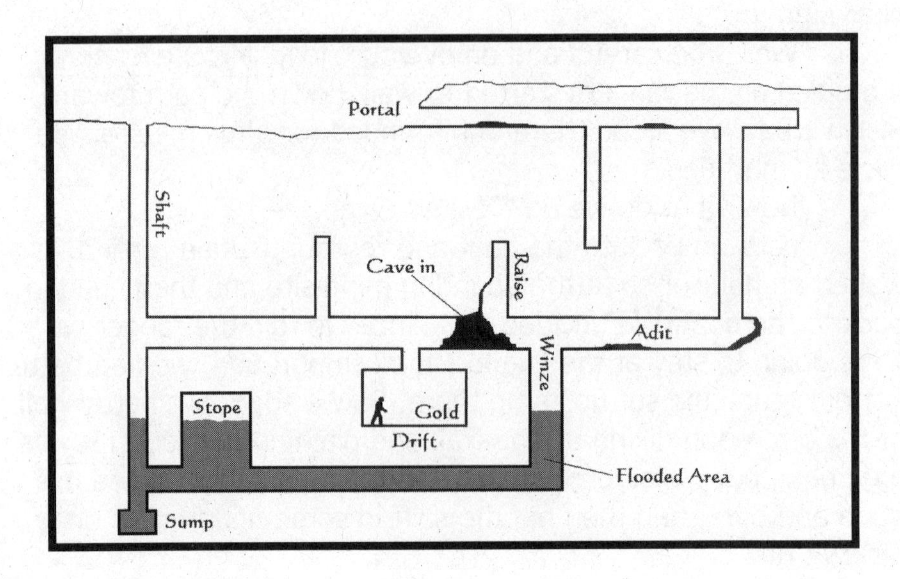

and Paige had to accompany us into the mine, for we needed all the help we could get. After entering the mine, we tried to disguise the portal as best we could. The four of us carried all of the equipment down the treacherous adits and winzes. This dive was at best tricky, and at worst, deadly—even to the most experienced diver. Brian and I had never scuba dived in a mine shaft before—or for that matter—an underwater cave.

The women helped us put on our dry suits and scuba gear. Lastly, we donned our masks and gloves. The water was about thirty-four degrees. I knew we wouldn't last more than about fifteen minutes in that freezing liquid hell. Judging from the map, it looked like we had to descend about thirty-five feet until we got to the third level adit. We then had to swim horizontally for about ninety feet until we reached the main vertical mine shaft. Then we would have to swim up that shaft the same thirty-five feet until we got to the second level adit again. Hopefully, the water would be gone and we could continue our little adventure on dry land. We had to walk back to where the cave-in was and find the drift, or another hole in the ground where the gold was hidden. We had to pray that there wouldn't be any cave-ins on the way.

I grabbed the 'buddy' rope, attached it to my dry suit, closed my eyes and slowly plopped into the dark watery hole. When I opened my eyes, it was complete darkness. I couldn't tell if I was upside down or right side up. I started hyperventilating and panicking, listening to my heavy breathing through my mouthpiece. I started kicking my legs and waving my arms, and I felt like I was bumping into things. I sensed the walls of the winze were closing in on me. I wanted to take off my mouthpiece and swim up to the surface—only I couldn't figure out which direction the surface was. I had the horrible sensation that I was suffocating and being crushed by caving in walls at the same time. I got the profound feeling, for just an instant, that I was going to die. I felt something grab me and start to shake me. The entire winze was lit up by an immense light. I glanced through the murky water and saw the thing that grabbed me. It was Brian and I could see his mouth moving behind the scuba mask. I thought I heard sounds. He appeared to be saying, "Settle down! Settle down, Jens."

I felt like a fool jumping into the dark water without first turning on my flashlight. I guess I was too excited. I composed myself and started to breathe regularly again. I gave Brian the thumbs up sign, and he pointed downward. I nodded my head and waited a few moments for the sediment and mud that I had kicked up during my little episode to dissolve. I started slowly descending by releasing pressure from my buoyancy compensation jacket. I could feel pressure building up in my ears as we slowly descended the winze. I plugged my nose and mouth with my hand and started to gently exhale until I felt a slight pop and the pressure in my ears subsided. I couldn't hear anything except my deep breathing and I watched as a multitude of air bubbles swished by me. In no time I felt my feet bumping into the muddy bottom. I had misjudged how deep the winze was and when I did hit the bottom with a thud, a dark thick cloud of mud and sediment rushed by me, rising up like a cloud. Brian came down almost on top of me and we both fell on our back sides. We sat there for a minute waiting for the water to get clear again and shined our flashlights down the horizontal shaft. I got up and started swimming down the adit. I knew it would be almost a hundred feet before we came to the main mine shaft.

I looked at my watch. Could that be true? Three minutes? We had only been in the water for that long? It had seemed like almost half an hour. Man, how scuba diving in an abandoned mine can play tricks on your mind. I had to stop reminding myself how cold the water was and watch out not to touch any of the water-logged support timbers that were lining the adit. As we were slowly making our way to the main shaft, I could see old pickaxes and shovels lying about, as well as an old coffee kettle. I wondered when the last time human eyes fell upon this place. It was scary, but also a thrill, to be seeing it.

Two minutes later, we found ourselves at the main shaft. We slowly kicked our fins upward, and I released more pressure from my buoyancy compensator. When we got to the surface, it was a little difficult because there was a twelve foot difference between the surface of the water and the second adit level. Luckily there were a few outcroppings that we could use for footings to climb up and out of the main shaft to the adit. When I looked up the main shaft toward the surface, I saw a hint of sunlight wandering down through collapsed portions of the shaft and rotten timber supports.

We took off our scuba gear and tried to warm up by slapping our bodies and running in place to get our blood flowing again. We quickly walked down the adit toward the cave-in. Our hearts started to pound harder and heavier as we came to the small hole in the ground where the drift was located. I couldn't recall what a drift was, in a mining sense, but this particular drift was like a pit about eighteen feet deep. I shined my flashlight down the entrance and all we could see was more rocks and debris. Brian took his rope ladder out of his bag. This one was a fifty-footer and I knew it was more than we needed. We secured one end to some large rocks and threw the ladder into the hole. This time we could hear the ladder hit the floor in a few seconds. Brian said, as he made a motion with his hands, "I believe you have the honor, Jens."

I smiled and started down the ladder. As I was descending, I thought to myself, gold or no gold, what an adventure this had been! I felt solid ground and grabbed my flashlight. I surveyed the entire drift. It was about twenty feet high by about twenty feet wide and about forty feet deep. At one end I could see a partial human skeleton. I walked over to it and said, "Hello, Chester, you double-crossing bastard." I started to walk over to the other end of the drift, but stumbled and tripped over some debris lying in the middle. I looked down and saw more human bones, but it was hard to distinguish between the bones and the dirt. These bones had to be Odd's. A tear suddenly came running down my cheek as I thought about the wonderful stories Torbjørn told me about him. Okay, enough paying respects to the dead. I shined my flashlight at the mound. Slowly, I walked over to it and pushed some dirt and sediment from the pile. I saw some old, rotted wood that appeared to be from crates. I dug in further and felt something hard. My heart started racing and I actually felt sweat streaking down my forehead and temples. I dug around and felt a sharp object. I pulled at it and realized I was holding a bone. It looked like a part of a leg bone. My heart skipped a beat as I threw it down. Oh my god! Could that have been part of Torbjørn's leg? The one he claimed to have cut off when he was pinned down by the gold? I looked at the jagged end of the bone and imagined a crate edge smashing it. It seemed to fit.

I shrugged it off and started digging again. I felt another hard object with my fingers. I traced the shape of the object. It was a rectangle. I tried to pick it up with my free hand, but it was far too heavy. I thought my heart was going to burst as I positioned my flashlight under my chin and grabbed the object with both hands. It took a few tries, but by wiggling it back and forth, it finally dislodged from the dirt. I picked it up and couldn't believe how heavy and dense the object was. I set it down on the ground and shined my flashlight on to it. Brushing off more of the dirt, I bellowed out a colossal scream. It was a bar of gold!

Chapter XXIV

Brian came running down the ladder when he heard me scream. "What's wrong? Are you hurt, Nilsen?" He saw me jumping up and down, and dancing back and forth like a crazed punk rocker. Then he noticed the twenty-seven pound gold bar I was holding in my hands. He too started to scream and dance as I tried to hand him the bar. Grabbing it, he was taken aback by how heavy it was. I ran over to the pile and found another bar. We were still jumping up and down when I finally said, "Do you realize Brian that between the two of us, we're holding over $300,000!?"

Brian and I calmed down after another minute of exhibiting mindless enthusiasm. We ran over to the mound in the corner and started to feel around for more bars. After we found a few more, we started to stack them in the center of the drift so we could more easily hoist them up to the second adit level. Twenty minutes later Brian asked me, "Nilsen, how many so far?

I quickly counted the stacks we had compiled, each having twelve bars. "Let see... two... four... six... two over there... um... six... OK times twelve... that's seventy-two. Wait a minute. Torbjørn said there were eighty bars. There must be more around here."

"Let's look around," Brian said. After another ten minutes or so, we did find all eighty bars of gold.

"Jens, there's a lot of gold bars here. Do you think we'll be able to sail back to Madeline Island okay?"

"I think so..." I said, as I was jolted a bit about what he had said. I was trying to do the mental math in my head... let's see... eighty bars at twenty-seven pound a piece... That would be about 2,200 pounds... "Oh my god," I said a bit too loudly.

"What is it?" Brian asked.

"What?" I said, shaking my head, trying to get those figures out of my mind.

"Will the *Peer Gynt* take the weight of the gold, Jens?"

"I think so. Maybe we'll have to throw some things off the boat to compensate for the additional weight."

"Well, let's see, Nilsen. Don't you weigh about 200 pounds? Maybe we can throw you off." He said with a sarcastic smile.

"Oh my God!" I blurted out.

"Now what?" Brian asked

"The women! We forgot to check in with them after a half an hour. They probably think we're dead or something!"

We tried the walkie-talkies, but—as I had suspected—they weren't getting through this far underground.

We quickly ran up the rope ladder and donned our scuba tanks, flippers, buoyancy compensators, and masks. We got our guts up again, jumped into the shaft and followed the guide rope we had run between the winze and the main shaft. I saw Brian starting to shake the rope back and forth, apparently to let Nora and Paige—who were undoubtedly anxiously waiting and wondering if we were still alive or not—at the other end.

Ten minutes later, Brian and I broke through the surface to the surprised and relieved looks of the women. "What happened to you guys? What took you so long?" Nora said in a relieved, but irritated voice.

Paige was a bit more vocal, "We thought you assholes were dead! Why didn't you let us know that you were at least alive? Do you know what it was like for us just waiting and waiting? Couldn't you guys just have the common courtesy to let us know what's going on so we don't have to keep tearing our hair out?"

I was about to say something when Brian nudged me with his elbow to be quiet. A small smile emerged on his face and I could see he was taking a little pleasure in letting Paige ramble on before he would tell her the news. Paige was still swearing like a marine, punching Brian in the stomach when he looked over at me and said, "Jens, show them what's in the bag."

Paige immediately stopped yelling and Nora's eyes transfixed on the bag that I had strapped to my belt. I slowly reached in and took out the gold bar. The water had cleaned off the dirt and sentiment and it was glowing in the artificial light we had set up in the adit.

"Oh my God!" Nora exclaimed.

"I don't believe it," was Paige's reply. "Is that real?"

"Of course it's real," Brian said.

"How many bars are there?" Paige demanded.

"Eighty." Brian said. We all started yelling and dancing. Brian started to dance the jig—just like in the John Ford movie, *Treasure of the Sierra Madre*, and Nora kept on saying, "I can't believe it... I just can't believe it!"

Paige added, "We're rich! We are all filthy rich!"

•

That night we all got a good night sleep. The next morning I knew we had to contend with the other park ranger, Ms. Harvey, who would be making her three-day rounds. We thought it best to hang around the campsite all day and continue tonight the difficult work of bringing the gold bars to the surface. However, in the afternoon, I made a solo reconnaissance hike back to the skiff at Siskiwit Bay and motored the five miles or so to check on the *Peer Gynt,* moored at Hay Bay. When I got there, the sailboat appeared to be okay, and the lock to the main cabin was undisturbed.

On my way back to Siskiwit Bay, I scouted around the Island Mine Trail, near the beach where we could secretively and temporarily store the gold bars, until we could at night move them on to the *Peer Gynt*. Lastly, I hiked past the Siskiwit Bay dock and saw that the park ranger's patrol boat was there—just like clockwork.

That night, Brian and I went back to the mine, scuba dived back through the flooded adit, and removed all eighty bars from the treasure drift. We used a make-shift basket with a steel rope to raise the gold bars up from the drift —two at a time—to the second level adit and then we carried them the sixty feet or so to the main shaft, where we stacked them neatly. This operation took most of the night, and when we got back, we both collapsed in our separate tents and within moments we were fast asleep.

•

The next morning we got a visit from the park ranger. She hiked up to the campsite and appeared to be surprised we were still in the area. I woke up from a deep slumber, hearing Nora talking to her. The women had gotten up early and I could smell the pleasing aroma of coffee brewing on the campfire they had started. I sat up and tried to listen in on the conversation, though the wind traversing through the trees made it a little difficult. Nora was charming the park ranger, asking astute questions which required ten minute answers. After about half an hour and a few cups of coffee, Ms Harvey said, "Thank you for your time." She finished her last sip of coffee, handed Nora the cup, and went on her way.

That night we started to extract the gold bars from the mine. First, Brian and I carried a couple of lightweight tubes and a make-shift winch. We were going to use this as a crude hoist to bring up the gold from the main mine shaft. The main mine shaft was out in the open, and the darkness was our only friend. We all prayed that there would be no midnight hikers, or worse yet, park rangers taking a walk around the area. The basket was large enough to hold two gold bars, but small enough to maneuver its way through the various stages of cave-ins, and decaying timber support walls. Brian and I donned our scuba gear and for the last time—hopefully—swam through the flooded adit and winze to the gold bars neatly stacked up. It was up to the women to crank up the basket with the two bars about eighty feet to the surface. Once it got to the surface, the women had to swing the basket away from the hole, pick up the bars and hide them in some nearby undergrowth. We would have liked to help them, but we didn't want to take the risk of one of us swimming alone in the flooded adit and back up to the surface. It took about five minutes for them to raise the gold bars to the surface and another five minutes to hide the bars and bring the basket back down again. At this rate, and taking some much needed breaks in between, it would take six or seven hours. In fact, it was broad daylight before the last of the bars was taken from the mine and discreetly hidden.

We started carrying the bars at about three p.m. after we tried to get some rest. We were all on edge and it was difficult to sleep. Most of all, we needed to relax our sore backs and shoulders. Nora and Paige were extremely stiff in their shoulders and arms after winching up and hiding the gold bars. They appeared not to care too much about that, though. In fact, I noticed we all displayed an alarming intensity. We were short-tempered and shot back unnecessary and childish comments to each other. I knew we were tired, stressed, dirty and sleep deprived, but this was getting ridiculous.

The four of us could carry a total of twelve bars in our backpacks per trip. Brian and I carried four each and Paige and Nora carried two each. That meant we would have to take a total of seven trips. Each trip took about two hours. If we took a half hour rest in between the hikes, the entire operation would take about seventeen hours. We wanted to spread it out for two days, so that meant about three trips a day. The first three trips were long, tiring and blister infested, but on the whole, uneventful.

Coming back to the mine on the beginning of our fourth trip the next day, we encountered a youth church group, who were singing the contemporary hymn *Earth and All Stars* while hiking along the trail in the other direction. The adult counselors gave us a congenial nod as the group continued marching on, not skipping a beat, praising God.

Nora and I smiled at each other and at the same time said, "Luther League." Brian and Paige looked a bit perplexed. Nora smiled and said, "If you've never experienced it, you'd never understand it." Nora and I enjoyed a few more chuckles.

Later, in the cold and dark of a moonless night, I slowly and carefully—with all running lights off—navigated the *Peer Gynt* around Point Hay to about fifty feet off the sandy reddish beach of Siskiwit Bay. There I waited for a flashlight signal to anchor the boat just off of where we had stockpiled the gold bars. After a few elongated moments and unsuccessfully trying to contact them with our forty-year-old, Army surplus walkie-talkies, I saw the signal. I attempted to maneuver the sailboat, oh so slowly, toward the signal, praying not to scrape the bottom of the boat. I knew they were waiting for me with a load of about fifteen gold bars on the skiff. I quietly lowered *Peer Gynt's* anchor as I watched Brian silently rowing the skiff toward me. I grabbed my binoculars and surveyed the bay and island hoping not to see any running lights of boats or campground fires. Fortunately, everything was pitch black. After six trips, the *Peer Gynt* was loaded down an additional 2,160 pounds. I knew that each new gold shipment would lower the sailboat in the water, so I moved the sailboat farther out into the bay after each shipment. My biggest fear was that the additional weight of the gold would accidentally beach the *Peer Gynt.* But that proved to be groundless—the boat was lower in the water, but not dangerously so. After the last load, we tied the skiff to the back of the sailboat and slowly trolled out into the deeper waters of the bay off of Senter Point.

We anchored the *Peer Gynt* and had a meeting in the main cabin, which was kind of a joke because there were gold bars all over the floor and benches. Paige wanted to set sail immediately so we could get back to Madeline Island within twenty-four hours. She said—"No offense, but then I can get off this hellish boat and take a nice long shower."

That plan was quickly voted down because I didn't want to navigate the treacherous Houghton Point passage at night, especially with the sailboat running low in the water.

•

The next morning we woke to an ominously dark sky. The wind had picked up a bit and the *Peer Gynt* was violently weaving back and forth. I immediately went to my navigation station and turned on the radio to hear the weather forecast. I began writing down the pertinent information in my log book, when I heard Brian yell from the deck, "Nilsen, get up here, we've got company."

My heart sank, and I jumped up (hitting my head on the ceiling in the process) and ran up the ladder to the cockpit. "What's going on?" I said as I grabbed my binoculars, which were always wrapped around the helm. I saw a long, sleek sailboat running easterly across Siskiwit Bay toward Hay Bay. As I was rubbing the emerging bump on my head, hoping that it wasn't bleeding, I said, "That boat looks familiar."

"Could it be that mystery sailboat from Devil's Island you thought you saw, Jens?" Nora suggested. My heart froze and I nodded. "Honestly, I never really got a good look at it... I just don't know."

"That's right, Jens," Brian said. "Let's not jump to conclusions. Let's just see what he does first and then think of a plan." We all uneasily watched the mystery sailboat slowly disappear past Point Hay on its way to Hay Bay. There the sailboat could do anything, undetected; hiding in the secluded bay with no trails leading to it. I started to pace up and down the deck, wondering what we should do. Should we make a break for it, or should we just stay put for a while? I wanted to take the skiff and motor over to Hay Bay and spy on what they were doing. Were they just on vacation and planning on staying there for a few days, or did they have more sinister plans? Brian didn't like that idea because if something did happen, he didn't want us separated. So we all sat there for another hour, trying to decide what to do. Finally, after much arguing and petty debate, we decided to go. We started to untie the main sail and were about to raise the anchor when suddenly, coming from Point Houghton, we saw the park ranger patrol boat heading toward us.

As we watched the park ranger come up beside us, I turned to Nora and said, "You've seemed to have gotten along with her pretty well. Why you don't talk to her and see what she wants?"

"Howdy strangers, you're all still here?" Ms Harvey, said in a pleasant voice as she came up to us and threw her mooring line to Nora, expecting to come on board. My heart started pumping faster. We hadn't even tried to lay a blanket or anything on top of the gold to hide it. It was all in plain sight in the main cabin. Nora helped her on board the *Peer Gynt* and then she looked around and said, "My, my, my, did you all gain weight or something?" We all looked at her and started to shake our heads in unison.

"It's just that your sailboat is sitting a little deeper in the water. That's quite odd, don't you think?" She was making us sweat and she knew it. She continued on another tack, "You know, we've been getting reports that some young folks were poking around the Old Island Mine up yonder," She pointed in the general direction of the mine. We all looked at her again and started to shake our heads in unison.

"You people haven't seen any suspicious activity in the area, have you?" We all shook our heads.

"Huh, I didn't think so. Mr. Stevenson said he saw you guys around the old abandoned Island Mine the other morning." She then started to move her right hand down near her hip and service revolver and then said, "You don't suppose I could go down below just for a few seconds and look around?" There was dead silence. None of us could muster a word. That's it, I thought. This thing was all for nothing, not to mention possible prosecution and the probability that Nora and Brian could be disbarred.

All off a sudden the massive doors of *Åsgard* opened and the glorious Norse Gods came rushing out in all of their generosity to help us. We heard Ms Harvey's walkie-talkie go off. It was a park ranger from the Rock Harbor Station telling her of an accident and possible injuries at the Daisy Farm campground and requesting immediate assistance.

"Damn," Ms Harvey said under her breath. She wanted so badly to go down into the sailboat, but lives were at stake. She turned and grabbed her mooring line from Nora and jumped back into the patrol boat. She looked up at us as she turned on the motor and yelled out to us, "You better still be here when I come back in a couple of hours or else I'll call in the Coast Guard on you. Do I make myself clear?" She then spun off in a northerly direction.

"We're screwed, there's just no way around it... we're screwed." Paige said to herself while walking around the deck in circles.

"Calm down, everyone. We can't come unglued, here," said Brian. "We have to think of a plan and we've got about two hours."

Then Nora said, "The way I see it, we either have to leave now and take our chances on the open lake, or dump the gold, right here in the bay, and come back later."

I said, "If we take off now, the Coast Guard will find us. They have radar and helicopters to track us down."

"Well, I don't know what to do, but I'll tell you one thing, I'm not going to get disbarred over this, that's for sure."

"I think the best thing to do is to take off," Brian said. "The accident over there at Daisy Farm could be really serious and maybe Ms Harvey will forget about us. Plus, if the injuries are severe, then won't they need the Coast Guard helicopter to pick up the injured and fly them to Duluth?"

"You're right, Brian," agreed Paige, "Let's do it. Let's go."

I looked at Nora's face and she shot me a glance like, okay, what the hell, let's do it. I nodded my head and said, "Okay, but let's wait until the patrol boat is completely out of sight so she thinks we're waiting for her."

Twenty minutes later, when the patrol boat was gone, I started the motor and Brian raised the anchor. I put the throttle into gear and we started to make our way toward Houghton Point Passage, when I heard Nora gasp.

"Look!" she yelled and pointed toward Hay Bay. There was the mystery sailboat coming right at us. I grabbed my binoculars and saw little orange and red colors spitting up from the rear cockpit area. Suddenly, I could see the entire rear portion of the sailboat engulfed in smoke. The smoke was thick and dark, like oil ablaze. I said to myself, "Oh my God, this can't be happening."

Chapter XXV

"I don't like the looks of this at all," I said under my breath as I watched the mystery sailboat approach us at a frightful speed. I scanned over to the rear of the boat and saw smoke and flames intensifying.

"What was that you said, Nilsen?" Brian asked.

"I said I don't like the looks of this—it's too convenient. They're trying to get us to let our guard down, help them, and they'll somehow steal our gold."

"Well, that fire doesn't look fake, Jens," Paige said in a condescending tone. I continued to steer the *Peer Gynt* toward Point Houghton passage, trying to ignore the incredulous stares burning at me. The sailboat was now in yelling distance from us and we all turned and looked as a dark and stocky, solitary figure was on the deck jumping up and down and screaming "Help... help!"

"Jens!" Nora said in an uneasy voice. "You just can't ignore it. You have to help him. He looks like he's in real danger. And besides that, don't you have an obligation as a licensed charter skipper to help out another boat in distress?"

"Come on, Jens, Nora's right. You just can't leave someone who is in mortal danger to die on the lake like that. Can you?" Brian said.

"I'm with Jens, here," Paige said, "It looks like a trap."

"That man could die, Paige. Do you want that on your conscience?" Nora said. Paige gave an indifferent nod and Nora rolled her eyes.

I stood there for a few moments, shaking my head and then said, "Okay, I'll do it. We'll go over there and help him. But..." I said as I pointed to all three of them, "Be on your guard!" They nodded as I turned the *Peer Gynt* in the direction of the smoking sailboat.

"Should we use the radio to call the Coast Guard?" Nora suggested. I thought for a few moments and then said, "No. We can put out the fire with our fire extinguisher. If the Coast Guard comes, they might want to snoop around on our boat."

"Okay Jens, but I will personally call the Coast Guard or the park ranger if there are any serious injuries on that sailboat," Nora informed me. As we advanced on the distressed sailboat, I noticed that the weather was just as turbulent as our current situation. More ominous dark clouds had started to move in and the wind was definitely intensifying from the northeast. Whitecaps began to emerge. A few seconds later we were within a few yards of the mystery sailboat. Brian threw the stocky man a mooring line as I yelled at him to use his fire extinguisher. He yelled back that he didn't have one, so I cut the motor and ran down the ladder to the main cabin and grabbed an extinguisher stored under the galley bench. I ran up to the deck, jumped onto the mysterious sailboat, aimed the extinguisher and put out the fire in ten seconds. I did a double-take at the origin of the fire. It was in a cut-down oil drum. It looked as if the fire was intentionally set and placed in the drum to contain it, so it wouldn't spread to the rest of the sailboat. It appeared that someone wanted to get our attention. And they succeeded.

Before I had time to warn the others, a familiar face, holding a revolver, slithered from the cockpit entry. It was Brett Ruud.

"Well, if it isn't the asshole college boy who stole my uncle's treasure map."

"I didn't steal it," I said without thinking.

"Oh... no," Brett said with a smirk as he pointed his revolver at my head. "What would you call it then?"

"Torbjørn gave me the map. He wanted me to have it. You never visited him at the nursing home, did you? You neglected him like you do your wife and kids. Torbjørn decided to give the map to me," I said. I could feel pure rage boiling deep inside me. I took a step toward him and then he cocked the trigger of the revolver.

"Screw you," was his witty reply.

"Gentlemen... gentleman," Brian interrupted, "Let's all calm down now and talk rationally. We don't want anyone to get hurt.

Perhaps we can work out some type of arrangement that can satisfy everybody."

"What are you offering, sleaze-ball?" the stocky man said as he produced his own gun and pointed it at Brian's chest.

"Well," Brian continued, "Why can't you guys put down your guns so we can have a nice, safe chat?" The revolvers stayed pointed at us.

Brian went on, "I guess we all know what's inside our sailboat. How about if we give you guys... say... five gold bars each. That's about $750,000 for each of you. We'll give it to you, then you guys can go on your way, and we'll forget this little scene ever happened."

"I want it all, dickhead. Boy, you're a piece of work. What are you, some kind of sleazy lawyer? Because you certainly sound like one."

"Go to hell, you lazy bastard!" I snarled at him. "If you think I'm just going to sit here and let you take this treasure away from me, then you're stark raving mad. I was the one who planned this expedition. I was the one who figured out the supplies to bring, what equipment was needed and sailed the boat to this island. Then Brian and I risked our lives to go down into that mine and get the gold. If you think I'm going to see you take it all away from us, you have another thing coming. Sure, you'll get this gold—over my dead body. Come on shoot," I said as I raised my hands and made a bigger target for myself. "I dare you to shoot me in cold blood. You don't have the balls, do you? Sure, you and your pal may be rich for the rest of your lives, but you'll have a murder rap on you. You'll always be looking behind your back for the law... come on, I dare you, shoot me, you wimpy bastard, shoot!"

"Jens... stop it! Just shut up!" I heard Nora scream out as I heard Brett's gun go off and a bullet whistled past my ear. I ducked and fell onto the deck. Brett took another step toward me and said, "Why don't you tell your lady friend to come on over to my boat? We'll make beautiful music together."

"Okay, okay, let's all settle down here. There's got to be a way that we can make a deal," Brian said.

Then the stocky guy said to Brett, "Come on, Brett. Listen to the man! I don't want no murder happening here. Come on, man, hear what he has to say."

"Okay, man." He said to the stocky guy and then turned to Brian and said, "Okay sleaze-ball, talk. And don't insult me by saying we can have ten bars."

"All right, how about this: We'll give you half of it."

"Well, how much is half?" Brian shot me a glance and I gave him a hint of a nod. He then lied and said, "We have a total of forty bars, so that means we'll give you and your partner here twenty bars."

"How much money is that then?" The stocky guy inquired.

"It's about $3 million," I said. Brett stopped for a second and then looked over to the stocky guy. They exchanged glances and, by their facial gestures, we could all see they were carrying on a conversation. It looked like the stocky guy liked the deal, but Brett needed convincing. I threw in, "If you take it all away from us, then, when you leave, we'll call the park ranger and the Coast Guard and we'll squeal. We'll tell them the whole story. They'll have you in jail before you can get to land."

"Who's to say you'll all be around to tell them anything?" Brett said slowly and diabolically, as he pointed his revolver at my head again.

"Come on, you're no killer. You're not going to kill four people in cold blood, are you? You're many things, Brett, but a murderer, you're not. Think of your wife and kids. Are you really willing to go to jail?" I added.

Five minutes later the stocky guy had tethered the two boats together and Nora, Paige, and Brian were sitting down on the front deck of the *Peer Gynt.* Brett told them to sit on their hands and volunteered me to carry the gold bars onto his sailboat. The stocky guy was helping me and Brett was closely watching all of us straddling his legs on his sailboat's cockpit with revolvers in both hands. The stocky guy and I went down into the *Peer Gynt's* main cabin and I showed him where the bulk of the gold bars were located. I couldn't tell if he thought there were more than forty gold bars lying about—he didn't seem to notice. He told me to grab one and carry it up onto the deck. When I did, he followed me up and jumped over to Brett's sailboat and then stretched out his hands.

"Here, hand it to me," he said. I could tell by his gyrations and his cussing under his breath that he was surprised at the weight of the bar. A broad smile enveloped Brett's face as I turned and walked toward the hatch leading down into the main cabin. As I was about to step down, I looked up at Brett and asked him, "How did you find out that we were sailing to Isle Royale? And how in the world did you know we had gold bars?"

Brett smirked and said in that obnoxious, cock-sure voice of his, "It was easy. Somehow I just couldn't believe that the four of you were going down to Central America to do missionary work. Ha, no way, don't make me laugh. I had to bite my upper lip when your boss... Norm? Yes? Norm is his name, right?... when he told me on the phone where you had gone on your vacation. So then, I looked up your parent's address in St. Louis Park and went to visit them."

My body froze. To think this disgusting creature, this freak of nature went to talk to my parents. It made me feel like I was going to throw up.

"Of course your sweet little mother told me the truth. You couldn't lie to your sweet little mother now, could you?"

"Go to hell!"

"She told me that the four of you were sailing to Isle Royale. I told her that my uncle Torbjørn had left something important for you and that you needed it right away. She was gracious enough to give me a copy of your neatly typed itinerary. I knew exactly when and where you would be at all times... thank you very much."

I felt cold stares coming my way from my crew members. I had given my mom an itinerary—not mentioning the mine or gold, mind you—so if we got lost or in trouble, she could let the authorities know our approximate whereabouts. So much for that idea, I thought to myself. I looked at Brett again and said, "What about the gold bars?"

"Oh that. That was also easy. You see, after Torbjørn died, I went over to the nursing home and the hospital and had some interesting chats with some of the staff. One nurse in particular told me that on the last night of his life, Torbjørn muttered in his sleep about some men named Odd and Stig, and he kept on saying a few words she didn't understand but she remembered them because she had heard Torbjørn say it so many times. He kept on saying: '*gullet... hver er gullet*?'"

"Gold," I whispered to myself. "Where is the gold?"

"Then," Brett continued, "The nurse said he kept on saying something like: '*Sjøkart. Jeg trenger sjøkartet.*'"

"Sea chart," I whispered again under my breath. "I need the sea chart."

"Now, I never stepped one foot in a college class, see," Brett went on, "but I can put two and two together. So I figured it all out. And then I asked myself, 'Why should I risk my life trying to find and get the gold? Why don't I have that smart-ass college boy find it for me? Then I can rightly take what was mine to begin with, see.' So I call up my old friend Cliff over here," he pointed to the stocky man, "who was in the Navy and knows all about sailing, and tell him he should come up to Lake Superior and rent a sailboat with me. I told him it would be well worth his while. So he did. Now get going, I don't have all day," he said as he looked up towards the looming dark clouds.

After I absorbed all he said, I walked down the ladder to the main cabin. I grabbed another bar and made my way up to the cockpit. Cliff extended his hands. Just then, a large wave whacked against the sailboats. It sent a spray of water up onto the deck, startling Cliff, and he began to fumble the heavy gold bar as I put it into his hands. For an instant, I thought to myself this was another sign from the Norse Æsir from *Åsgard*; this was my chance. I did something that I would regret for the rest of my life. As Cliff was trying to get a better grip on the bar, I shoved him off the sailboat and into the freezing, turbulent water. I can't tell you why, but for some reason, in that split second, I decided I didn't want Brett and Cliff to have any of the gold. The gold bar shot out of his hands and disappeared into the water.

The next thing I heard was Brett yelling something and feeling a bullet whiz by me and scrape my sweatshirt sleeve. I immediately fell down on the deck and felt pain throbbing from my arm. I looked up to see Brian jumping up from the deck and pushing, with all of his might, the mast boom, swinging around and catching Brett unaware. The boom smacked the front of his chest and threw him overboard.

For an instant, time just froze. I instinctively grabbed my right arm with my left hand and felt around for any blood. I thought for sure that I was shot. Nora came running over in hysterics and asked if I was okay. Brian jumped over to the other sailboat and picked up Brett's revolver, which hadn't fallen into the lake. He pointed it at Brett, who was dog paddling in the bone chilling water, telling him not to come close to the sailboats.

I quickly determined that the bullet had just grazed my skin and that it was just a minor flesh wound. Nora ran down into the main cabin to get the first aid kit. Brian told Cliff to swim over near Brett so that he could keep an eye on both of them. They appeared to have some difficulty trying to stay right side up in the large waves coming from the bay. Then Brian said, "Well Nilsen, what do we do next?"

I paused and thought for a second. Nothing came to mind. Nora had come up from the cabin, quickly helped me take off my sweatshirt, and started bandaging my arm.

"What are we going to do with them, Jens?" Nora asked as she was finishing up with the bandages. "We just can't let them drown, can we?"

"Why not?" Paige interjected. "They didn't care much about our lives."

"They'll die of hyperthermia in no time," Brian said.

Then I quickly said, "Okay, this is what we're going to do." I ran onto Brett's sailboat and started the motor. I pulled the line up from their skiff, which was tied behind the boat and jumped in. I disengaged the small outboard motor at the back of the skiff and threw it overboard with a loud splash. I took the two small oars lying on the floor of the skiff and threw them overboard, far away from the dogpaddling men. I jumped back onto Brett's sailboat and untied the skiff and pushed it toward the exhausted and freezing men. I yelled out to them: "Get into the skiff. The waves will push you to shore." I told Brian to start the *Peer Gynt's* motor and follow me. I took the helm of Brett's sailboat and headed northeast, toward Point Houghton passage. Brian followed in the *Peer Gynt*, about fifty feet behind me.

As the sailboats were motoring toward the passage, I turned around and saw both men wriggling into the skiff with their waterlogged clothes. Brett was shaking his hands at me and his head was shuddering back and forth like a big league manager barking at an umpire's bad call. My heart was pounding and my mind was mixed with emotions, just like the storm that was starting to brew. I didn't know what my plan would be from one moment to another, nor could I understand what I had just done. All I remembered was that I felt good about myself. I felt alive.

After another fifteen minutes, I motioned for Brian to come up next to me. I tied the steering wheel when the boat was pointed north of the passage, toward the Siskiwit Islands and the inner reef of Long Island. My hope was to just let the sailboat smash into the rocks. As I moved toward the rail, I noticed the gold bar lying on the deck. No sense leaving that behind! I picked it up, motioned Brian to come a bit closer and then I jumped onto the *Peer Gynt*, timing the level of the decks from the waves.

As we navigated the *Peer Gynt* through the now more difficult—thanks to the wind and waves—Point Houghton passage, we could see Brett's sailboat slam up and into the rocks and shoals of the tiny Siskiwit Islands.

Once we had gone through the passage, I headed straight east onto the open lake. I wanted to get away from Isle Royale, fearing we might bump into Ms Harvey's patrol boat if I sailed north along the coast. I also didn't want to sail south, fearing I might bump into Mr. Stevenson near the Windigo ranger station. No, I wanted to get away from the island and take my chances on the open lake.

I started to breathe more freely. I took a deep breath and tried to relax. Relieved at what had just transpired and thinking that we had just lost only one gold bar, I felt pretty good—considering the circumstances. My mind was crudely shaken, though, and came rushing back to reality when I glanced out at the vast horizon and saw a black curtain of clouds and sheets of rain falling down in front of us. I quickly closed my eyes and I pinched myself in disbelief. When I opened them again, I could see a full force gale enveloping us out on the open lake.

Chapter XXVI

In all of the commotion, I had completely forgotten to listen to the weather station. There was a density in the air and I could feel the foreboding calmness before the storm. I could see the dark clouds looming toward us, and it seemed for a moment, everything was moving in slow motion. There was nothing to do now but batten down the sailboat, warn the crew and tell them to stay below. I put on my foul-weather suit, lifejacket and, of course, my safety harness. Judging from the darkness of the clouds, the wind, and the height of the waves—which in some cases were reaching six feet—I decided not to look for any shelter back on Isle Royale, but to try to ride the storm out. Now, I read somewhere that if the winds exceed thirty miles an hour, then you've got a gale on your hands. After I had taken down the jib sail and reefed the main sail, I looked at the wind speed indicator on the helm. It was reading up to twenty-five miles an hour. The rain came, pouring down in heavy sheets, and I thought I may have felt some hail. The main sail, even though it was reefed, was making a terrible cracking sound.

After about ten minutes, the wind and the waves were definitely intensifying. The *Peer Gynt* was bobbing up and down with the waves and water was now washing over the deck and cockpit. I opened the latch door and shouted down to Brian to turn on the bilge pumps and the weather station and find out when this blasted storm would end. He yelled something back at me, but the wind and the rain were way too loud. I closed the latch and slowly made my way back to the helm.

Part of me wanted to slither on down into the rear cabin and roll up in the berth, close my eyes and pray for the storm to end. The other part of me wanted to stand on top of the cabin deck, lash myself to the main mast and ride out the storm. What should I do? I clamped the helm on a nice, straight easterly course—out toward the open lake. I then opened the lazarette hatch in the cockpit and got out a bunch of bungee cords and walked onto the cabin deck holding on to the main stays. I tied the bungee cords around the main mast and then to myself. I then leaned forward and stared right down into the 'soul of the storm.' I could feel my body riding up and down, pitching and rolling with every wave. I was riding high up on the crest of the wave and then I would smash down and see nothing but water in the troughs. Water spray was constantly washing over me, and between the rain and the waves, I felt completely drenched. It was better than any amusement ride. I was staring nature and death right in her eyes. I was amazed at the raw power and danger of the storm. I never felt more alive. I started to laugh like a madman, like I had never laughed before. "Come on lake; give me your best shot! Come on, Death, let me see you, so I can laugh and spit in your face, you bastard, you!" I yelled at the top of my lungs. I had reached another peak in my life where time seemed to stand still. I then saw something out of the corner of my eye. I turned and saw the schooner *Valkyrie* sailing next to me, riding the same wild waves. I looked at the rear of the ship and saw Grandpa Jens at the helm. He was smiling and waving at me. I smiled and waved back. I never in my life felt so at peace with the world as I did at that moment.

•

The next thing I knew, I felt Brian shaking me and saying in disbelief, "What the hell are you doing, Nilsen?"

I opened my eyes. It was daylight. I looked around and saw the lake was relatively calm, although the skies were still overcast. I had forgotten the previous night for an instant, and then it all came rushing back at me. I gave a quick smile and said, "Oh yeah. I tied myself to the main mast last night so I wouldn't be washed overboard."

"You gave us all quite a scare this morning when we opened the latch and couldn't find you in the cockpit." Nora said with some fear. "We thought you had been thrown overboard last night—until we saw this body hanging on the mast. Just what in the world were you thinking Jens?"

"Like I said, I just wanted to be safe. An extra precaution, I guess." I then looked all around and saw water in every direction.

"Does anybody know where we are?" I was trying to change the subject and hoping that all those strange stares I was getting would go away.

"Isn't that your job, Jens?" Paige asked.

"I guess so. I'll just go down below and turn on the Loran and radar."

Five minutes later I was trying to warm up, sitting at the navigation station and sipping on some hot cocoa that Nora had prepared. That little storm last night had blown us approximately thirty miles east of Isle Royale and about twenty miles north of the Keweenaw Peninsula on the Michigan Upper Peninsula. I was amazed that the storm hadn't knocked out the radar equipment. It looked like now we had two options; either sail the twenty miles or so south to Eagle Harbor and risk the chance of getting caught with all the gold; or quietly sail southwest, approximately 140 miles back to La Pointe on Madeline Island.

I posed our dilemma after we ate. Surprisingly, it was a fifty/fifty split. Brian and Nora opted to stop at Eagle Harbor, and somehow get someone to drive Brian back to Madeline Island to retrieve the Suburban and then drive back to get the gold. The storm and Brett Ruud was enough for them to never sail on the lake again. I thought this plan was far too risky and the possibility of getting caught too great. Paige and I, on the other hand, agreed that sailing back to Madeline Island was worth it for financial independence for the rest of our lives. We could easily sail back to Madeline Island and proceed with our plan of sneaking the gold bars off the sailboat at night and then drive back to Minneapolis.

We moved up to the cockpit and continued our little discussion as I took the helm. After a few more minutes of yelling and screaming at each other, Nora went on that the gold bars weren't worth our lives and Paige came back and said we've gone this far, why don't we just try to pull it off? After another twenty minutes of bickering back and forth, it was decided that we would settle this little dispute by a coin toss. Paige said 'heads' as Brian flipped the coin and let it drop on the deck of the cockpit. "Heads it is," I said and then turned the sailboat to a southwesterly direction. We raised the jib sail, un-reefed the main sail and headed for Madeline Island.

•

So here is where my story picks up from the first chapter. I was all by myself in the cockpit and at the helm of a loaded sailboat, limping back to Madeline Island and praying for calm seas. It was dark again, night had fallen and my crew had gone below for the evening. The clouds had dissipated, and I could see the crescent of the moon shining above and shooting a dancing moonbeam reflection on the water. There was a breeze gently brushing against my face from the southwest. I could hear the placid slapping of the water on the hull of the *Peer Gynt*. The moon and the stars were my only companions. I thought about the look of utter frustration on Nora's face after our last altercation, and worried. I didn't think she would allow me to set foot in the rear cabin, let alone sleep in the same bed. Brian was also upset with me. I think the coin toss was the last straw. He wouldn't even look at me. What was surprising is that Paige and I were now allies. I agreed with her about taking the chance and sailing all the way back to Madeline Island. Somehow, I feel uneasy about that, though. Because ever since I've known her, I've thought she was a materialistic, social-climbing, slave to fashion, stuck-up woman. I believed I had nothing in common with her. Was I right on that? Had she changed, or had I?

Throughout the midnight cruise, I went down to the navigation station every now and then to check out the radar screen. I wasn't too confident yet about my sailing abilities at night. I didn't want to run up on anything unexpectedly. At about four a.m., I went down to check on the radar and see what the blip I had detected earlier was doing. It was moving on a similar tack as ours and it appeared to be moving far too slow to be a laker or a saltwater ship. I wondered who could be out this early in the morning. Was it a small commercial fishing boat, a coast guard patrol boat, or perhaps another sailboat? I just couldn't tell. I decided that I was going to keep a sharp eye on that blip.

By daybreak, my crew members had all come up from below to get some fresh air and sip hot coffee. The skies were still overcast, but the morning sun was trying to break out of the thick, gray clouds. I noticed that Nora and Brian were a bit standoffish toward me; however, as the morning dragged on, they both settled down and started engaging in conversation again.

I looked at the vast horizon in front of me and noticed that a dense fog was beginning to penetrate the area. I was getting a little concerned and told Nora to take the helm. I jumped down the hatch to the main cabin and over to the navigation station. When I looked at the radar screen I noticed that our little friend was gaining on us. It now appeared that it was only a few miles behind us and on the same heading. I ran up to the cockpit and grabbed my binoculars. I scanned the northeastern horizon behind us, but couldn't see much. The fog was beginning to get thicker, like pea soup. I took the helm and we made a large leeward tack. I sat for a few moments, praying that my newfound fears would not come to fruition. I went back down to the navigation station and saw to my great fear that the blip in the radar screen was now moving on the same tack as we were. As the morning progressed and the fog got thicker, I made a few more tacks with the sailboat. The blip on the screen changed course every time we did. I knew it was following us.

Chapter XXVII

By mid-afternoon, the fog intensified to a thick grayish soup. Visibility was down to about 100 feet. On top of that, the skies had grown darker and the swells were up to three feet and increasing. The weather station indicated another storm was moving in from the northeast. The situation didn't look good.

I tried to go about my business as calmly as possible to avoid raising the anxiety level of the crew. I subtlety changed course and headed southerly, toward the mainland on the Michigan Keweenaw Peninsula. I knew the *Peer Gynt* might not last long, if she had to endure another rough storm with the extra weight of the gold bars. I headed straight for the Ontonagon Lighthouse, some thirty miles south and prayed there would be some kind of shelter nearby where we could ride out the storm. There was no fooling around. This was serious.

After about ten minutes on this new tack, I decided to go down to the navigation station and check out the blip following us. Not to my surprise, the blip had also changed course and continued to follow us. At that point, I was beginning to lose it. Between the friction among the crew, the overweight sailboat, the thick fog, the looming storm, nightfall around the corner, and now this damn ghost ship following us, I was becoming extremely stressed. Who the hell could this boat be? It couldn't be that park ranger, Ms Harvey, could it? Maybe she tipped off a coast guard patrol boat to come after us, but that couldn't be right because the patrol boat is a lot faster than us and we would have seen it by now. I knew one thing; it certainly couldn't be Brett Ruud. I saw the damaged sailboat off the shoals near Point Houghton Pass. There was no way that sailboat could ever sail again.

We had about twenty minutes before the storm hit, which meant we still would be twenty miles from shore. I decided to make a few maneuvers with the sailboat to get closer to this ghost boat and find out what the hell they wanted. I started to make a few starboard tacks until I was making a large circle. Brian wanted to know what I was doing and I explained to him that the ghost boat would eventually catch up to us anyway, and I just had to find out who it was. I can't recall his exact response, but quite honestly, I really didn't care what he thought at that moment.

My tacks were getting smaller, the fog was becoming thicker, and the waves were getting higher. According to the radar, the ghost ship was right on our tail. The wind was gusting now and the storm was minutes away. The sails were making a crackling clatter in the wind and I knew it was time to take down the jib and reef the main. I told Brian to prepare for heavy seas and we both donned lifejackets and safety harnesses. I told the women to go below, batten everything down the best they could and put on warm clothes and lifejackets.

Holding on to the mainstays for balance, I made my way to the bow of the deck to take down the jib sail. As I bent down to grasp it, I felt a jet of icy cold water on my face as a wave slammed into the hull. Just then it started to rain. It was heavy, and stung when it hit my exposed skin. The waves were intensifying and I could feel the bow of the sailboat plunge down into the trough of the wave and then lurch upward toward the crest. It was like a rollercoaster ride. I was just about finished lowering the jib with one arm, and hanging on to the forestay for dear life with the other, when a colossal dark object filled the sky. Suddenly, the *Peer Gynt* pitched downward in the trough of a wave as I watched in horror as an enormous hull emerged above me on the crest of another wave. The hull slammed down, missing our boat by inches. It was a miracle that the two boats didn't collide. I quickly staggered back to the cockpit and took over the helm.

Brian yelled, because between the rain, waves, and whipping of the main sail, it was extremely hard to hear, "Did you see that? It almost hit us!"

"I know. That has to be the boat that was following us," I screamed at the top of my lungs as I leaned forward to compensate for the rough seas. I tried to get my bearings and steer south toward the mainland. I peeked behind my shoulder and was stunned to see the ghost ship bearing right toward us. A tingling sensation scampered through my body when I realized the ghost ship was the sailboat of Brett Ruud. By some unexplained freak of nature, the mystery sailboat had not been damaged to the point where it could not sail again when it ran aground on the rocks back on Isle Royale. Brett Ruud and Cliff had been resurrected to hunt me down and reclaim the gold which he believed was his. Brian and I just looked intently at each other with mouths wide open.

Then Brian shouted, "Look out, Jens, he's trying to ram us!" I quickly turned the helm as hard as I could and we again just missed each other by a few feet. As the sailboat passed by, I felt like I was so close to Brett that I could reach out and touch him. I glared at him—he looked different, somehow. He looked like a man who was possessed by the devil. I glanced into his flaming eyes and it gave me a chill down my spine. Deep in those smoldering eyes I saw hatred and wickedness, the kind that I've heard slumbers in everyone, waiting for an opportunity to emerge when unfortunate situations arise. He personified all the hate and evil in the world. I got the impression that either he would succeed in stealing the gold or die trying. His bloodcurdling eyes reminded me of the legendary Norwegian Sea monster, *Sjøormann*. Legend had it that if you saw him, it meant bad luck and death would surely be around the corner. That just wouldn't do. I turned the helm toward Brett's sailboat, preparing to ram it amidships.

"What the hell are you doing, Jens?" Brian barked out.

"I have to do what I have to do. Don't you understand? He's screwing with our happiness—our financial independence. That just won't do!"

"So, you're going to kill him, Jens?" Brian pleaded.

"I'm going to do to him what he is trying to do to us. Why is that so hard to figure out, Brian? Can't you see we're so close? So close—and you don't even realize it. Wake up man!"

"Don't you realize that you're just as crazy as he is, Jens?" And with that I smacked Brian in the jaw and he went down like a ton of bricks on the cockpit deck. I wasn't proud of what I did, but I had to do what I had to do, right?

I concentrated on finding Brett. I looked around and thought I spotted a black object off the port beam through all of the rain and rough seas. I steered toward it and was shocked to see it listing to one side and the cockpit was filling up with water. I guess the sailboat did indeed sustain some damage on the grounding at Siskiwit Bay. I saw Brett and Cliff frantically bailing water out of the cockpit with plastic buckets. Just then a large diagonal wave hit the *Peer Gynt* and the bow soared high up on the crest of the wave. When the bow started to descend, it slammed right on top of the cockpit of Brett's sailboat, crushing it in two instantly. With the additional weight of the gold, the *Peer Gynt* was like a big fat battleship. It broke the mystery sailboat in half and I sadly watched the two halves, along with the two bodies, descend into the liquid abyss.

I felt so helpless. All I could do was watch as Brett and Cliff slowly sank. To try to save them would be sheer suicide on my part. I quickly thought about what Torbjørn had said about the curse of the treasure. He said too many people had died because of it. Now there were two more dead people that I could chalk up to this curse.

I looked up from the lake and surveyed the horizon. The storm was getting worse. The seas were definitely intensifying and I couldn't tell the difference between where the lake ended and the sky began. It was like I was sailing into the gates of hell and there was no turning back. The waves were splashing over the deck and accumulating in the cockpit. I was scared. I didn't know what to do.

I looked over at Brian, who was beginning to stir. I opened the hatch to the main cabin and yelled for Paige and Nora.

"What was that horrible crash just a few minutes ago, Jens?" Nora asked as she peered out from the hatch way.

"Oh, that," I said, trying desperately to think of a good explanation. "We must have hit a huge wave or something."

"I thought we must of hit land or a rock or something and we were about to sink. Paige is really seasick down here and has been throwing up all over the place. I'm a little ill myself. How much longer is this storm going to last?" I just looked at her and shook my head and said, "Brian slipped up here and hit his head. He'll be okay, it's just that we have to help him down to the cabin, okay?"

Ten minutes later, I was alone in the cockpit watching the storm from hell swaddle the *Peer Gynt*. I gave up trying to head south and find cover near the coast. Instead, I took down the mainsail and decided to ride the storm out. Every time a huge wave washed over the deck, I wondered if that was the one that was going to sink the sailboat. It got so bad I was praying to a God I didn't even think I believed in to save us from the storm. But funny, that didn't happen.

The piercing reverberation from the wind and the rain slamming against the sailboat started to make a certain kind of music. If I listened carefully, I thought I could hear the earsplitting percussion and brass of a Wagnerian Opera. I thought I heard the *Entry of the Gods into Valhalla* from his opera, *Das Rheingold*. I now could distinctly hear the loud trumpet blasts and crushing cymbals emanating above me. I looked up to the sky as the *Peer Gynt* was rolling and pitching back and forth and thought I saw a bright light shining down at me. The music was getting louder and I thought I saw the God *Heimdall*, the watchman of the Æsir, who stood guard at the top of the rainbow bridge at the entrance to *Åsgard*, home of the Norse Gods. He was blowing his hefty trumpet horn called the *Gjallarhorn* at the top of his lungs, which meant there was danger ahead. Maybe it was the beginning of the *Ragnarrokk*—The Twilight of the Gods—the beginning of the end of the world. Or possibly it was the beginning of the end for me.

Then I saw nine golden haired maidens riding horses, flying out of *Åsgard*. Those women must be the *Valkyries*—choosers of the fallen heroes. The warrior maidens would fly around the world and choose which warriors would die in battle. Then they would bring the fallen warriors to *Odin's* great hall, *Valhall*, where the fallen warriors would party until the end of time. I wondered if any of them were coming for me?

My mind was brought back to reality when I saw the dreaded 'three sisters' heading right for the sailboat. The old Great Lake mariners tell of the frightful Lake Superior legend called the 'three sisters.' It has to do with a series of three consecutive enormous waves during severe storms. According to legend, and shape and size of the lake causes these three huge waves to hit a ship right in a row. The first wave hits the ship's deck. A few moments later, the second wave hits the deck before any back-wash can clear from the first, then the third wave hits the deck and, it is said, sinks or capsizes many vessels.

I can remember it now as if it were yesterday. I saw the first wave hit the *Peer Gynt*, pushing the bow of the boat down, then the second wave hit and I saw the sailboat move sideways. When the third wave hit the sailboat, it completely flipped over. My harness was attached to the cockpit so when I was thrown overboard I was still connected to the boat.

When I opened my eyes, I was surprised that there was, somehow—and don't ask me how, because it was night and the storm had made the skies pitch black—adequate visibility. As I was looking at the overturned sailboat, I watched in disbelief as all of the gold bars fell from the floor of the main cabin and smashed right through the ceiling of the main cabin deck. My heart sank as I watched seventy-nine gold bars, worth just under $11.9 million; gently glide down to the bottom of the lake. I watched as all of my dreams of independence, my plan of walking into Norm's office next week and telling him to 'shove it, because I don't need this job no more,' and all of my plans of becoming a marine archeologist and exploring the underwater mysteries around the world sink along with the gold bars.

Then I saw Brian and Paige fall out of the front cabin where they had been lying in the v-berth. Somehow, and don't tell me how, the gold bars had missed them and they were now quickly floating up to the surface wearing their lifejackets. I swam over to where my harness was connected to the cockpit. If the sailboat sank, I would sink with it! I fumbled around, but I couldn't find where to release the harness. My lungs were about to explode, so I gave a few kicks and went up to the surface. I took a few deep breaths and filled my depleted lungs with fresh air. I looked around and saw that the seas were still rough, but I could see that our skiff was floating right side up, a few feet away from me. I swam over to it and untied the line leading to the sailboat.

I yelled to Brian and Paige, who were bobbing up and down like corks in a shaken bottle about twenty feet away from me. I pushed the skiff toward them and yelled for them to get into it. I looked around for Nora, but she was nowhere to be seen.

I swam over to the overturned hull of the *Peer Gynt*, hoping that she was on the other side of it. No such luck. I started to yell, "Nora... Nora... Where are you, Nora?"

No reply. I quickly swam over to the skiff. Brian and Paige had already gotten into it. "Have you seen Nora?" I yelled to them.

"Oh my God, no!" was Paige's reply. Then all three of us started yelling at the top of our lungs—but there was no reply. I released my line to the harness and my life jacket, took two deep breaths, and went under again, fearing that maybe she was trapped inside the sailboat.

I made a few kicks with my feet and then opened my eyes; I thought I saw a marvelously beautiful woman deep down in the dark greenish water smiling and holding a great big fishing net which she used to fetch all of our sinking gold bars. I shook my head in disbelief and looked again. She must be *Rân*, the Norse goddess of the sea, who is married to the old sea god, *Ægir*. *Rân* was the goddess who gathered the drowned sailors and collected gold and other valuables from the countless number of shipwrecks throughout the world and put it in her huge fishing net. At the end of the day she took the sailor's misfortunate loot back to her great underwater hall.

Behind her was an ugly creature, which I immediately recognized as the horrible *Sjøtroll*—sea troll. He looked just like the famous painting by Theodor Kittlelsen. He was an enormous ogre with a bulky head and disproportionably large mouth with sharp, shark-like teeth. His nose was stumpy and troll-like, as was his body with large muscular arms. He was dressed in a greenish, seaweed shroud that was oversized and fluttering in the water. In his massive and muscular arms I saw he was holding the bodies of Brett Ruud and Cliff. The division of labor was evident; *Sjøtroll* had the dirty work of collecting the drowned sailors, while *Rân* gathered the fallen valuables.

I then looked up at the capsized sailboat and thought I saw Nora trapped inside the rear cabin in an air pocket. She was screaming and panicking as her head was jammed up against the floor where there was only a foot or so of the air pocket. She looked like she couldn't decide whether to stay inside the air pocket or hold her breath and try to swim out through the damaged main cabin and up to the surface. My heart stopped as I saw the repulsive *Sjøtroll* look up and spot the terrified Nora. He smiled and immediately dropped Brett and Cliff and started to swim toward Nora, undoubtedly wanting to add her to his catch of the day and take her down into the bowels of the lake.

Chapter XXVIII

I closed my eyes and took two strong kicks toward the upturned *Peer Gynt*. I had to get there before the *Sjøtroll* took Nora away for good. I was running out of breath and I thought I wasn't going to make it to the air pocket. I started to panic, franticly thrashing my arms until I felt someone seize me and pull me toward the sailboat. It was Nora. She had been watching me swim over to her from the air pocket and when I had started to panic, she held her breath and swam out to save me.

"Jens, are you crazy? Why did you come here?" Her voice sounded desperate as we both squeezed our heads in the increasingly dwindling air pocket near the ceiling.

"What do you mean? I'm here to save you."

"Jens, you really are a fool. There's no way we can get out of here. And if we do, we can't stay in the water much longer. I'm already feeling numb all over."

"Nora, listen. Brian and Paige are safe and on the skiff, right above us. They're waiting for us," I said as I pointed to the surface.

"I'm sorry Jens. I can't. I just can't do it. This is how it's meant to be. It's that curse Torbjørn talked about. It's the curse of the treasure, Jens, and I'm the next one in line to die."

"Nonsense! Look, Nora. The gold bars—the treasure, it's gone. It all sank to the bottom of the lake. That means no one can get the treasure, so the curse is gone."

"Still, Jens, we should have never gone after it. We should have never woken up the ghosts that protect that treasure from greedy people like us." I shook my head and grabbed her. I felt like shaking some sense into her, but then said forcefully, "Okay, Nora. This is what we're going to do. We are going to take in three large breaths. I'm going to take your hand and you are going to follow me. Do you understand?"

"But Jens... I can't..."

"I'm not going to take no for an answer. Do you hear me?" I counted three breaths and then we were off. We made our way down past the jagged edge of the main cabin ceiling and I began to kick upward. Nora also began to kick and, just before we reached the treacherous surface, I peeked down into the murky, greenish water to see if *Sjøtroll* was still coming. I didn't see a thing. Just as Brian was helping Nora and me into the small skiff, we saw the over-turned *Peer Gynt* plummet under the water.

•

I'd calculated it had been about twelve hours since Nora and I joined Brian and Paige in the skiff. It was daylight again, and the storm was subsiding. The four of us were huddled together trying to stay warm. On many occasions, a large wave would gush icy water into the flimsy, inflatable skiff. We had to use our hands to bail the water out, and I was fearful that the prolonged exposure to our hands would induce hyperthermia.

Einar Tviet was smart enough to equip the skiff with a portable homing beacon, which we had turned on. We knew it would be just a matter of time before a coast guard boat or helicopter would home in on our position. The four of us were surprisingly quiet. I think we were getting just a little tired of each other. None of us had the energy to complain about who did what and who made the biggest mistakes. I had a sneaking suspicion that I would lead the way in the mistakes category. We just sat there, huddled close together, like zombies, staring off into the vast horizon. I think we were all astounded that we hadn't perished in the hellish tempest.

•

Four hours later, we were sitting in the coast guard station in Houghton, Michigan, with blankets over our heads, sipping coffee. A coast guard helicopter had spotted us and picked us up. The coast guard officer kept asking why we were sailing in such a tremendous gale. Hadn't we listened to the weather forecast on the radio? The officer was especially hard on me, since I was the captain. He was demanding to see my charter's license and other credentials. I told him that I wished I could show him that stuff, but it all went down with the *Peer Gynt*. We all froze when the officer asked if we saw another sailboat during the storm. He said that a certain sailboat, named *Revenge*, out of Bayfield, had also gone missing in the storm. He thought there were two on board and a search and rescue operation was underway. We all looked at the floor and shook our heads. I heard Paige say that we hadn't seen anybody since the park ranger on Isle Royale. I guess we all felt that it wasn't worth going there, not now at least.

•

I think one of the most difficult things on the entire trip was seeing the expression on my dad's face when he came to pick me up in Houghton. Now mind you, my dad is a man of few words, but his face can speak volumes. The look he gave me—after he found out that I and my friends were okay—was that he thought I was an utter failure. And maybe you could mix in stupidity. He looked at me like he was saying: 'Haven't I taught you anything? Do you possess an *ounce* of common sense?' Now his expression he couldn't hide. But what he said when he came walking into the door of the coast guard station was, "Are you all right?" in a very concerned and loving tone. He then said, "Your mother and I were worried about you."

Nora's parents came to pick her up, and Paige and Brian rode back to Minneapolis with them. I think they were all trying to avoid me, not even giving me the satisfaction of eye contact. When it was time to go, I walked over to Nora and gave her a big hug. She responded by giving me a somewhat less than lukewarm sign of affection and, turning away and staring down at the ground, said she would call me. I smiled and thought... well that's it. She and I are history. Looking back at it all, that was the hardest thing to experience in this entire adventure. Not the scuba diving in the mine shaft, not the storm, or the near drowning, not even getting shot at a couple of times by Brett. It was the way my friends acted toward me at the coast guard station. To think they were probably blaming everything on me.

Now, I know that maybe some of it was my fault, but come on, no one's perfect. Not to be outdone, as my dad and I were preparing to leave, the coast guard officer ran up to my dad's car and wanted my address and telephone number and told me I had to return to the station in a few weeks to be interviewed by the

Marine Board of Investigations to see if any disciplinary actions were needed. I rolled my eyes and said, "Great."

The drive home was the longest and loneliest ride I've ever experienced. My dad only said a few words to me, so I was left to go over, in vivid detail, the entire adventure, one slip-up at a time. It was then, watching the lush pine trees whiz by me on the highway in the Michigan Upper Peninsula that I realized that I would have to return to the dull and ordinary world I was so accustomed to. I turned my head toward the side of the passenger car window, put my hands up to hide my face, and silently wept the entire way home to Minneapolis.

•

It's been a few months since the sinking of the *Peer Gynt*. I've only talked to Nora a couple of times on the phone. The conversations didn't go well. She said she still needs 'time' to sort things out.

Brian did forgive me for that sucker punch, but I think our relationship has never really recovered after that. Last week he informed me that he and Paige had decided to find a place to live together and he told me that at the end of the month he'd be moving out. I, of course, can't afford to pay the full rent of our apartment, so I guess I'll be moving out at the end of the month also. Where will I go? I've got no clue. I'll have to worry about that later.

I had to kick myself though, for stooping to a new low and begging Norm to give me my job back. You see, the two-week vacation turned into over a three-week expedition with all of the complications we encountered. But what can I say? I'm broke. I've spent all of my money and savings on Torbjørn's funeral and the sailing trip.

A few weeks ago, I met my cousin Mickey at Ole's bar for beers and a greasy dinner. After a few beers, my treasure adventure story came rushing out. I didn't leave anything out. I even told him about Great Grandpa Jens, and even *Rân*, the goddess of the sea, and the *Sjøtroll*. I'd figured since he was family, he would understand that I was half raving mad. He was surprised and hurt that I didn't tell him about the gold. Why didn't just the two of us try to get it? Oh well. He got a little upset, also, when I told him about my situation with Nora and Brian. Paige I don't even care about. I can remember him saying: "Those stuck-up bastards. Why do you even waste your time with them?" He asked me if I knew where the *Peer Gynt* had capsized. I told him I had a pretty good idea, but not exactly. Then he said, "Who knows, Jens, maybe someday we can go looking for that gold on the bottom of the lake!" I just smiled and nodded my head.

•

So if you ever happen to be in south Minneapolis, somewhere near Cedar Avenue, why don't you drop by Ole's bar? Don't worry if you're not Norwegian. The owner, Ole Myhre, says it's all right—he needs the business. If you do, you might find me sitting in a dank booth, tucked way back in a corner of the bar. I'll be there drinking an *Aass* beer.

You see, after I told Mickey about this little adventure, he suggested that I write down everything that happened. He also said to be kind when I was talking about him and put in a good word or two. Well Mickey, I have. And I have been writing for a few weeks now, and things are becoming clearer. I still don't have a good answer for why I pushed Cliff in the water when I was handing him that gold bar. Wasn't nine million dollars enough for us? Why did I want it all? I also regret smacking Brian and slamming my sailboat into Brett's. A few days after I came home, I read in the newspaper that two men, a Brett Ruud and a Cliff Wilson, were found half dead in a skiff on Lake Superior off of Houghton. So they didn't go down with the *Revenge* and they did survive, but I think one of them had severe frostbite. So much for Torbjørn's curse.

All I know is that I wasn't really myself at the end of the trip. That gold did something to me. I guess it was the sickness of wanting all that money. Something transformed me, like an addicting drug. I had to have it all.

But all in all, did I regret it? Did I regret going out and finding Torbjørn's gold? No way. Did I regret meeting and finding out about his life, his brother, his wife Ida? That's a definite no way. When I think back on it, I realize that I was never happier and I never felt more alive than I did in those few short months of my life.

There's a Kinks song that I can't get out of my head lately. It's from the 1975 album called *Soup Opera*. The song is near the end of the album and called *(A) Face in the Crowd*. It's about a guy finally realizing after all of his grand illusions that he's never going to amount to anything of greatness. He's never going to be rich, powerful, popular, or successful. He finally understands that he's never going to get all the women and be the center of all the parties and all the latest trends. He realizes that he's just going to be average. And when he dies he'll possibly be remembered for a few years, and then he will be forgotten. He's invisible, just like the rest of us. Man, how I can relate to that song. The song ends by with: "Mister, can you tell me who I am? Do you think I stand out? Or am I just a face in the crowd?" Lately, I've been thinking that maybe it's okay just to be average.

I'm only working part time now at the appraisal office. It's something like freelance work. The money is not good, but it frees up my time to do other things, like working a few nights a week at Mickey's record shop. I've sold my expensive Saab and bought a 1973 Volvo P1800ES. Mickey has helped me fully restore it back to its original configuration. I've also moved into his small two-room apartment. I took the bedroom he used as his 'music room' with the thousands of record albums. It's cramped but 'cozy.' Since Mickey's apartment is so close to the U of M campus, I've decided to take out a school loan and take a few classes. I've enrolled in a marine archeology class and an English Comp class. Who knows what will happen after that?

•

It was late, about ten o'clock on a boring Tuesday night. The bar was practically empty, except for the usual suspects. I was probably becoming one of them. I had written a few more pages of my story and I started to rub my eyes, I was so tired. I glanced over at the bar and saw that same old Norsky sitting at the bar. The one I noticed when I brought Torbjørn here about a year ago. He had a drink in one hand and a cigarette butt in the other. He was smiling and trying to say something to me from across the bar. A bartender walked over to me and handed me a beer. "What's this for?" I asked.

"It's from the old geezer sitting up at the bar." He said as he pointed to the old guy and started walking away. The old Norsky raised his glass and his face was lit up and I could faintly hear him say, "*Skål!*"

Did Mickey tell that old dinosaur about my misadventure? Or maybe my story got caught swirling around in the air, mixed in with the stale smoke and musty smells of the bar, and happened to land his way. I couldn't tell. I smiled, raised my beer glass, shook my head in disbelief and said back to him, "*Skål!*"

Just then the front door of the bar opened and I saw Nora. She looked around the bar and then saw me. She smiled and began to walk toward me...

The End

Other Novels from Singing River Publications:

With Malice Toward All by Roger MacDonald

A Drama of the Caribbean by William Brennan sj

It Happened in Minnesota by Tony Bridwell

Young Adult Novels:

Britta's Journey, An Emigration Saga by Ann Mershon

Bo Bear... The Journey Begins by Connie Loisel